D1614827

AN ITALIAN ELEGY

M. BLACK

Knights Press

Stamford, Connecticut

Cover designed by Christopher Karukas ©

Published by Knights Press, P.O. Box 454, Pound Ridge, NY 10576

Distributed by Lyle Stuart, Inc., 120 Enterprise Ave., Secaucus, NJ 07094

Library of Congress Cataloging-in-Publication Data

Black, M.
    An Italian elegy / by M. Black.
      p. cm.
    ISBN 0-915175-31-2 : $9.00
    I. Title.
    PS3552.L336I8 1989
    813'.54—dc19   88-29258
                             CIP

Printed in the United States of America

Acknowledgements

No book is its own creation, no writer his own creator. Among the many people I am indebted to for this particular story, my deepest love and gratitude go out to my friend and sister, Carole, who made Trento possible for me; to Michael Guillen, whose affection and encouragement over the years have inspired me to go on writing; and to my old friend Dennis Kruszynski, whose energies were drawn into this book with no assurance of reward, or even cooperation — no one could have had a better editor. And no one could have better friends than these.

Special thanks are also due my friends from Trento: Luciana, Roberto, Maria — and above all Claudio, who opened his heart and his city to me. *Vi voglio bene.*

AN ITALIAN ELEGY

I   The Vatican Spy

It sometimes happens on the bus that I lapse into daydreaming in Italian. This fact in and of itself is not so surprising. I am Italian and the bus ride is often a long and boring one. What is interesting, for me, is the effect this internal distraction has on my ear for the English language. Although it is my second language, I have lived in America for almost seventeen years now and even before then I spoke and understood English with some degree of proficiency. So it is not easy for me to remember how English first sounded to me before I comprehended words and meanings. But in those minutes of reverie in Italian I am struck suddenly alert by the voices I do not understand, and I remember.

Of course I can't remember the very first time I heard English spoken. In Trento, the small town in Northern Italy where I was born and where I lived until I came to San Francisco, there were always a few English-speaking tourists about. In the winter they come to ski on Monte Bondone and in the summer they sometimes stop en route to Austria and Germany, or coming from there, stop en route to the more alluring cities of Italy. Trento, and I speak as a native, is not a major city on anyone's map. The town sits on the railway line between Rome and Munich, and if not for this happenstance almost no one would ever visit it. The Council of Trent is important in the annals of the Catholic Church, but the history of the town is familiar to few tourists, and its attractions are less than spectacular: a castle, a cathedral, other churches, some old walls. Nothing out of the ordinary for Italy. But it is in a very pretty setting in a valley at the foot of the Italian Alps, and it is not, again I speak as a native, without its charms. For me, certainly, the memory of Trento is rich with a personal reality that is at times joyous, at other times heartbreaking.

Probably I first heard English as a boy in the narrow streets of the historic center. They were never packed with tourists as in Rome or Venice or Florence, but still it would have been unusual not to eventually overhear the conversation of passing strangers and notice the difference. Perhaps at first German and French and English were all the same for me. But at a very early age I must have detected the surface differences among these languages. Later at school each would take on the form of "language," but before then I already had a particular impression of the *sound* of each language. All of this takes place for Italians, I should emphasize, when we are very young, as we are all bilingual practically from infancy owing to the vernacular spoken in each province along with standard Italian. I never had occasion, for instance, to *speak* Trentino, the dialect of Trento, but there was never a time, in any meaningful sense, when I did not understand it. In addition to this bilingualism, it is difficult to live anyplace in Europe and not have an acquaintance, even as a child, with the concept "foreign language."

The English I most probably first heard spoken in Trento would have been British. There always seemed to be something strangely soft, indistinct and mumbly about their English, as though they were creatures newly come to language, and thus somewhat reluctant to utter anything that might be contradicted by someone who knew what they were *trying* to say. They often spoke through their teeth. When spoken by Englishmen, especially, it sounds to many Italians an effeminate language. It was, in any event, the most curious of the languages I heard growing up, and maybe for that reason I found it specially enchanting. Having to make a choice many years later, I naturally took it as my first foreign language in school.

More rarely heard in the streets of Trento was American. It is even possible that I originally heard some snippet of what was to be my adopted tongue in a film or on television. However I first encountered it, I remember clearly thinking, "That's English?" The general impression is of course very different from British. Though not as guttural or consonantal as German, American shares with its distant cousin certain superficial phonetic similarities as well as a kind of round, growling sound more appealingly — and carelessly — indulged than its German counterpart (as always, dictatorially precise). Because of these harmonies between the two languages, I would have thought American was a dialect of German had I not known it was called *inglese.* Or rather, Americans sounded to me like tomcats who had been taught to imitate human speech (probably German), and who practiced this artifice with considerable pride.

British or American, there was something innately odd and amusing about this language, further incentive to study it at school. Its somewhat comical sound was more compelling to a boy such as myself than even its usefulness in the modern world as the "universal language." We were encouraged at school, however, to follow British pronunciation, and with this snobbism tucked neatly under my chin by the time I got to high school, I would often refer to the American "meowing" of English. This is the sound I hear once again on the bus.

I have since, it should go without saying, had the opportunity to listen more closely to many languages. Simply by getting on a bus in San Francisco one is likely to be exposed to Spanish or Chinese or Japanese or Russian or Vietnamese — or even Italian. And besides speaking English, Italian and French, I have a linguist's ear for syllabication; I recognize word forms in languages I don't even know. Consequently, I have had to revise some of my more naive opinions. Nonetheless there is still some mystery for me in this matter of the sound of languages. For one thing, Spanish still sounds like a flabby, lazy Italian to me — notwithstanding its breathtaking speed. Chinese sounds even more like cats in heat than American ever did. But it is that masculine, feline quality of American, alien and unfamiliar for one brief instant, that disturbs my self-involved bus ride to or from the private high school where I teach Italian.

Shaken from my daydream, I am awakened from yet a deeper dream. This apparently accidental trip over an ancient memory of foreign languages jolts the sleepwalker (which I have become) into an immediate consciousness of the loosened dream state and the reality it conceals. It is a reality of memories, like my memories of Trento, as full of happiness as of sadness. For when I think of the initial impact of American pronunciation upon my senses, I am invariably led to thoughts of the first American I ever knew. And these memories echo with a terrible resonance that is sweet, painful and unending. But I cannot be sure that it is not specifically to stir these memories that I take the bus to work instead of driving my car. My course is all the more suspicious when I have forgotten to bring a book to read.

These days of course the name of Clayton Hayes will be recognized at once. Even if you have never read a single one of his books, you will surely know the name from a general cultural osmosis that sometimes sucks up certain popular authors whether they are read or not. But he *is* read, and some of his books are widely respected for their beauty and intelligence. My bias in the matter restrains me from commenting more thoroughly upon his work here. That is not the purpose of this book.

Perhaps if the name has somehow escaped your attention up to now, you may have seen the movies *The Piper Dances* or *Kidnapping of a Modern Hero,* both successful films taken from two of his most famous novels. In the latter, in fact, there appears the character of Andrea Sapetti, a name not ingeniously different from my own, Luca Savelli, and a young man, I state without modesty, based in large part upon myself. But that was all to come later. When I first met Clayton Hayes, fame had not yet descended upon him.

Over the years I have tried to reconstruct in my mind that first meeting with as much verisimilitude as I can muster from my failing memory. Maybe I have preoccupied myself with this effort in an attempt to divert my sometimes morbid fascination from the later recollections and their frightening clarity. At any rate, I must begin not with our first encounter, but with what I first heard about this American, or rather what I *thought* when I first heard about him.

In the winter of 1971 I was twenty-two, attending the University of Trento, and still living at home with my parents and my older sister Claudia. I would not have to write "still" living at home for an Italian audience, as it is more common than not for Italians to live at home until they marry, even into their thirties. In America it is very different, though, and I want to make it clear that at that time my life, in all its particulars, big and little, was normal, unremarkable and, not infrequently, boring.

I was studying economics at the university and my greatest ambition then was to make money. I imagined I would eventually end up being an officer in a bank or even owning my own business. My best friend was Marco, with whom I shared this ambition, along with more easily realized interests in skiing, soccer, and girls.

My girlfriend, Antonella, and I had just decided that winter to start seeing less of each other. There had been an undeniable physical attraction between us — consummated more than once in my father's Peugeot. But we were not in love and too young to waste our pride on anything less. Still, we were able to remain friends and even continued to enjoy, in those rare moments when a young Italian couple could be alone, a variety of petting perhaps more playful than passionate. By January, though, she had ceased letting me go "all the way."

Then, too, there was Marie in France, whom I had met two years before in Paris. Besides being very pretty, her sly exuberance always made her fun to be with. We kept up a close correspondence, but I only saw her once every six months or so.

I had other friends, but these were the most important to me. The only other acquaintance I would mention at this point would be Francesco. We had been best friends when we were fourteen, fifteen, and sixteen. He was a pleasant boy, with black, expressive eyes, but when we met in the streets after having grown and gone separate ways, we would only smile and say *ciao* and pass on. I could not look at him without feeling some unexplored dread and guilt, and I think it was the same for him.

Claudia, my sister, was four years older than me and had already graduated with a degree in English Literature. She had a job teaching English in a private school in Rovereto, a small town about twenty miles south of Trento. Her boyfriend was a younger Englishman whom she had met during her studies abroad. It was obvious that they were very serious about each other and no one doubted that they would someday marry. But as it was a long-distance romance, there were innumerable difficulties — the least of which possibly being the phone bill. He was still studying at Oxford and Claudia wasn't sure about committing herself to living in England. America was considered as a compromise, but he had yet to graduate, and emigration to the United States is never easily accomplished. For now, they had to be content visiting each other regularly in Italy or England, while leaving a thousand indefinite proposals floating in the air. Only later was I to learn the intense level of frustration Claudia had had to manage those many months.

Our relationship I suppose was very typical for a brother and sister. We fought about everything. There was also what I imagine is a very ordinary rivalry with our parents. It had always seemed understood between us that I was my mother's favorite, and Claudia my father's. Our parents would have denied it, of course, but it was there, and the charge of favoritism often reared its ugly head in any argument that our mother or father stepped into in order to arbitrate. But it would never have occurred to me that Claudia didn't love me, and I was as bound by love to her. This admission, *ti voglio bene,* would probably never have been dared if not for the tragic turn of events.

The one quality of Claudia's that would have been admitted by everyone was her sincerity, and because of this everyone liked and trusted her. Indeed, everyone loved Claudia. She is one of those warm, gentle people who seem to be everyone's best friend — whether these friends can stand one another or not (they often cannot).

Her sensitivity and easy affability did not in any way affect a keen intelligence. It is discretion, knowing what to say and what not to say, that is as much the basis of friendship as a *simpatica* nature. A dull mind cannot bring this off. Remarkably, she listened patiently to everyone's problems and was never made cynical by them.

Though not exceptionally beautiful, with her large and lovely gray eyes she was pretty enough to have had her share of boyfriends — if they had not become the kind of close friends that thought of her as a "sister." After mentioning my own quarrels with her, I use the word advisedly. Not until she went away to England, and broke through this protective, insular layer of friendship, did she find a boy for whom she was much more than a sister.

One of her closest friends in Trento was Alessandro. They had met in their college days at the University of Verona. From the beginning I can't say I much cared for him. But he was good to Claudia and his sense of humor was sharp enough that he even made me laugh sometimes. They studied together often, and his face became a fixture about our house for many years. My own deduction is that Claudia was infatuated with him at one time, so it may be that my distaste for him had always been colored in some small measure by a peculiar form of jealousy. Why is now hard to figure, for Alessandro never treated her as anything other than . . . a sister.

Alessandro had made a trip to America a few years earlier with another friend from Rovereto. It was a journey on which Claudia was to have joined them, but at the last moment a financial crisis in our family prevented her going. She had been extremely disappointed about her misfortune and remained dejected for weeks afterward. Some recompense was made when they returned and told her all about their adventures so often and in such detail that she felt, as she continued to say years after, that she had taken the trip with them after all.

The highlight of the trip for Alessandro and Stefano, the boy who had gone with him, had been their stay in

San Francisco. There they had met a wonderful American who had been both host and friend to them. The stories of their good times together could not help but filter down to me, so that by the time Claudia informed me that Alessandro's friend Clayton was coming to Trento, I already had a fantasy, however genially amorphous, of what this American must be like.

Alessandro, unlike most young men his age in Italy, had his own small apartment in the old center of the town at that time, just near one of the ancient city walls. It was there that Claudia had met the American shortly after his arrival. Claudia told me later that he was planning to get his own apartment in Trento and stay for six months.

"Trento?" I had asked incredulously. Yes, it was the center of my universe, but why should this American make it the center of his — even for six months?

"Because he has friends here," she had said. "Besides, he's already been to Italy a couple of times and seen most of the rest of the country. And don't forget that Trento is a cheaper place to live than Rome or Florence."

I must have been silent for some time before asking, accusatorially, "And what does he intend to do here for six months?"

"He says he wants to learn Italian. Evidently he speaks a little already," she answered, and then added: "And to write. He says he's here to write. . .in English."

"What's he doing for money?" I'm sure I demanded this information in a rather indignant tone, for her response was short and irritable.

"I don't know!"

I think we had both assumed by then, in our naivetè, that he was simply another rich American vacationing in a poorer, for him practically third-world, country. I knew just enough then; in those days: Now that it is the U.S. which is virtually a third-world country — while Italy's economy thrives — this "distancing" is unavoidable. I had often met abroad a distressing attitude of condescension towards "provincial" Italians. But we were — *are* — an advanced, technological society. Modern European civilization is as much a product of Italy as of any country. But of course Americans *had* to be the best. And, in fact, weren't they all rich? This notion, mixed for me as it was with envy and resentment, seemed to belie any suggestion that the American had come to Trento because it was cheaper to live there than in Rome or Florence. Surely the excitement of Rome was worth the higher price, quickly dispensed with, as I was convinced it could be, by a credit card or two. And what kind of writer was he anyway?

The mystery took on new complications.

"How old is he?" I asked.

"Oh, thirty, I think Alessandro said," Claudia replied. "He seems our age though. He's really very nice."

I said nothing, but I know my mind was whirling in a way I cannot today fully fathom: No one, I thought, comes to Italy at thirty years of age to learn Italian. Where was his family, his wife, his children? Was he divorced? Was he Italian-American? Did he have relatives in the area? Was he truly one of those rich American playboys I had seen in movies? Was he going to school in Trento? No, I remembered that Claudia had said Alessandro was going to give him private lessons.

It was none of my business, but I was intrigued nonetheless. How could a grown man arrange to have *six months'* vacation? And what did Claudia mean, "he seems our age"? With some exasperation I thought, *Americans!*

These questions were not unraveled immediately, nor when I met him, nor even, completely, in the months that followed. The amorphous fantasy in my mind, however, was slowly giving way to a more concrete image touched by some random facts, and something of romance.

I met Clayton Hayes a week after the conversation with my sister. He came to our house with a group of friends in one of those casual, impromptu gatherings not uncommon around Claudia. He had arrived with Alessandro and Stefano and Stefano's girlfriend, Erica. Already present, besides me and my parents, were more of Claudia's friends — Michela, Luciana, and Paolo. They were all making themselves comfortable in our dining room. My mother and father were getting ready to go over to our aunt's (her sister's) for the evening, while I sat in the living room by myself watching a soccer match on television. It was Sunday. As you see, I have been able to establish with some certainty, and with sufficient satisfaction, the setting of that night. Not all the attendant performances come back to me so readily.

The first thing that struck me about Clayton, and it may seem funny to the reader unfamiliar with my region of Italy, was his height. He was not really short, but neither was he tall. He was only a few inches taller than Claudia, who was indeed considered short by local standards. I watched through the doorway between the living room and the vestibule as he entered the house, and as *ciaos*'s and *buona sera*'s were exchanged all around I could not quite believe that *this* waOthe American.

I must explain that my shock extended from a particular ethnic prejudice. In the northern region of Italy where I come from there has been a great deal of German influence historically. Our people, too, are very tall and often fair. I myself am six-foot-one and blond, with green eyes. We like to think of ourselves as a breed apart from the darker, shorter, *wilder* Neapolitans and Sicilians who have given America its stereotype of Italians. I have in two decades of expatriation had to forego this racism, born of the foolish conviction that Trento *was* the center of the universe, and now find myself more and more the kinsman to those swarthy, excitable Italian-Americans of movies and television.

In Trento, though, anybody short and dark was naturally suspect. We had a saying: *Altezza metà bellezza.* Tallness is half of beauty. The heroic dimensions the American must have taken on in my imagination may be judged by my genuine surprise that he was under six feet. No one so important, so dynamic, could be so — not tall. I had expected him to be much taller than me. (Months later I would find on his California driver's license that he was five feet, eight inches tall.)

His handsome face, being of dark complexion with chestnut hair, could not at first redeem my almost regretful discovery. I was at least relieved to see, as he took off his coat, that he was not fat. That would have been too much at once. He was solid, but not *fat.*

Claudia introduced us and I half-rose from the sofa to shake his hand. He smiled and spoke, and instantly I felt a friendliness more startling than my disillusionment over his height. His voice was deep, but clear and light and intimate.

"*Ciao*, Luca," he said. "Claudia tells me you speak English."

"I hope that it were so," I answered in a futile endeavor to maintain my cool composure. I realized my nervous solecism at once and blushed. But he seemed not to notice at all and went on.

"I know you must speak very good English with Claudia in the house. Her English is *perfect.*"

As Claudia humbly demurred (to an unequivocal fact acknowledged by everyone), Clayton's subtle brown eyes fell on me with a warmth that embarrassed me, but that did not linger as he turned with the others to go into the dining room.

He was older than me of course, but years younger than thirty I would have thought. I have since learned that this trait of youthful preservation is common to Californians, as distinct from other Americans, and certainly from Italians, whose physical vanity after thirty, especially the men's, is predicated primarily on self-delusion.

My parents were running late, but my father took the time to insist on opening a bottle of very good spumante in honor of the American. My mother, meanwhile, rushed about the kitchen pulling out every cake, every fruit, every nut, every sweet and candy, and offering it to Clayton. None of the other guests seemed to mind this extravagant display of homage to the American. No one else had come so far to be our guest. And as I have noted before, Americans were a rare species in Trento.

Clayton kindly declined most of what was proffered, except the spumante, and after exchanging a few words in Italian with him my parents finally left. Even as she exited, my mother continued her solicitous generosity with an invitation to dinner, *"la prossima volta."* Next time.

The soccer match I was watching was a crucial one, but my attention was drawn repeatedly to the happy, animated voices that emanated from the dining room. I found myself waiting anxiously to hear the American speak again. Minutes would go by, during which my mind would begin to wander back to the television screen, and then suddenly I would hear him laugh, a laugh of such obvious good nature, and he would say something that fixed my eyes to the half-closed door to the dining room.

His English was so clear that I could hardly believe that he was American. It sounded nothing like the other Americans I had heard in Trento, who had seemed to speak in one long modulated slur — like a cat's meow. Clayton's pronunciation was sharp and even and spoken at a pace slow enough that even I could understand most of what he said. For though English had long ceased to be one fluid sound for me, devoid of words and sentences, I did not in fact speak or comprehend it with anything like fluency. I had studied it for five years, but years more would pass before I realized exactly how vast my ignorance was at that time. I was often content then simply to know that there were real English words there in the language I heard spoken by native speakers, even if I couldn't make them out. That night, though, I strained to grasp every syllable.

It occurred to me after a while that Clayton was speaking slowly deliberately, for the benefit of those around the table whose English was no better than my own. I surmised this from the way he would interrupt the general conversation at times and say something very fast to Claudia or Alessandro. The cascade of words was an incomprehensible torrent to me, and perhaps to the others as well, for only Claudia, Alessandro, and Clayton would end up laughing after one of these asides. There would be a quick Italian translation and my full ignorance of English would begin to dawn on me.

Clayton's Italian, on the other hand, was even worse than my English. Although it improved over the months, he was never to speak it without a fracturing hesitation. (There was a time to come when, alone with me, he would speak Italian with confidence and expressiveness. And certainly when I was angry with him he understood me well enough. But then vulgar Italian is always the first learned and best remembered.) His pronunciation was not bad, but he was never thoroughly comfortable speaking the language and his mistakes were always plentiful. He could read Italian well and even write it with some wit, but when he first came to Trento his listening comprehension was very poor. For this reason, I think, most of the conversation that night was in English.

I remember early in the discussion Clayton's intention to learn Italian came up.

Michela, who was Claudia's best girlfriend at the time, commented, "But you already know some Italian;

it won't be so hard to learn it living here with so many Italian friends."

"Oh, he can speak it, believe me," Alessandro said.

"*Io so la grammatica, ma parlo un italiano bruttissimo, veramente bruttissimo.*" I know the grammar, but I speak a really awful Italian. Clayton could always speak the truth with absolute assurance.

"*Non lo credo,*" Michela said. I don't believe it. "*Ti sento parlarlo benissimo.*" I can hear that you speak it very well.

"*Non'e vero,*" Clayton persisted. "*Mi dispiace, ma non'e vero.*" I'm sorry, but it's not true. "*Spero che sia vero,*" he added, at least avoiding any error like my own: I wish it were true.

"Look, Clayton," Alessandro said in English, "you are in a grace period now. We're speaking English now just because you're new here. But in two weeks *everyone* will speak Italian and only Italian to you."

"Okay, but I won't understand a word," Clayton answered. "Or barely a word."

"Don't believe him!" Stefano announced to the others. "He understands *everything*. He's a Vatican spy!"

Everybody laughed. But during his stay in Trento Clayton continued to speak mostly in English, and we all always responded in English.

After the soccer match was over, I casually strolled into the kitchen to get something to drink. I told myself I couldn't care less about the American. Who was he to me anyway? But in the kitchen, which opened onto the dining room, my calm, brittle disinterest shattered under the weight of sheer wonder. I felt excited just to look at him. If his eyes happened to catch mine for a second while I watched, he would smile kindly before I stupidly jerked my eyes away. What power one glance of his seemed to have. More often, though, he was obviously involved in the lively conversation at the table, so that I could study him at my leisure. My curiosity had me running in and out of the kitchen all evening, under one pretext or another, with a boyish agitation that makes me laugh today. And I had thought myself so mature and self-possessed at twenty-two!

My first taste of the American was, on balance, exhilarating. Let down initially by his stature, I was thankful that some piece of my fantasy was left intact. I could sense even that first night that he had a "presence." He was, in spirit, not less than he should have been, but more. With more pride than was my due, I looked forward to his stay in Trento, and to his visits to our home.

Many nights later I lay in my bedroom trying to go to sleep. Unlike many men my age, I look on my early youth as more troubled than my middle age. Across a great distance, this memory sometimes comes to men as a dream worn clean of any worrisome details, a vision of imperfect, yet perfect, bliss. Not for me. I see even more clearly now that this time of my life was rife with miseries that can only be diminished by an effort of will within someone who no longer has to live them. That night, in particular, there had been a long, loud and savage argument between my mother and father. Perhaps to forget that disturbance, and other hurts I could not name, my thoughts had turned to the boy Francesco, whom I had once called my friend.

Shortly I heard voices and laughing out in front of our house. I went to my window and opened the shutter slightly. Walking up to the house through the snow were Claudia, Alessandro, and the American. The men were bringing my sister home after having gone out for a late pizza. They had all plainly had something to drink with dinner as well. Alessandro and Clayton had locked their arms through Claudia's and were lifting her up every few steps as they walked. Their giddy voices rang with an uninhibited merriment that sounded to me in that moment like nothing so much as pure happiness.

I sank onto the window sill and stared out at the friends enjoying themselves. I watched the American laugh and throw his head back. His darkly beautiful face was partially lit at that angle by a street lamp. It was more completely and attractively illuminated by a light I could not see. I began to feel a bitterness well up inside me, a childish bitterness for what I felt was being denied me. I had no one, really. My heart was empty and ached with a hunger that neither Marco nor Antonella, nor Francesco, nor even Marie in Paris could ever fill.

I sat looking out upon the white blotches of snow in the night long after Claudia had come in and the two men who had hugged her good night had gone away.

II A Car. A River. A Father.

My father had retired that winter from his position in the local juvenile justice system. He was sixty-one, almost fifteen years older than my mother. Over the years I have tried to recount to myself as many incidents of their relationship as I could in an attempt to throw some light on later events, but my understanding is a fleeting, incoherent montage of remembered feelings. Every family has its story, but mine had never seemed extraordinary to me. There were problems, yes, for all of us, and sometimes vociferous confrontations between my mother and father. But, as much as these scenes pained me, I thought ours was a really very ordinary and adequately content family.

One development that had noticeably altered my father's life had been the stroke he'd suffered ten years earlier. It had been a "minor" stroke, from which he had recovered with amazing speed. But his left arm and leg, and most apparently the left side of his face, had been left with traces of paralysis. In the hospital I had been frightened by the immobile grimace on that side of his face, and the drooping frown his lips could not lift themselves from. Between arduous physical therapy and tedious speech therapy, though, he had been able to return to a virtually normal way of life within a few months. His limp articulation and sibilant shuffle were not, in fact, any true hindrance to him. But the unmistakable vestiges of his stroke were never utterly dismissable, least of all to himself, and my mother and sister and I saw in him a psychological change, a defeat only partly masked by an energetic return to his work and family, and a defeat from which he never really recovered. Maybe because of some shame attached to these changes, physical and psychological, and because of the now dramatically visible discrepancy in their ages, my father and mother did not go out much together except to visit family. My mother did maintain her own circle of younger friends, with whom she indulged a vivacity more befitting her years.

My own relationship with my father was not special, but neither was it unsatisfactory. Being my mother's favorite, I knew at a very young age how to manipulate any disputes in her direction. My father was, nevertheless, a man I could respect and I would not have hesitated to call him a good father. He could be too strict — certainly not unusual in Italy — but he was a good deal more intelligent than the fathers of many of my friends, and capable of genuine kindness.

I remember one summer I had gotten a job washing dishes at a restaurant in Rimini. Rimini is a popular seaside resort on the Adriatic. There were nights when I would have sworn that every single tourist in town, and possibly all the native residents as well, had dined at the restaurant where I worked. The dirty plates and pots seemed perpetually stacked in discouraging towers surrounding me, as in a cartoon — to no comical effect. My schedule was a grueling one of long hours and no days off. After a week I determined to call and tell my mother I was giving up and coming home. I didn't care about the money. As it turned out, however, my father answered the phone, and before I could stop myself I burst into tears and blurted out that I wanted to come home.

My father received this information calmly, but told me that he could not come and get me the next day — it would have to be the day after. Perversely, in those two days I found myself making lots of new friends, attending late night parties and enjoying the novelty of independence. With the erratic willfulness of a child I changed my mind, and when my father showed up to take me home I would not have left Rimini for anything. My summer there had already begun to look preciously short.

Far from being angry, as I had feared, my father took my capriciousness in good humor and even spent my few hours off with me filling me in on all the gossip from back home. As he was getting ready to set off on the long drive back to Trento, he must have seen something in my face, for he turned reassuringly to me and said, "It's all right. I've told your mother that I was going to Bologna on business. You were to have been a surprise for her."

I think only a loving father could have had such care for the silly pride of a boy. My humble re-payment of this debt was never to boast about the good times I'd had in Rimini that summer — at least not in his presence.

In the days following his retirement my father rambled about our house in an aimless, ghostlike existence. He simply did not know what to do with his time. As might be expected, more than the usual number of arguments broke out between him and my mother. His presence in the house during the day was depressing for me, a constant moping, so I thought, unfairly imposed on the rest of us. I spent more and more time away from home.

Of course, even if this had not been the case at home, I would rarely have been found there. I was after all a student with a rather full social life (even if that social life left something deep inside me unsated). I went to bars and movies and discos, or just for a *giretto* about the town with friends. I trooped up to the mountains to ski and played soccer when the weather permitted. I eventually removed my studies from home to the university library, where I always met someone I could go out for a coffee with. It was not surprising that my grades took a slight dip.

The one subject that I really began to worry about was English. I had an important exam coming up in April and I knew I was not prepared. I had tried studying once with Claudia, but a brother and sister do not make the best student and teacher.

"Why don't you ask Clayton?" Claudia suggested to me over lunch one day. "I know he's looking for private students to tutor."

"For money?" This had come as something of a shock.

"Of course for money *scemo*. He says he's going to need a little extra cash to make it through six months."

"But *you* don't pay him anything." I knew that once a week she and Alessandro and Stefano, and sometimes others, had already begun to meet with the American for lessons that were referred to as "English at the postproficiency level." Supposedly these were general discussions on a variety of topics, punctuated by the occasional dictation, all intended to expand the "students" vocabulary and fluency. I began to suspect it was all just an excuse for a party once a week.

"I don't know why he doesn't ask us for money. I guess because we're friends. He's certainly worth it; he's a good teacher. Very clear, very organized — and yet it's still interesting. Sometimes a native speaker's knowledge of his own language is so. . .sloppy."

"You should take him a bottle of wine or something," my mother advised at that point. My father nodded.

"Yes, maybe I should," Claudia said thoughtfully, "but I don't know if he would accept it. He told Alessandro that the lessons are his way of repaying our 'kindness' — though what I've done for him I can't imagine. At any rate, he really does seem to enjoy the lessons."

I finally voiced my own doubts. "Even an American can't charge guests at a party."

"I can't deny we all have fun sometimes," Claudia answered defensively, "but it's not as informal as you seem to think. Clayton takes it very seriously. He's astonishingly thorough — and his patience seems inexhaustible. I've learned a lot I didn't know."

She rose from the table with her empty plate and I made a humphing sound of skepticism. She ignored it.

"Anyway, if you like I can ask him for you." She looked down at me. "Do you think you'd be interested?"

"How much does he charge?" I asked.

"Well, I know he already has one paying student and I think she pays eight thousand lire an hour, once a week."

"Eight thousand lire!"

"He's mother-tongue, after all. And actually he says the lessons usually run more like an hour and a half."

"I don't know. . . ." I started to mumble.

"Look, do you want to pass the exam or not?" she said more sternly. "Here you have the perfect opportunity to be tutored by a native speaker. Forget about the exam — think about your *English*."

"Okay, ask him — just to see what he says." My mind was quickly calculating the discount he might give to the brother of such a good friend.

"You'll have to pay for private lessons yourself," my father warned.

I was not sure that could be managed. At that time I was giving lessons myself, as a swimming instructor at the one public indoor swimming pool open through the winter. My father knew a man in the city's recreation department and I had been recommended by him to be one of the instructors. In government affairs in Italy it always helps to know someone. I was given free access to the pool — which, in addition to the lessons — I used for laps of my own along with unlimited privileges in a gym adjacent to this facility. I was thus able to keep my swimmer's body in good shape while making a little money. But even when I had a whole group of kids to teach, the sum I earned was negligible by any accounting. Eight thousand lire a week would take a chunk of my income scarcely smaller than the total itself.

By chance I ran into Clayton and Alessandro in the center of town a couple of days later. It was only the third or fourth time I had seen the American, and these encounters had never consisted of much more than an exchange of *ciao*'s. I was always glad to see him and he was always friendly and relaxed with me, but we had never had anything to say to each other — I out of nervousness; he, I thought, from an undeviatingly sincere lack of interest.

That day, however, he enthusiastically broached the matter of my lessons. He was willing to begin immediately, but he insisted that he could take no money from me. I protested, saying I had to pay *something,* but he would not hear it.

"Listen, all of you have made me feel so welcome and comfortable here I can't ask money of you for something I enjoy — I can't," he said very earnestly, almost pleading. And then without pausing he asked, "Is Friday okay with you? Three o'clock? Okay? And don't forget to bring a pen and paper and whatever books you use at school. Claudia has the address."

I had of course relented, nodding dumbly to all of this.

We parted and he and Alessandro rushed off in the direction of Alessandro's apartment in the Seconda Androna. I heard Alessandro say with alarm to him, "But you can't give free English lessons to everyone in Trento!" But Clayton appeared to be unmoved and commenced intently explaining something to him. I could not hear what.

I was left standing in the street watching them disappear around a corner, having forgotten where I had been headed before meeting them. More than the relief I felt over the cost of the lessons, I was thrilled with the conceit that I had been admitted to an honored inner circle of the American's.

On Friday afternoon I also had a swimming lesson, so I had to race from the pool to Clayton's. He had rented a fifth-floor apartment in a large condominium complex in Via Chini. I had not been invited there before, but it was not far from our house and I had often seen the buildings from Viale Verona. I arrived a little late, afraid not that he would be cross but that he might have forgotten the lesson altogether.

He didn't seem to mind my tardiness in the least, and while I apologized profusely, he began gently directing me through his apartment on a little tour. I must have been babbling quite senselessly, for his faint, bemused smile at last blossomed into a laugh, and he said, "Okay, I'll show you the apartment some other time — since your English lesson already seems to have begun."

"I'm sorry," I sighed abjectly, finally looking around. It was a large one-bedroom apartment, fairly modern in design though some of the furniture was very old. Its most pleasing features were its spaciousness and its big

picture windows that faced out onto the mountains above
Trento. "It's very nice. Did you rent it with the furniture?"

"Oh, yes. I couldn't very well run out and buy a
whole set of furniture for six months," he said, leading
me to a table in the living room. "And when the Italians say
furnished, they mean furnished. I even have sheets and
silverware."

The table where we were to sit for our lesson was
set beneath the largest of the windows, which included a
glass door opening from the *salotto* onto the balcony.

I looked out upon the snow-patched peaks and
pointed: "You see that mountain? We call it Dante. You see
how it looks like the profile of Dante sleeping, with his face
looking up to the sky?"

He nodded and said, without irony, "Yes, I think
someone else mentioned that." I realized then that *everyone*
must have already told him that. My self-consciousness was
complete. But he did not exhibit any impatience, nor did
his watchfulness betray the kind of wary evaluating one
might expect of a teacher sizing up a new pupil. Only the
innocent warmth of his eyes. He offered me a glass of white
vermouth and matter-of-factly explained, "I like to give all
my students something to drink before we start. It helps
loosen their tongues."

"Yes, thank you, a little. . . . I mean, yes, please." And
we laughed.

"You can say 'yes, thank you' — even before you've
been served. Americans say it all the time. Only the British
are so *pignolo* on that point of usage." He withdrew to get
the Martini and I sat at the table.

The lesson went by very swiftly. I was startled to
look at my watch and see that almost two hours had
passed. Clayton had checked my university text to see where
I was in it, and then we had gone over some of the relevant
grammar. He prompted responses from me in English and

I had to concentrate as hard as I could to speak correctly. Although there were only the two of us in the quiet room, I felt like there were a million noisy distractions about me. But his praise, encouraging without being effusive, kept me on the right track. By the end of the lesson I could hear myself speaking English more freely than I ever had before. It had simply become a conversation between friends.

"Do you ski?" I asked him after glancing at my watch.

"No, but I'd like to try one of these days," he said.

I invented an expedient lie: "I was planning on driving up to Monte Bondone tomorrow. If you'd like, we could go up together and I could teach you to ski. Or at least start." I had no idea how I would borrow my father's car for such a last-minute excursion — on Saturday no less.

"Thanks, but I have some writing I need to get done tomorrow. Next time though." And I could tell that he was genuinely pleased that I had asked him along. There would be a next time.

I had not been humiliated; still, I felt my spirits somehow dampened by his polite postponement. I wanted to ask him what he wrote, but said nothing for several seconds. Then the door bell rang.

"That will be Alessandro," he said, rising. He quickly gave me a writing assignment for the following week.

Alessandro and I met at the door of the apartment as Clayton was showing me out. I saw that Alessandro was surprised — unpleasantly, at that — to see that I was still there. I, in turn, looked upon him as an unnecessary interruption in what had been amiably unfolding into a delightful afternoon. We were civil to each other. Clayton made nothing of all this, though he couldn't have failed to notice it, and turned to bid me good-bye with that smile and cast to his gaze that made me dare to think that I was someone unique to him, someone of value.

The next few weeks spun by smoothly, if busily, for

me. Things at home settled down a bit and I was able to study in peace. Another class of swimming pupils descended upon me, and I resolved to buy Clayton a bottle of Martini with some of this money. I anxiously looked forward to my lessons with him, and did not sleep well on Thursday nights. I unconsciously began shifting my English to an American pronunciation. During the lessons I longed attentively for some. . . sign, a key veiled in the man's words and gestures to unlock the mysterious feelings inside *me*. Vainly, sifting his simple, unaffected tone for I knew not what, I was inevitably jarred to earth by the ring of the doorbell and the arrival of Alessandro, or sometimes Claudia and Alessandro. I was tempted to view these "crashers" with a shade of paranoia, as if Clayton might *want* to get rid of me, a goal attained with the carefully orchestrated collusion of his friends. I knew in fact, though, that I would not have been bothered with them at all if Clayton hadn't allowed our lessons to run over so late.

On the Friday I was bringing Clayton the bottle of Martini, I was again late to the lesson. It was February 19, 1971. I detected a strange uncertainty when he answered the intercom downstairs. I wondered what was wrong. Upstairs he opened the door, but didn't stand aside to usher me in.

"I think you better go home, Luca," he said, his face tensed with concern. "Your mother was just here looking for you. She was very upset. I couldn't understand her; she was all excited and talking too fast. Something's happened, but I don't know what. All I caught was *macchina, fiume,* and *padre.*"

Car. River. Father. I couldn't grasp any significance from these words and would have thought Clayton was joking if not for the pained expression on his face. It was that look of very real sympathy, more than the garbled message, that made me turn for the stairs. Suddenly I remembered the bottle in my hand and ran back to give it to Clayton. I gave him no explanation for it, but only told him I would speak to him later.

"I'm sorry," he called after me in a voice that apologized as much for a presentiment as for any incoherently relayed message.

I ran home, and when I found my mother sitting by the telephone weeping into her arms, I felt my worst fears confirmed. I was certain my father had had another stroke. But the first thing my mother asked me, hysterically, was if I'd seen my father. Fighting back my own tears, I asked what had happened. She grabbed me, pulled me into her arms and sank her head onto my shoulder. Between sobs she breathlessly related what had transpired that afternoon in my absence. And at last I began to cry, too.

I had not eaten lunch at home that day, but instead had had a pizza in town with some friends so that I would not then have to rush to the swimming pool. My mother had come home from her secretarial job in a real estate office as usual to fix lunch for my father and sister. As in much of Southern Europe, we have long breaks for the noon meal, and normally my mother had from twelve noon to three o'clock off. But that Friday my aunt was sick, so after preparing lunch for my father and Claudia, she had hurried off to her sister's to help with lunch there. She had intended to go straight back to the office from my aunt's, but she had forgotten some papers at our house and had to return home to fetch them.

At home she had found my father gone. When she asked Claudia his whereabouts, Claudia told her that she didn't know; that he had sent her on an errand to the post office and when she returned home he had not been there. Perhaps my mother would not have thought this so odd if she hadn't seen lying on the dresser in their bedroom his watch and his wallet, including his driver's license. The car, of course, was gone.

In the incipient panic my mother had demanded that Claudia go out looking for her father while she stayed at home and tried to track him down by phone. Claudia had enlisted the aid of a neighbor, and together they had driven about Trento seeking out some trace of our father. Eventually they found his car parked down by the Adige River, the driver's door open. They had phoned my mother only after thoroughly searching the area. Then, as Claudia and our neighbor proceeded to the police station to report my father's disappearance, my mother had run to Clayton's in hopes of catching me there, and maybe even my father.

One's first reaction in such a drastic situation is always, I think, incredulity. I simply could not believe that anything as horrible as we were all thinking could possibly have occurred. On the basis of the barest circumstantial evidence we were not about to lunge at the most cogent conclusion. Such a determination would have required an effort not cognitive, but visceral. Our minds — and our hearts — were not ready for the effort. We could not immediately know what had happened, definitely, and in that there was hope and, as the weeks were to draw on, a kind of terror.

I could not stop crying. I began to blame my mother for the emotion of the moment. If only she would calm down and compose herself, I thought, we could all sit down and reason the events out till a logical, less-than-tragic explanation presented itself — or until my father came home.

But what had merely caused hysteria in my mother produced in Claudia a devastation bleaker and more complete. Returning from the Questura that evening with a pair of detectives, she had me too scared to cry. Her face had already taken on a thin, haunted look which was to grow more dreadful in the coming weeks. Her voice was hoarse from crying and her eyes deathly blank. The detectives asked questions and went through my father's effects. Claudia would break down crying every few minutes. But her tears, unlike my mother's, seemed even then to tire her, as though every last drop of energy and emotion was flowing out of her into those tears.

When the detectives finally left with some photographs of my father, I think we all felt as if some hot, dry wind had just swept through our lives, scorching our sensibilities raw. And Claudia had lain most directly in its path. My mother lost years in the next weeks, but Claudia was to lose, at least temporarily, any hint of her youth — and, almost, any glimmer of life.

None of us slept that first night, and after a week had passed and neither my mother nor sister had slept more than a few minutes between them, they at last succumbed to a powerful sleeping prescription forced upon them by our doctor.

Our confusion was in the beginning a private matter. The first week we kept everybody away from the house. My mother did not go to work. She waited by the phone for some word, or else impulsively called the closest of her relatives and friends to talk — nervously, volubly, straining for the word or phrase that would vanquish her own jittery anxiety, for something to dispel the apprehension, magic somehow wielded by madness. Or she would call simply to cry. My sister stayed home from work too, and together they sustained the stifling atmosphere of doom that had with frightening suddenness enveloped our lives.

All of us continued to sleep poorly, my mother and Claudia only under the influence of pills. But after the first week friends and family began to come over, and the house seemed to have a tide of guests forever coming and going, bringing what sympathy or light they could to a home inhabited by the undead. We ate practically nothing, and again it was Claudia from whom anxiety exacted its heaviest toll. She ate little more than crumbs of bread in the course of two weeks. My mother and I became increasingly worried about the state of her health. She lost twenty pounds, and the gaunt, pale mask that had replaced her face floated listlessly through the house. It was like the apparition of a victim of some experiment in torture, upon whom the last cruelty had been the burning out of her eyes. . .to leave two grim, black holes.

Why Claudia was touched most deeply by the developing tragedy was, I think, due not only to her sensitive nature, but to the special relationship she felt with our father as well. As I have said, she was always clearly his favorite, and the extinguishing of an intimate and essential relationship, I have learned, is the sharpest wound that human beings ever suffer: thirst, hunger and sleep are feeble rivals in comparison. That my mother suffered brutally was also true, but next to Claudia she had displayed relative equanimity. It may be that her grief was tempered by maturity and experience, or perhaps even by some unspoken guilt. And maybe because of that guilt, she never participated in any of the later psychological speculation about my father's action.

It was a time, understandably, when the three of us drew closer together. What remained of our family became a tightly knit unit of three hearts in despair. The renewed feeling of kinship and affection was to mark all of our lives forever, as much as the loss we had so unexpectedly been dealt. Never again would there be any shyness in the confession *ti voglio bene, ti amo.*

In the meantime, religion and the Church to which we had all felt securely bound until then failed us miserably. Which is to say that it did not seem to mitigate in any way our anguish. We prayed around the clock, and any one of us could be found in church most any time of the day or night. But there was nothing soothing in all of this, nothing to alleviate our burdened hearts. Only unanswered prayers. The vivid, blatant silence of our God only added to our sorrow. For the faithful these trials might have been perceived as a test, but that season of bitterness had claimed too many sacrifices from us. Our faith was just one, its loss the least painful.

(My mother is still a member of the Church, and when I go back to Trento to visit her I take her to mass. Her one-time complacency, however, has been whetted to a finer, more cynical edge. She sees such last-ditch maneuvering in the details she and her fellow supplicants attend to. My sister and I have, without any formal renunciations, never remanded custody of our souls to the Church.)

The day my father's car had been found Alessandro and Stefano spent the night at the car, hoping that my father might have simply wandered off in some kind of absent-minded daze. He had not. The bottom of the river was dragged and my mother even paid for a special underwater camera on a rig that cruised the river looking for evidence of my father. None was found. We put notices with his photograph in the paper and on TV, asking for any information about him. From these ads we received several anonymous phone calls telling us that the man in question had been seen only yesterday in such-and-such piazza. But they were all cranks and nothing concrete ever came from the ads.

The phone calls were especially upsetting to Claudia, and it was around that time that Alessandro stepped in and, at least in those weeks, redeemed himself in my eyes. He was the one who persuaded her to go back to work. And being an English teacher himself, he would often make a point of conferring with her about school assignments and his students' homework. More than once he almost physically pulled her out of the house to go to the movies or on an outing to the mountains. Alessandro was her most constant companion in that period and was at our house every day. It couldn't have been easy for him. I remember in particular one day when he had stayed for lunch with the three of us. Claudia was by then at least nibbling at food on a regular basis. Things were going along well enough — we had even laughed — but then all at once a silence fell across the table. Without any warning, Alessandro was faced with three people sobbing over their plates.

Even more than Alessandro, however, the arrival on the scene of David, Claudia's English boyfriend, was to prove a boost to her wearied spirits. He had been in telephone contact with Claudia from the beginning, but he had not been able to get away from his studies until late March. His presence provided the most comforting consolation Claudia was ever to benefit from in her inconsolable bereavement. But after he had to return to England, she seemed struck anew by a double loss, as we all should have guessed would happen, and lapsed into bizarre fluctuations between crazy fits of tears (angrily crying, "Why! Why! Why!") and the incredible fantasy that our father would be returning soon. "I'll buy that for Papa," she would say in front of a shop window, with eerie calm. "I know he'll like it when he gets back."

I had to salvage what I could of my own life in those weeks. I had made myself go back to school before either my mother or sister had returned to work, perhaps stung by their pitiable examples. I tried to surround myself with old friends, in the desperate pretense that everything was as before. I went skiing with Marco and even began seeing my old girlfriend, Antonella. Once, after coming back late from the Waikiki Disco in Gardolo, where she had taken me in a futile attempt to cheer me up, she offered herself to me in the car. We were in my father's car and that is probably why I was at first disgusted. Only after a moment's reflection was I able to understand what she was doing. I refused her offer as graciously as I could.

At the end of the first week of my father's disappearance, as my mother, sister, and I were giving to the world our firmest intention of wrapping ourselves in a cocoon of self-destruction, Clayton had come to our house. It was three-thirty on a Friday afternoon. He told me I was later than usual for my English lesson.

I was appalled by his gross insensitivity and wailed pathetically at him, "Don't you know what's happened!"

"*Lo so*," he answered in Italian. I know. "Get your pen and notebook and come on."

I did, and followed him back to his place.

Upon recommencing, my English lessons with Clayton became, in a sense for the first time, only English lessons. My schoolboy infatuation with him had been suspended by graver concerns, and my time with him came to seem safely routine, automatic. . .careless. I had to be grateful though for whatever diversion I could wring from them. And if the student Clayton now found himself with was worse than the one before, he did not let on.

Entering his apartment on that Friday after our one missed lesson, I was puzzled to see the bottle of Martini still in its bag on his kitchen counter. "You left that here last time," he said.

When I explained that it was a gift in thanks for the lessons, he thanked me without any unnecessary words and put it in the refrigerator. Nothing more was said of it and we went on with the lesson.

Towards the end of my family's ordeal Clayton had asked me to write a composition in English on anything I felt like writing about. I composed a few lines about my father, thinking that writing what I felt for him in a foreign language would exorcise some of the pain I could not express in my own language. And, in fact, while writing the composition I felt perfectly lucid and under control. But when Clayton asked me to read it aloud during our lesson, I was not able to get through it without choking. I lowered my head, and as tears dropped onto the page I fumbled for the strength to go on. My vocal cords would not oblige me.

Clayton stood up and put a hand on my shoulder. "That's okay. We'll read it some other day." His hand rested on my shoulder until I had recovered somewhat. I got up to leave and he went with me to the door. Instead of saying goodbye he embraced me and whispered my name, "Luca . . ." I was crying again in his arms.

I did not weep long, but when Clayton at last pulled away from me there was a troubled, baffled look on his face. I couldn't understand how I could have fazed *him*. I thought maybe I had embarrassed him with my bawling. He smiled as warmly as ever, though, and said that he would see me the next Friday.

Occassionally Clayton would come to visit Claudia, or would accompany her and Alessandro out someplace. What solace he gave her I do not know. Certainly, the trio I had watched so jealously from my window had lost most of its flash and verve. Any joy that despair had not bled dry survived at all, I think, thanks only to the more desperate tenacity of endangered friendship.

Even the loyalty of friendship was taxed as time went on and the conjectures as to the fate of my father became wilder and more irresponsible, which they did with each passing week. Only Michela, with typical candor, persisted from the beginning with the notion that our father had killed himself. "He's dead," she had told Claudia, "and you just have to face facts." Suicide of course had been the readiest assumption all along. I do not mean here to summarize all the outrageous speculation that friends and family toyed with; I wish merely to suggest the liberties people were not afraid of taking in order to "help" us figure out what had happened. Not all of these ideas were stated to us directly, but we eventually heard each of them.

Crazy Uncle Ugo, my mother's brother-in-law, asserted that our father must have been kidnapped. The fact that no ransom note was ever received could not dissuade him from his theory. My cousin Marta thought he might have been the victim of some unspeakable crime, the perpetrators of this foul play being either gamblers my father was known to associate with, enemies he had made while working for the local justice division, or drug addicts. Marco was also sure that my father had killed himself, but the provocation for his act was supposed to have been some entangled plot involving a mistress who had rejected my father for another lover. Luciana's boyfriend, Paolo, was to have the last word on the question of suicide. He said that if our father had killed himself, only the three remaining members of the family would ever have any real inkling of why. We, meanwhile, knew nothing.

My mother finally turned to the supernatural in hopes of obtaining a definitive account of her husband's disappearance. She talked with mediums and clairvoyants over the phone, or sent them personal items of my father's by mail. She and Claudia even drove to Milan once to see a noted medium there, but with vacant faces came back as unsatisfied as when they had left. All the psychics were equally nebulous in their pronouncements. He was either dead or alive, usually dead, but no adequately precise or verifiable clue as to how or why was ever given. Invariably, however, each week brought us the name of a new psychic whom we just *had* to consult.

I was very skeptical about this dalliance with parapsychology, the more so because it had yielded no results. So it was with some reluctance that I joined my mother and sister on a trip to Venice to see yet another mystic.

Venice was shrouded in gloom that day, I remember, and the little room in which we were received by "Signora Buonocuore" was even drearier. La Signora herself was rather distinguished-looking, but the cramped, ill-lit *monolocale* was further depleted by the suffocating stench of a canal below. As usual, nothing was said that could not have been gleaned from newspaper reports. But I have never been able to forget the preternatural voice issuing from her mouth that answered her entranced call for Bruno Savelli, Signore Bruno Savelli: "I am walking into the water. It is cold. I am going deeper and deeper, walking. The water is over my head. It is cold."

Mercifully, a week later on April 11, Easter Sunday, my father's body was dredged from the Adige near Ala. It had clearly been in the water a very long time. I had insisted on going with my mother to identify him.

I do not know with what shred of willpower I was able to take my English exam before the funeral. It was a minor miracle when weighed against the fact that I had never felt so irresolute in all my life. That I passed seems the less remarkable accomplishment.

At the funeral, my father's body in the ground, Claudia had thrown herself on his grave and once more cried, "Why! Why! Why!" — until she had to be carried away by Stefano and Alessandro.

I was standing next to Clayton. "I think she'll be all right now," he said. "The long nightmare is over."

I knew he was right. The nightmare was over.

I kept close to Clayton the rest of the afternoon, as if to cool myself in the shade of some broad, life-giving tree. And when later at our home it came time for everyone to leave, it was Clayton I most regretted seeing leave. I was afraid of the empty, withering glare I would be left standing in. He kissed my mother and Claudia good night in the

Mediterranean style, on both cheeks. Claudia, steady now, was already looking healthier and stronger.

Clayton came to me and took my hand and started to kiss me in the same manner. I instinctively clasped him in my arms and he returned my hug. He tightened his hold. I did not want to let go. When finally we disengaged, he said to me, "You know, you don't have to take an English lesson to come and visit me."

I nodded and he left, smiling sadly. I then went to my room and cried one last time for my father.

III   Dante's Dream

There are those who will always say that Clayton was merely a father figure for me — as though that, even if it were the entire truth, could explain any relationship. And they will point to the timing of our friendship as indisputable proof of their hypothesis. Beyond the irrelevance of all this to the understanding of a personal relationship, I could argue that our ages had never seemed so disparate to us, or that his affection for me was never tainted by paternalism. But I do not feel it is necessary to defend myself, or Clayton, and I do not care to argue any particular viewpoint. Those who want to drown our feelings in a sea of analysis will go on doing as they choose regardless of what I say or write.

In the wake of my father's death my family had to contend with many problems, some emotional, some financial, but the nightmare was indeed over. How strange it seemed even then that death, tangible and capable of being buried, had come as a relief. My father's death had sliced through my callow youth with a neatness, and cruelty, inseparable from the indifference of the universe. What I experienced as a loss of immeasurable proportions, however, was in fact an expert cut by the forces of reality to implant something more lasting where my own complacency had been. The cut was healing, quickly; I was still young, still hopeful, still eager for new experiences. I did not let myself brood over my dead father or the question "Why?" But within me there had germinated a sense of life as something with an approaching, irrevocable end. Those things that must be had, had to be gotten *now*.

A few days after the funeral, after a morning class, I stopped by Clayton's and asked him out for a coffee. He was writing, but did not hesitate to grab his jacket and join me at a nearby bar. He told me it was a welcome break from a tiring morning. I asked him what he was writing and he told me he was working on a novel. (This was destined to be *Organ of Conceit*.) I could not understand what was so tiring about writing. He tried to impress upon me the energy and discipline, and sometimes the pure stamina, it took to get through another day of writing. The story lurched onward, at times, only out of his ability to heedlessly tell himself that it was the greatest artistic achievement since *The Brothers Karamazov*. But then imagination, however perverse, was the name of the game. The characters became like old friends, he said, whom he looked upon with a kind of weary patience. He secretly hoped, without hope, that they would perform some act of their own volition, preferably to finish the novel themselves and leave him to bask in the acclaim and honors. He laughed and said it was all really only a madness, a peculiarly literary malady, a fury of words in the mind that could only be dissipated with pen and paper — and hours of work. But what evidence, substantial and irrefutable, did he have to show for his work until he was published, which had yet to happen? He complained lightheartedly that he knew most of his friends in Trento, and even back in the States, were of the opinion that when he said he was writing, it was just another way of saying he was doing nothing. I'm afraid I was among that number, at the same time feeling, self-consciously, that I was taking Clayton away from something more important.

It was the first time Clayton had ever really talked about himself to me and he soon changed the subject. He asked me how I was doing and we talked about my family. He was glad to hear that things were getting back to some semblance of normality. As discreetly as possible he inquired about our money situation and I strove to sound responsible and concerned. My mother, in truth, was the one wrestling with that monster. I had no clear idea then, or for some time to come, how completely she had borne the brunt of its blows. I assured Clayton that we had money in the bank and that we would keep on receiving my father's reasonably comfortable pension. The fantastic debts incurred by my family in the previous two months went unmentioned.

In typical Italian fashion I had downed my cappuccino in two gulps. Clayton still sipped his. He apologized for being so slow. When he had done, he suddenly looked at his watch and, realizing it was lunch time, invited me to come back to his place for lunch. I let him know in a nonchalant, studied manner that I was expected at home for lunch, that I had work to do myself, that I was very busy.

"Of course," he said, disappointed. He did not politely extend the invitation a second time.

We parted at the bar and I immediately regretted not having gone with him. I was so angry with myself that I almost ran after him. But I was sure such childishness would have repelled Clayton; I would have appeared to him at once excessively flighty, and even stupid. So I went home and spent the afternoon thinking about him. I went over in my mind his expressions of that morning, everything I could remember him saying, and the way he said it. Again and again I visualized his face before me, telling me something without words, his eyes bright with interest.

Our formal English lessons had ended. I used this as an excuse in the following days to call on him. I needed to keep up my perfect English, I joked, and he always seemed happy to have me visit. Sometimes we went out to a bar, or had tea at his apartment, or just took a walk together. I scheduled my visits at what I thought were decent intervals, but even if I had weakened in my resolve not to make a nuisance of myself, there was always Claudia, or Stefano, or Michela, or more usually Alessandro, to tempt him away in his free time. I was of course annoyed with their demands upon his presence, but concealed from Clayton the selfish irritation brewing inside. Once or twice he had asked me to join him and the others, but I had become used to being the sole object of his attentions when I was with him and had no intention of sharing this privileged place with anyone.

Our morning coffee breaks together evolved into a regular thing, and eventually I was again asked to lunch at Clayton's. I accepted — promptly. He made messy cheeseburgers and mounds of fried potatoes, an authentic American meal we both relished with abandon. Although I cannot remember what we talked about, I know it all seemed to go by too fast. We laughed and relaxed with each other in a way I don't believe we had ever managed before. I suppose I am including his feelings with my own. Perhaps he had always felt at ease with me — except that one time at his door when he had hugged me. I know that *I* was beginning to feel for the first time like an intimate friend of his. The bigger-than-life persona that I had held in awe for so long was being supplanted by a real and appreciable person. More and more was casually revealed to me of his personality, qualities fresh and sensitive, which ultimately increased the esteem I had for him — and for myself, as his good friend.

I left his apartment the afternoon of our lunch together with the feeling, yet again, that something had ended prematurely. I knew he had to write, but my own needs started to press their urgency upon my heart. The time I spent with him was never enough.

I could not cease thinking of Clayton that spring, and my days seemed filled with the persistent echoes of his voice, with images of the man that would not fade. At night, especially, my thoughts were troubled by sentiments I had no means of untangling. I knew I wanted to be with him and that was all.

Meanwhile, in my home the general truce that affairs had reduced me and my sister to was broken. The signal that normality was finally being returned to after my father's suicide was surreptitiously received by us all with some gladness, but the divisiveness itself was also aggravated by his absence. In this I feel my mother was to blame mostly, though perhaps it is fair to excuse her under the circumstances. I was certainly only too ready to take advantage of her misjudgment, and can think today of my behavior then only with a deep shame. But I was little more than a boy; my mother should have foreseen the jeopardy into which she pushed our delicately balanced relationships. Yes, we had all grown much closer during the tragedy, but peril — averted, deferred, lusted after or inundated by grief — *is* life.

Because her favorite child was now also the only man in the house, my mother began to lavish upon me a care, and carelessness, of such extravagance as would not have been tolerated previously by the other members of our family. In that exquisite English phrase, she spoiled me rotten. She not only foolishly indulged my every whim, but also released me from any of my usual household duties that I found odious. And of course they were *all* beneath me. What Luca needed, what Luca wanted, what Luca said and did were never long from her own lips or thoughts. And while her slavish devotion to me welled imprudently, she and Claudia lapsed into their old quarrelsomeness with accelerating frequency.

In Italy we have a word for the exaggerated inter-relation of mother and son, and Claudia was not afraid to use this charge against me when she found herself washing dishes for the twenty-first time in a week: "Oh, by all means," she would yell sarcastically at my mother, "Luca can't be allowed to dirty his hands or raise a finger around here. No, Luca mustn't be bothered with anything so petty. He's too busy studying the finer points of *mammismo*!"

My mother could give as good as she got in these exchanges, which only worsened matters. Within weeks of my father's funeral vituperative discord once more became a staple of our family life, and with it well-traveled extremes for both my sister and mother: loud, bitter arguments, blood-curdling in their ferocity given the recent events of our household; crying jags, by one or the other; or, most terri-fying of all, angry silences between them that lasted days. I was blithely unalert to the deteriorating state of their rela-tionship, and only intervened if I was distracted to peevishness by their screeching — or by the unearthly quiet of the house. I would usually then attempt some tentative rapprochement with my sister with a kind word or some small gesture of affection. By then, though, my ministra-tions were without sufficient moral force to make for a lasting peace, and these early fights were merely the harb-inger of a belligerent estrangement, between me and my sister and between my sister and my mother, that would endure for months.

After dinner one evening I had rushed to leave the house while Claudia cleaned up. I asked my mother for the keys to the car and she started to hand them to me when Claudia began to protest that she had already been promised the use of the car that night. On a different evening I might have acquiesced, but that night I had a date with Marco and some friends to go to a concert in Rovereto. We hadn't bought the tickets yet, it was true, and I could have attended the same concert the next night. But I had seen so little of my friends lately (other than Clayton) that I felt compelled to grant some importance to the evening. I lied and told my mother and sister that we had already bought the tickets. Claudia could not argue with this, but because my mother had absently promised the car to both of us, she had an easy target for her frustration.

"*Porca puttana!*" she cried angrily. "Why don't you just *give* him the car, along with everything else!" (She was not calling my mother a "pig whore"; this expression, rather colorful in English, is an altogether pedestrian expletive in Italian.)

"Don't you speak to me like that!" my mother shouted back at her. "It's still your mother you're talking to!"

"I was under the impression you had only one offspring these days," was my sister's retort.

"I told you to watch your mouth!"

"I'm not a baby anymore — even if Luca is. I'm an adult and you've got to treat me like one if you want my respect."

"You're not too old to do what I say in *my* house."

"*Ma, scusa,* should I move out into the street? I'm sure at least I'd get a warmer welcome from strangers there than I do from my own family."

"Shut up!"

"*Porca puttana!*" Claudia cursed again. She ran to her room and slammed the door.

Neither one of them would apologize to the other

and a storm-beaten silence hovered in the house for many days. My guilt in this instance had me doing my best to placate both of them. I only succeeded, however, after forgoing my rights to the car for two weeks, and by giving my mother (in Claudia's presence) a lovingly stern, self-humbling and insincere lecture on the necessity of treating her two children equally.

If Claudia had any comment upon the time I was spending with Clayton, I was never privy to it. She must have known about these hours, although I was not the one to keep her apprised. Not being the jealous type, she would naturally not have dwelled on my time with him, as I did about the time she, Alessandro and the others spent with him. I may have worried that they all laughed about my worshipful attachment to him, but I cannot remember such feelings with any clarity. Only the memory of a certain look on Alessandro's face makes me think of them at all.

Clayton's own feelings seemed to me to become increasingly transparent as the weeks of spring progressed. I knew he liked me. I cannot explain, though, why the "like" of one person is so often worth much more than all the adoration of many others. That Clayton desired my company was always exciting to me. And vaguely surprising.

I even dared at last to visit him twice in one day, something I had up to then deemed too bold. As much as I thought about him, I had been able to control this urge. I had had lunch with him one afternoon and, as usual, had exited the building afterwards feeling oddly unsatisfied. That evening there was a party he was invited to with Claudia and Alessandro and the others, and so I was content, in my discontent, to know at least where he would be and with whom. But after dinner at home, just as she was getting ready to leave, Claudia told me that she had heard from Alessandro that Clayton had decided not to go after all. She didn't know why. She shrugged and went out the door, leaving me to ponder my own intentions. I sat in front of the television with my mother for several minutes before I worked up the courage to get up, put on my coat, and tell her I was going into town for a walk, maybe to see some friends.

"*Disturbo?*" I asked anxiously as Clayton opened his door to me.

"No, no, I was just reading," he said. And in fact he had that dopey expression on his face that people often get after reading for too many hours.

"English or Italian?" I asked.

"English, I'm afraid," he said smiling. "My mind isn't quite sharp enough at the moment for Italian." He offered me a Martini.

"Are you sure it's okay?" I asked again. "I heard from Claudia that you weren't going to the party. Maybe you'd rather not have guests?"

"You're not a guest, Luca," he said. "*Accomodati.*"

I took off my coat and relaxed, as well as I could anyway, on the old worn sofa in the living room. He brought me the drink, and one for himself as well. We saluted one another with our glasses.

"Why didn't you go?" I asked after taking a sip.

"I don't know, just didn't feel up to it," he said, leaning back into the opposite corner of the sofa. "To tell you the truth, it was Michela's invitation to a friend of hers: There were going to be a bunch of people there I hadn't met. I don't mind meeting new people, but . . . I had the feeling it was going to be one of those evenings when I would be paraded about as the 'American,' a novelty, an exotic bird. A rare import. But the novelty's worn off for me. I mean, I can't complain; I realize it's the main reason a lot of people have been so kind to me here, have treated me so special."

"I understand," I said, wondering if I had been one

of the culprits, and at the same time wanting to say out loud, No, no, not me, Clayton . . . .

"Of course, I do have real friends here. You, Alessandro, Claudia, but . . . ." He didn't finish, but looked into his glass as though he had said too much. His pensive face looked up at me and smiled. "Maybe you've caught me on a bad night."

A train rumbled by outside. Beyond his windows were the elevated tracks used exclusively by the Valsugana *locale* to Venice.

"Would you rather I go?" I asked.

"No, please stay." He looked at the disappearing train and said softly, "*Ciao*, Venezia!" And then he looked at me and smiled as if I really *did* understand. I took strength from that.

"Come on, Clayton," I said standing up restlessly and putting down my glass. "Let me buy you a drink someplace."

"But you've already paid for this one," he said, indicating the remaining vermouth in his glass. It took me a second to remember, and then we laughed.

I said, "In that case, I'll have another one, thank you. But I can get it," and started for the kitchen.

"No, I'll get it for you. You turn on the radio."

There was an ancient German radio that had come with the apartment. It sat in the living room, a huge, slickly polished wooden cabinet with dials and knobs and switches I could not begin to make out. I had seen it before of course, and heard it, but I had never been asked to touch it. When Clayton returned with the drinks, I was still trying to figure out how to turn it on.

"It's my favorite thing in the whole apartment," he said pushing a button. "It takes a moment to warm up, but the sound quality is incredible. It must have been made before the war."

I agreed. His eyes were again cheerful and confiding.

I playfully nudged his side and said, "You're really going to get fat and lazy sitting around drinking and reading and listening to music all the time." And then added, mischievously, "I forgot, that's right . . . and writing all day. Great exercise."

He took it well, laughed, and shoved me back saying, "And you, what's a skinny kid like you got to say about it?"

"Skinny?" I did not remember at once what this word meant, and when I did, I was only half-correct. I thought it also necessarily implied weakness. I put down my glass, bent down to grasp Clayton's legs below the knees, and started to lift him.

"Hey, what are you doing! Put me down!" For balance he was waving the hand that did not contain his glass. I placed him back after having raised him a few inches off the floor.

"You want a fight, do you?" he challenged me, putting the glass on top of the radio. "Okay, you'll get a fight, We'll just see who the lazy one is." And he grabbed me about the waist and would have thrown me to the floor if I hadn't braced my leg and pushed him off his balance. I was able to wrap an arm around his head while he readjusted his hold, but before I could apply any leverage he lifted me bodily off the floor and flung me around. When my feet touched the floor again, I broke from his grasp with an upward thrust. We attacked each other again, laughing, until we fell back onto the sofa in a single heap.

"All right, Mr. Smart Aleck," he said, pummeling me with mock punches.

"Mr. Smart Aleck?" I tried to ask through my convulsive laughter. He was on top of me trying to get his arms under me to lift me up and off the couch.

"Yeah, Mr. Smart Aleck, you think you're such

hot shit. Now we'll see who the brave one is." But he only laughed when he finally got his arms secured around me.

"Let me go!" I laughed, still struggling in his clutch. My height was no advantage on the sofa.

His face was above mine. Suddenly we both stopped laughing. Slowly, slowly, as I watched expectantly, he lowered his lips and kissed me. Our mouths opened, and passion, which I thought I had known before, entered my life for the first time.

Our wrestling holds were swiftly transformed into caresses, as his body pressed down warm and hard against my own. My legs wrapped around his and my arms groped for an embrace that would bring him closer to me. His mouth left mine and we stared into each other's eyes. He smiled, that smile that was forever telling me I was unique. . .the *one.*

"I've wanted you so much," he said. I lifted my head to take his lips again with mine. The words told me that my desire had not been one-sided. The kiss told me with what power he had been restraining himself.

"I. . .I. . . ." I started to murmur, but could not think what to say. His lips covered my face with kisses. As his mouth moved hungrily down my neck, his breath quickened. My own breathing was even heavier when I heard myself say, "Clayton. I love you."

He looked back into my eyes, not smiling this time. He seemed to be plumbing their depths for some corroboration, some secret story that only they could tell. We then kissed again, violently, until he whispered in my ear, "Let's get these clothes off."

We went to the bedroom. The open window that looked out upon the mountains was too high above the other buildings to require curtains. The bluish glow reflected from the mountains cast a cool light into the room. Clayton turned on the warmer light of the bedside lamp and we began to undress. I was never away from his side, nor my lips ever far from his, so I cannot quite imagine how we arranged this feat. But we were soon in bed together, naked, making love.

And here I must draw a kind of curtain that did not exist for us that night. Even in those days it was almost mandatory for famous writers and movie stars and government officials — i.e., virtually anyone in the public eye — to speak of their private sexual acts with an explicitness bordering on the clinical. So much more so today. But I cannot fulfill the anticipation — not out of any prudish modesty, though certainly I do not consider modesty in such matters a vice, nor because my memory fails me on these erotic details. On the contrary, my memory on the mechanics of our love-making is exceedingly accurate and precise. And herein lie my reservations.

I have tried to convey something of the magic Clayton brought into my life. The glory of our love was emotional and spiritual *and* physical. The electric excitement it stirred in our bodies would in a sense be derogated by trying to encapsulate it in a few graphically athletic descriptions. What he gave me, and what I know I gave him in return, was more powerful, more pleasurable, more climactic than mere orgasm. By stressing the overwhelming magnitude and symmetry of our attraction, I hope not to exclude any aspect of that relationship, least of all the physical — his touch would always set me on fire, regardless of who did what to whom, in which position.

Not unrelated to my attempt to preserve the *truth* of our intimacy is a psychological factor that may be purely personal. For me sex as such has never had a profound emotional resonance. I have enjoyed it, pursued it, languished for lack of it, but the *memory* of sexuality carries no significance for me beyond the erogenous clamor of my glands. Even with Clayton the moments of poignancy, of meaning, of love and arousal, are never remembered tied to an actual act of sex. Rather, in my reminiscences I am moved by a particular image of his face, by his inflection of a certain phrase, by a typical gesture of his. In the end his eyes more than his cock (as much fun as I had with it) were the real stimulation.

And perhaps for this reason I was never to feel divided or guilty about my love for Clayton. Whatever social complications we were to have later, even when instigated by my own duplicity, I never felt capable of denying our physical and emotional bonds. I might have fretted from time to time about what my mother or someone like Marco would say if they saw me making love to a man (I would be dishonest in omitting these qualms), but my heart never wavered in its dedication to the man who would change my life forever. I did not then try to sort into categories or classifications all that I was feeling. I did not, for instance, feel I had stopped liking girls. What I felt was that I had met someone, a man, whose very presence made me feel loved; whose touch and look ignited overpowering desires in me; whose body and soul I wanted to clasp to my own. I loved him.

None of these meditations, of course, was in my mind that night. My senses were being flooded by new experiences, new sensations. I surprised myself a little by the degree to which I submitted to passion in endeavoring to sate it. I took everything Clayton gave me and craved for more. Passion itself was never consumed, only our own mortal energies.

We lay in bed after a while, silent, and it came to me with a thrill that I had never lain totally naked with anyone before. Clayton's body, warm and moist, enclosed me in security. I settled into his arms. He finally spoke, softly, in Italian, to ask me how I felt. I didn't have to answer. He smiled. I kissed him and ran my hand down his back and over the firm, round buttocks. He told me in Italian that I made him very happy, that I was beautiful, that I was everything that he had ever wanted. *Ti voglio.* I nestled my lips against his ear and whispered again, "I love you, Clayton." We kissed.

He got up to go to the bathroom and for the first time I saw his naked body as a whole. I was startled to see how perfect he was. While making love I had hardly been conscious of the beauty of his physique or its well-defined muscles and finely proportioned form. What I had taken to be simply "bulk" under his clothes was exposed in the low light of the bedroom to be hard and smooth, a classic build of baroquely developed and toned musculature. All of a sudden I was intimidated by the man I had made love to. His body, once examined more fully, provoked in me a new sense of awe. (It was not to take me long, however, to learn to appreciate and hunger for it in all its wondrous perfection.)

While he was in the bathroom I began to think of my own body. I was *not* "skinny". I had a slim, broad-shouldered, swimmer's build. What had not been kept tight and strong by swimming or *calcio* or skiing, I had taken care of at the gym. But next to Clayton I felt like the proverbial ninety-pound weakling. I vowed to start working out at the gym more regularly.

As Clayton crawled back into bed with me, I made some stammering remark about his beauty.

"You call this good shape?" he said, amused. "I really am on the verge of getting a little flabby. But I haven't been able to afford to go to a gym here. I've tried to keep up with calisthenics, but I know when I get back to the gym in San Francisco, my body's going to be screaming for mercy." And, then, as if reading my thoughts, he said. "You're not as skinny as I thought though. You're beautiful, Luca. Really."

And to emphasize this sentiment he clambered back on top of me and ground his hips into mine. "Your thighs alone were worth coming to Italy for," he smiled. We rubbed our erections together and kissed. He said, "The strange thing is, you're not really even my type. I mean, I don't normally find myself attracted to tall, slender blonds — even when they're as good-looking as you. I usually prefer my men a little darker and more compact."

I told him about my reaction the first time I saw him, and how stunned I had been by his height. We laughed. He told me how he had fought against falling in love with me. As handsome and sexy as he had found me, he felt he had almost succeeded in erasing from his mind his sexual attraction to me. Then I understood what that look on his face had meant the day I had cried in his arms. I told him he had made me practically sick with longing. And we talked and laughed about all our missed opportunities and misunderstood cues.

We made love again and afterwards I thought: If I must die, let it be now, in his arms.

It was almost eleven o'clock by then. Clayton asked me if I shouldn't call my mother.

"To tell her what?" I innocently asked.

"That you're spending the night with me," he said in what I thought was a half-serious tone.

"It's not the first time I've come in late," I said, smiling.

"But what if you come in *very* late?" He pulled me closer to him.

I hadn't thought of this. How long did I intend to stay? I felt like I never wanted to leave that bed. "Oh, well," I said, "she has to go to work early in the morning and I have no classes, so if she doesn't see me till lunch tomorrow, she won't think anything's wrong. There's no reason for her to check and see if I'm in my room."

"I just don't want her to worry about you."

"Anyway, she's probably asleep now. Like I said, it will have not been the first time I've come home late." I was elated to have gotten a negative future perfect verb right. "Besides, how can I tell her I've spended the night in another house five minutes away?"

He said nothing. Presently he offered me something to drink. I requested a glass of water. He started to get up to get it.

"I know!" he exclaimed as he sat back down on the side of the bed. "Let's have a hot chocolate with Amaretto."

"*Che schifo!*" It sounded disgusting to me.

"Come on," he said, pulling the covers off me, "get up and help me make it, lazybones."

As the apartment was a bit chilly, he put on a T-shirt and his pants. He threw me a T-shirt of his and I reluctantly got up and pulled on my pants. I was cozy in bed, but I didn't want to be away from him. Wherever he was, I wanted to be there next to him. When I stopped in the bathroom to piss, he stopped with me and enthusiastically reeled off the savory virtues of the treat before us: the dark, rich chocolate, the sweet, almondy liqueur. I nodded skeptically. Then as I finished, shaking my penis slightly, he interrupted himself in midsentence and commenced rhapsodizing about how sexy I looked. In the kitchen we couldn't keep our hands off each other. We turned off the heating milk and went back into bed.

"You're a very horny young man," he said afterwards. He had to explain the word "horny" to me.

"You're not doing so bad yourself," I said with, I hoped, an appealing leer.

"Well, I don't want you to think it has anything to do with you," he teased. "It's just that I've been deprived here in Trento for so long." He grabbed me and kissed me and wrapped my hand around his penis and testicles. "Everything I have is yours," he said, this time in total seriousness.

We lay resting quietly for many minutes, Clayton moving his fingertips sensually over my abdomen. "Have you done this before?" he asked.

"What?"

"Had sex with a man."

"No," I lied, partly, and added instantly, "but of course I've had girls. I've fucked plenty of times." And felt immediately ashamed for having sought to flaunt my masculinity.

"You didn't even play around with the other boys when you were a kid?"

"No." The lie was more complete now. I was flustered. "Oh, maybe. . . ."

"Anyway," he said, skipping over my evasiveness, "you go to it with a good deal of gusto."

"And you?" I asked after a pause.

"Well, girls a long, long time ago. Young men I haven't as yet been able to give up."

"Have you had many?" I ventured shyly.

"Enough to know something special when I come across it." He reached down with his tongue and licked one of my nipples, as if the impulse had preempted any thought in his head. And then he kissed me. I fondled his penis as he lay back against the pillow and held me in his arms.

"I like it," I said. I meant the sex.

"Yes, I know." he grinned. "Italians all love *cazzo*. Crazy for *cazzo*. *Cazzo* this and *cazzo* that. *Che cazzo vuoi*?" he demanded ironically.

He was referring to the propensity in the Italian language to overuse the word for "cock" in the same way that Americans overuse the word "fuck": *Che cazzo vuoi! Che cazzo dici! Non capisci un cazzo!* What the fuck do you want! What the fuck are you saying! You don't understand a fucking thing! As I have noted, the vulgar elements of a language are always easily learned and well remembered; the motivation to learn dirty words is so earnest. Clayton had already done quite well.

I tried to explain that *cazzo* doesn't really mean "cock" when it's used in this way. *Che cazzo vuoi?* doesn't mean, "What cock do you want?" Clayton explained that "fuck" didn't mean "fuck" either in a sentence like, "What the fuck are you doing?"

"But, of course," I went on, "you can't ever translate these expressions literally. Look at the French word *merde.* It's not as strong as the Italian *merda,* and nowhere near as obscene as the English 'shit.' More like golly, gee whiz, gosh."

"Oh, that I know very well," he said, keenly interested in the subject now. "For instance, I will never understand your expression *Porco Dio.* Alessandro says it's the filthiest, most objectional phrase in the whole language. But in English it only means 'Pig God.' A mild blasphemy, maybe, but nothing like mother-fucker."

Again I tried to make him understand that *porco* doesn't simply mean "pig." It might more properly be compared to the British curse word "bloody," or even the more general oath "damn." *Porco cane, porco puttana,* and even *porco* by itself, carry with them an emotion that cannot be automatically transferred to another language. The obscenity *Porco Dio,* in particular, has a harshness that has always offended me. Even now that I claim, in good conscience, no religion, its severity as a figure of speech is powerful to me. I was perturbed that Clayton wouldn't just accept its force and leave it at that.

"Are you a devout Catholic?" he asked.

"No, not at all," I answered in my hard-earned, and bruised, apostasy.

"Do you believe in God?" he continued.

"I don't know," I muttered. There was nothing appetizing to me in this line of investigation.

"Well," he said, "if you're not sure about God, how can a blasphemy like *Porco Dio* affect you? It can't, unless subconsciously you still really do cling to the idea of some omniscient, avenging Lord of the Universe. You have to believe in the Wizard to believe in the power of his mumbo jumbo."

"And you? What are you?" I snapped defensively. Maybe I also wanted to say, *Non capisci un cazzo!*

"I'm agnostic. I know nothing. Oh, look here, Luca, don't get upset with me," he said soothingly. "I just don't understand how all these people who say they aren't Christians can be offended by the 'Pig God.' "

I had no, or few, intellectual pretensions at that time, and for me the conversation had taken a decidedly unromantic turn. I did not want to — nor did I know how to — articulately rationalize my criticism. I mumbled something about it all being hypocrisy and suggested that we have that hot chocolate after all. Amaretto and all, it was beginning to seem a better, albeit unpleasing, alternative.

He gently mussed my hair and kissed my forehead. All at once I was madly in love again. They say we Italians are an impetuous, volatile lot. Maybe they're right.

We had our hot chocolate — which, as it happened, I liked with the Amaretto — and talked late into the night. We spoke of so many different things. I talked of my childhood in Trento. Clayton told me about his life in San Francisco and informed me that he had made it his home for many years after moving there from Louisiana, where he was born. He had then worked as a waiter in order to save the money to come to Italy and write. This shocked me somewhat, but he said that after working in offices and banks and shops (a mobility unusually common to Americans), he discovered working in restaurants paid him the most money. He didn't like it, but then he laughed and said he didn't really like writing either. It was only the irreplaceable satisfaction of creation that redeemed the boring drudge work.

The light of dawn appeared in the east. The mountains more than ever resembled a silhouette of the sleeping giant Dante. We lay in bed looking out the window. Clayton was lying behind me, my back to him, my body cupped in his. The chatter of birds crescendoed as the brightening sky darkened Dante. A blue-white mist hung below the crags of his face, seeming to enshroud the sleeper.

"You see," Clayton said, "Dante's sleeping. This is all his dream. The world's a phantasmagoria — illusions and phantoms, and the hallucinations of those phantoms. All Dante's fantasy. We are only creatures of an enchantment."

But was the dream Paradise? Or Hell? Or Purgatory? There was no question in our minds or hearts that morning. He kissed me and lay his cheek on mine.

"But who knows the answer for sure," he said drowsily. "The only meaningful dreams are the ones that keep you guessing."

And the meaning?

"To keep the dreamer asleep."

We at last fell asleep to dream our own dreams. I was only dimly, happily conscious from time to time of Clayton's hand moving from my stomach to my chest, or back to my stomach, to draw me closer to him.

IV   The Kiss

About an hour later my mother did in fact have cause to look into my empty bedroom. Marco had called early to see if I wanted to join him, Antonella and Cinzia for a day at Lake Garda. This telephone call not only disclosed the fact that I had not spent the night at home, but also intercepted what would have been my most plausible alibi. I could not now very well tell her that I had spent the night at Marco's.

My mother had gone to bed early the night before, and so was unaware, as I knew she would be, of my failure to return home. I had never spent the night away from home without advising her first. She was perhaps justified, therefore, in overreacting to my absence. After the phone call she was distraught to the point of tears, and debated whether to go to work or call in sick and hunt down her missing son. Claudia persuaded her to go to the office, promising to call her the second I came in. In the meantime she would call some of my friends to find out where

I was. Even if he had had a telephone, I don't think she would have ever thought to call Clayton.

All of this was unbeknownst to me of course. After a few hours sleep Clayton and I awoke and made love again. Then I hurried to make it home by lunchtime. I asked him if I could come and see him again that afternoon. He looked at me inquisitively, then smiled and told me I was lucky he was letting me leave for a couple of hours to cover myself at home. I kissed him and he patted my butt as I went out the door. Before he closed it I pivoted around and asked, "Would you have charged me for the English lessons if I weren't. . . . ." and trailed off into an ellipsis.

"Beautiful?" he filled in. His look was both impatient and loving. "*Senti*, Luca, I meant what I said. You were my friend even before I fell in love with you." I shuddered, agreeably, to hear him say it. More lightheartedly, he asked as an afterthought, "Do you play tennis?" I did. And the weather was just turning fine enough to begin playing again. "Good. Bring your racket when you come back and we'll go out to the courts."

Fortunately I reached home just before my mother. Once having rebuked me for the worry I had thoughtlessly caused, Claudia warned me that Marco had called that morning. So when my mother came in I told her I had stayed at Roberto's house because it had been so late. His family lived on the other side of Trento and had no access to a car. I was to realize only later what an ally Claudia was for me. She did not contradict me, though after my mother left again for work she informed me, without elaboration, that Roberto had been one of the friends she had telephoned that morning. She never pressed me on my true whereabouts.

My mother had naturally been irate. It was the kind of grateful anger that often follows the summoning, and dissolution, of one's worst fears, as a hot gust of wind often follows a stifling, expectant stillness. She made me promise to call her next time, even if I woke her. But when she yelled that I had no business sleeping anyplace in Trento but my own bed — unless I meant to take up residence with the drug addicts off Piazza Duomo — I testily replied, "Okay, if you want to keep an eye on me the entire twenty-four hours, every day, you're going to have to pay the price. You'll have to watch *everything* I do — and what you don't see yourself I'll tell you about. I'll tell you *everything!*"

This made her stop and think. Not even she supposed that a young man's private life was a book to be meticulously read by his mother. That might prove too embarrassing an experiment for anyone's mother. In retrospect, I would have been glad if my mother's angry possessiveness had been the only problem Clayton and I were to face.

Clayton and I played tennis that afternoon. It was a difficult game for me. I was continuously distracted by Clayton's body, though *his* concentration on the game was relentless. Nor did his play seem affected by the minimal amount of sleep we'd had. His muscular legs flexed in the sunlight was arresting sensuousness, and the curve of his twisting torso or tightened buttocks excited me immodestly. Since there were other people on the courts, several times I had to turn away from the net and walk very slowly to the base line to try to discourage a hard-on. Only a day before, such "trigger-happiness" with Clayton would have bewildered me.

I played very badly. Neither of us let the poor match deflate our high spirits. The two sets his, Clayton casually draped his arm over my shoulder and we walked back to his apartment side by side.

Back at Clayton's we took care of the things that had to be taken care of, then showered separately. Clayton went first as I watched. Little did I suspect that I was about to witness what remains for me one of the funniest rituals I have ever seen. There was no shower, in the American sense, in the bathroom. The European designers had provided a large, modern bathtub, and on the wall about a foot above the side of the tub hung a metal hose with a shower head. No shower curtain or partition to protect the rest of the bathroom was thought necessary. One could either take a bath or hold the hose and carefully shower oneself while standing in the tub, or employ some combination of these two methods.

Clayton grabbed the shower head and got under way with a vigorous, frenzied exuberance that sprayed water all over the bathroom. It was like watching a horse splash wildly about in a fountain. I finally had to step outside to keep myself from getting drenched. He apologized but said he had never gotten the hang of the system.

When I went back in, the bathroom tiles, even in the far corner, were dripping. The floor was a lake. I then proceeded to show Clayton how one could take a shower and *not* hose down the bathroom. But throughout his stay in Trento he persisted in taking these ebullient showers that required two towels to mop up after. Nor could I ever get him to use the bidet for genital hygiene. He preferred to go all the way and take a shower. For him the bidet was merely a convenience for washing out his clothes.

Spring that year was colored with a bright, new happiness for me. Everything seemed to shimmer warmly in the vibrant breeze Clayton had brought with him. His enthusiasm for anything previously untried was inspiration for me. I taught him how to windsurf on Lake Garda. When we heard that there was a late snow in the Dolomites, we went up to Val Gardena and I gave him his first ski lesson. We went to a beach on the Adriatic and raced in the cold waters offshore. In Venice we lost ourselves with carefree adventure in *calle* after *calle*, until coming into a small, empty *piazzale* Clayton would pull me back into the shadow of a wall and kiss me. And in his apartment in the evening, where I always lingered even if I did not stay the whole night, we were both eager to express our love with fresh, unbridled passion.

And from his centered vitality and independence I drew strength, strength that was to sustain me even when I pitted it against his own will.

All the while, Clayton stumbled merrily through our language. His efforts were a self-replenishing source of entertainment, sometimes to his chagrin, more often to his own amusement. Invited to dinner at my aunt's once, he listened appreciatively to an Italian folk song she sang in the kitchen, and then turned to my cousin Marta and instead of saying, "What a beautiful song," (*Che bella canzone!*), he declared rapturously, "*Che bella cazzone!*" What a beautiful big dick! He was immediately embarrassed, though everyone quickly, and stealthily, brushed aside any notice of his gaffe. He and I had sneaked boyish smirks across the table. He would also often mistake (I wondered sometimes if it were deliberate) the words *pochino* and *bocchino.* Which is to confuse "very little" with "blow-job". And in English, he came to habitually curse, "Oh, Pig God!"

Of the humorous contretemps occasioned by his partial knowledge of Italian, I remember specifically one morning when I had stayed over. I still lay in bed while Clayton stood naked at the window (its height preserving all public propriety to anyone below). He was looking out onto the beautifully clear May morning, or, more precisely, he had gone to the window to see what was making the grinding noise that had awakened us. It had turned out to be some workmen with a motorized basket crane tending to repairs on the roof of the building opposite.

Now it so happened that there was an empty apartment on the top floor of that building, and on one of its windowsills there had lain, for three months, a dead pigeon.

The body of the pigeon had first been spied by us during one of my English lessons, as Clayton was teaching me "Expressions of Encouragement". From that time on the dead bird had become associated for us with the phrase "look on the bright side," and any bad news might be greeted by one or the other of us with a glance out the window and an exclamation of, "Look on the bright side!"

This morning Clayton determined once and for all to get rid of the rotting bird. He began shouting to the men in broken Italian to please, please take my dead bird away; knock it out of the window; it's been dead for three months; it's a nice bird, yes, but it's dead, so let's clean it away; take my bird, please! When the workmen would not stop laughing, and I too was laughing, Clayton was suddenly reminded that the word for bird, *uccello,* is also common slang for "cock."

(Later we would actually see other pigeons "courting" the dead bird, doing their mating dance about the corpse as though she were only being slyly coquettish.)

In the course of our burgeoning love affair Clayton's writing suffered tremendously. Under my auspices, he would neglect his work for days at a time. I too had been derelict in my studies, but for Clayton it was a different matter. I admit that his writing had never constituted one of the romantic components of the otherwise dashing figure I had come to admire in so many ways, nor did writing seem an important human enterprise in itself — my own ambitions lying elsewhere at the time. Writing was obviously not profitable enough to be really noble. It did, nevertheless, retain some air of mystery. Even in my youthful selfishness I began to fret about the hours I was "robbing" from him, if only in dread of the blame that might later fall on my shoulders. Clayton assured me that I was more vital to him and that the work would be returned to in good time. He knew his mind with singular grace. He did need me, as I needed him. The truth was plainer with each day. But he also began to steal back some of the hours I had hoarded. He was clever enough to make it seem like I was giving them back.

One day, having allowed the demonic possession that writing seemed for Clayton to reclaim him, I arrived late at his apartment to find him in an exceptionally good mood. I at once congratulated myself for having seen fit to sacrifice our being together for the sake of his writing. When I asked how the day had gone, he chipperly replied, "Oh, the typical day of a great artist: writing brilliant literature and washing out my underwear."

He laughed, but I saw another chance to do something for him. "Why do you waste your time doing your clothes by hand?" I asked. "My mother will be happy to do them for you."

Clayton had long been discomfited by the nuisance of hand laundry; his joke aside, seldom did toiling over a bidet full of dirty clothes impinge upon his time with anything like mirth. Public coin-operated washing machines, a rare thing in any part of Italy, were nonexistent in Trento. I had seen "laundromats" in England during a family stay there, but in Italy a washing machine is an indispensable appliance to every individual family (because there were no alternatives — a "catch-22" Clayton called it), and it was always one of the first purchases a young married couple made. Single people had to do their wash by hand — or, more usually, took it home to their mothers.

I was surprised to see Clayton receive this friendly suggestion irritably. What I felt had been an act of generosity he viewed as a less than generous assault upon my mother.

"Luca," he said with soft-spoken vehemence, "I don't expect you to help me with my laundry. I'm a big boy. And don't propose making more work for your mother in my name."

We dropped the subject, but the dispute over "letting" my mother do things for *us* was not to be terminated so summarily. It would crop up again.

Despite Clayton's gradual return to work on his novel, we were still together much of the time. My mother was distressed to see me spend so many nights at "friends." Upon catching me reenter the house after having barely seen me in the preceding days, she might acerbically ask, "Oh, did you remember you had a family?" If she pressured me more purposefully as to where I was spending all my time, I would vaguely answer, "I've been out with Marco," or "I went to see Antonella," or even, "I was visiting Clayton." Sometimes I stretched my time at home as much as I could, trying to make it seem longer and fuller than it was, knowing that I intended to gorge the next few days with Clayton.

On the other hand, my absences from home ameliorated the general atmosphere between my mother and sister, and between my sister and me. Our bickering, for a change, was only that. The tensions did not entail the kind of prolonged suppression that whipped up real storms. None of us had time. I thought it was because of this welcome respite from contention that Claudia did not display much interest in my activities. I assumed that she was simply glad to have me out of the house. I could not imagine that even she, being a close friend of his too, knew how much of my time I was bestowing upon Clayton. Meanwhile, another sort of rivalry was simmering between us. Or so I was inclined to think.

There was one set of days during which I had seen little of Clayton. For different reasons, mine familial (I had to go to Folgaria for a family celebration, among other things), his personal (including a book-shopping errand to Venice with Alessandro), we had not even had time together for a *sveltino,* a "quickie". My body seemed to ache sometimes when I couldn't be with him.

Finally I was able to get away from my home one afternoon, telling my mother I was going to see Clayton. She had called after me, somewhat petulantly, "Don't you think maybe you're starting to pester the poor man!"

Perhaps because of that sour note, I arrived at Clayton's already mildly piqued. I found Clayton trying to make tea after a morning of writing. But he was having trouble lighting the stove. The matches either wouldn't strike, or kept breaking. I was, as I had learned to say, horny, and thus without the patience for any nonsense.

"How come you Italians," he breathed crankily, "can't even make goddam matches that work?"

"What do you mean!" I declared hotly. "You think you Americans are the only one who know how to do anything! You think you're all such —"

"Hot shit?" he finished for me with sarcastic pedantry. This was too much. That he was attempting to perfect my English at such a time! But before I could let loose with a string of Italian epithets, he added, "And speaking of which, why can't you make a decent toilet? The shit doesn't even hit the water — it just goes sliding down the porcelain. And the shower! Let's not even talk about the shower! Let's face it, you're not the most modern nation on the face of the earth." And then with utter disgust, "Not even fucking matches."

I furiously took the box of matches and struck a match. It lit the first time.

"There, Mr. American," I said triumphantly. "And, yes, we have blenders, food processors, hair dryers *and* modern plumbing. Maybe you have us confused with those backward Sicilian dwarfs of the American Mafia. Or would you prefer to discuss *fashion*, which Italians are famous for, and which Americans don't know the first thing about. Nothing but blue jeans and plaid flannel shirts — even for *girls*!"

"Fashion?" he snorted. "Who gives a *cazzo* for

fashion — who but a bunch of people who have nothing better to do than sit around for three hours in the afternoon while everything shuts up tighter than a drum and eat pasta. Pasta! Pasta! *Basta!* I've had so much goddam pasta I could puke.''

Unable to control myself any longer, I launched into a volley of perjorative Italian, followed by a detailed oration on the shortcomings of one Clayton Hayes (''You weren't too good for pasta when you came here. You swore Italian food was the best in the world!''), in Italian also, and finally, when he tried to interrupt me in English, I hollered, *"Quest'é il mio paese. Nel mio paese parliamo italiano!"* This is my country. In my country we speak Italian.

"Va bene," he retorted. *"Vaffanculo."*

I was stunned into silence. Maybe Americans are an impetuous and volatile lot, too. But then I don't think he would have said ''Fuck you!'' to me in English. As it had been for him with *Porco Dio*, it was so easy to say things in a language one did not *feel* in. (Later I would hear myself matter-of-factly state the most incredibly blunt things, and only because I was saying them in English, which was not the language of my heart.) All of a sudden I felt a terrible pain inside of me. An icy chill gripped my chest where only a moment before there had been a raging furnace.

Clayton saw the damage he had done, we had both done, instantly. He took me in his arms and murmured words of regret, sorrowful words that I too felt. He kissed me and said, ''Oh, Pig God, I'm such a fucking idiot sometimes.'' I embraced him desperately and begged my own forgiveness. Fault was consecrated, and meekly petitioned by both of us. We vowed, in the solemn tone of two grown men who should have known better, never to fight like that again. A vow, too, which we should have known the value of then.

We made love, a deeply satisfying release for both

of us. Recklessness had elicited from us a greater care. And the sighs in each other's arms were the seal on that commitment.

   ·   I confess this quarrel seems comical to me today. I even think Clayton fixed us a marvelous tortellini dish with cream and bacon for dinner that evening. With hindsight I see a thousand little ironies in all this maneuvering, typical of the jockeying in the early stages of an intense bondship. May, indeed, was a month when our relationship continued on a relatively smooth and even course, albeit increasingly complex. We were still, after all, only "newlyweds," and love was still as improbable and delicious as dew. There would be time later to solidify and consolidate what we had staked out. Love *is* as effortlessly resolved as a dew, but its establishment into something lasting is *work* — as impossible, it seems at times, as preventing the blinding heat of the sun's rays from evaporating those dew drops.

   The end of May ushered in changes. As so often happens, troubles had been assembling in the wings only to make their dramatic debut all at once. The menacing spectacle that threatened hourly to make its appearance was inaugurated finally by a note from one of my professors. "Signor Savelli," it read, "is it possible that you have forgotten the paper due last week?" I of course had. It was not a difficult assignment to make up, one of the reasons I had left it undone so late, and the professor, being so kind as to jar my memory, was also kind enough to give me some extra time in which to submit my paper. But it was clear then that I would have to buckle down if I were to conclude the term respectably. I did not want my summer fettered by anxieties over school. To avoid this I would have to take more time away from Clayton.

   The two things that Clayton did *not* neglect then, to my consternation, were his friendships with Alessandro and Claudia. Although he saw less of them, he refused to deny them time altogether, and after a honeymoonish period of relative exclusivity with me, he began to reassert those friendships. Upon arriving at his apartment, intent on spending the afternoon with him, I might be told offhandedly that he had a dinner date with Alessandro, or that he and Claudia were going to a play together, or that he was just going out drinking with both of them later.

I had originally turned down invitations to their get-togethers as a matter of selfish pride. Then Clayton stopped asking me along at all. I began to read all kinds of ulterior motives into his keeping me apart from them. Soon resentment burned through me every time I was informed of one of these engagements. At that point I would not have joined them if Clayton had begged me. He never did. I never harangued him, but I did strive to make it obvious with my sullen silences that it was time for him to choose: It was me or them.

I don't know which of them I was more jealous of, Claudia or Alessandro. My sister, as my sister, was already under something of a competitive cloud. And though she could not know (I was sure) how completely Clayton and I had consummated our friendship, I was prepared to think that there was a conscious attempt on her part to undo our romantic liaison — maybe out of her own jealousy. I could not understand how Clayton could elect to be with Claudia, as nice as she was, over me, whom he was so obviously in love with. Alessandro, who was twenty-seven at that time and tall and very handsome, presented even further cause for alarm. There had always been a modicum of animosity in our feelings for each other, but whenever I saw him now he seemed especially cool towards me. I started to view him as my most dangerous rival.

One day after tennis I had asked Clayton, in passing as it were, if he and Alessandro had once been lovers. He had laughed and said, "But he's straight."

He had had to explain "straight," in all its sundry meanings, to me. My suspicions were still not allayed. I, too, had enjoyed sex with girls.

Whenever I was obliged to be with Clayton and Claudia or Alessandro, or anyone else, I was always circumspect in keeping my gaze off Clayton, as though I might be radiating some lethal ray from my forehead, in order to mute any sensual physical field we were unconsciously generating. I spoke to him in an even, modulated tone and never touched him. My presence in such cases was brief, aloof, and probably ludicrous.

My jaundiced opinion of Clayton's friendships may be incomprehensible, or just too juvenile, for the more mature reader. But I can even now vividly recall the pain, emotional and physical, which seemed to overtake me when I was away from Clayton for very long. At the bottom of my foolishness was desire. It must be remembered that I *was* very young and truly in love for the first time in my life. In my defense, no love has since measured up to it in any way.

Clayton himself was beginning to exhibit a growing irascibility then. Looking back I see it may have been my own haughty and erratic poutiness that was contributing to his ill temper. I never considered at the time that his grievances might be accumulating as feverishly as my own. The next eruption, however, unlike the argument initiated by the matches, was not directed at me and in fact redounded to my benefit.

He had had a date to go to a movie with some friends he had not socialized with for a while, among them Michela, Luciana, and Paolo. Plans for the evening out had been going on for a week, with a new crisis popping up each day. There had been repeated changes in people's schedules, necessitating changes in the time and date of the rendez-vous at the movie theater — or else some element of interpersonal politics to be cautiously navigated, or an individual whim to be catered to. Clayton often claimed that going out with a group of Italians was a major ordeal requiring the services of a professional social director.

The evening finally arrived. Paolo and Michela came to pick him up, but instead of hurrying out the door — they were late, as usual — they sat Clayton down and advised him that Luciana could not make it that evening; they should reschedule it for another night.

"All this mess for a fucking movie?" he had angrily asked. In spite of their contrite entreaties, he could not then even be prevailed upon to attend the movie at once as originally planned. He was fed up. He told them he was busy, had better things to do, and then "politely" asked them to leave.

This act of throwing two friends out of his apartment became a local scandal for a few weeks. In truth, it only polished the luster of his legend as "the American," a free soul daring even to be rude. He eventually made his peace with Paolo and Michela, but for me the immediate advantage was that I ended up spending the night with him. He had gone out and called me from a public telephone as soon as Paolo and Michela had left. I got to his place as quickly as I could, only to discover how black his mood really was. But even his bad company, however dismal, was precious to me then.

As if all these festering problems were not enough to cope with, my friend Marie came to visit the first week in June. Since our first meeting in Paris, the good times we'd shared together had been infrequent, but always memorable. Because of Clayton our correspondence had become rather one-sided of late, but I looked forward to her letters as much as I did to her coming visit. We liked each other very much — and from time to time our friendship had slipped into sexual play. She was only stopping in Trento for a few

M. BLACK

days in the course of a more general tour of Italy, but it would prove sufficient time in which to disrupt what veneer remained between Clayton and me.

Marie's beauty was as enticing as ever. She was also a bright, sophisticated woman, older than me by a couple of years, who was not afraid to speak her mind. She sensed that my relationship with Clayton was more intimate than platonic. Her disapproval was just as patent, though she had not as yet come out and said anything directly against him or our relationship. One evening I arranged for the three of us to go out for dinner. From the beginning there was probably some malice in this design, knowing what I did and, moreover, my ego still stinging from the day before, which Clayton had spent entirely "cooped up" with Alessandro at his apartment in Seconda Androna. I perhaps saw my chance to get back at him for all the abuses I had felt the victim of, and to incite a little jealousy of my own.

At the restaurant table I let — no, I *encouraged* Marie to flirt with me brazenly. I was just as flirtatious in return. Marie, who was conversational in English, was wont to say things that evening like, "When you're *our* age [meaning she and I], making love in public is as natural as love itself." Then we would say something to each other in French, laugh, and I would turn to Clayton and shrug as though it could not possibly be rendered into an English translation.

Clayton's face that night was an expressionless mask. He smiled occasionally, a false — to me frightening — smile. Only in his eyes did I momentarily glimpse reflected the humiliation I had successfully engineered for him. My heart cried out in torture, but I could not stop myself. Clayton said almost nothing all evening.

We dropped Clayton at his place and then returned to my house, where Marie was staying. No one else was at home. Still playing the game, fueled perhaps by the wine

76

we had had at dinner, I let her tumble me into my bed. But when she began rubbing my hardening cock through my pants, I panicked. My behavior that evening suddenly came back to me in all its cruelty. I jumped up and drunkenly spluttered that I had to go see Clayton, that there was something I had forgotten to tell him.

"Are you crazy?" she demanded. And as I ran out of the house, she called out, "That man is no good for you, Luca! It's sick!"

When I got to Clayton's, instead of automatically buzzing me into the building as always, he asked me through the intercom, "What do you want?"

"Clayton . . . Clayton, I've got to talk to you."

"You've been very cute this evening, Luca, but you're drunk and it's late and I think you'd better go home." He hung up the intercom.

I rang again. "Clayton, I've got to see you!"

"Go home, Luca!"

"What, what . . . what is it?" I stuttered stupidly.

"Don't be coy." I wanted to ask him what this word meant, but thought, *Non è il caso.* Now is not the time. I could guess what it meant.

"If you don't let me in, I'll wake up everybody in the whole bloody building," I bullied. There was a long pause and finally I was let in.

Wallowing in remorse, I had intended to apologize. But once in Clayton's apartment, he wouldn't give me the opportunity.

"What do you mean by coming here at this time of night and making a scene!" he barked at me. His face was more exasperated than angry. "Isn't one scene for tonight adequate?"

"What are you talking about?" I said, disingenuously.

"Don't start that crap!" he yelled. This I understood.

"Crap? Let's talk about crap! Who are *you* to tell me

what I can or can't do with Marie, or any girl I like —
or anybody!''

"Do what you like. But don't make me a *toy* in your
tricks. I've never tried to tell you what to do, with whom,
or how. But I did assume that the time you were spending
with me was because you liked me, not because you were
conniving to hurt me.''

"What time? You can be so generous only because
you *don't* spend time with me anymore." I was now pacing
the floor of his vestibule. "Of course you can be so liberal.
You don't care. You're too busy making your own scenes —
going off all the time with Claudia and Alessandro. But the
one time I flaunt *my* other interests —''

"Claudia and Alessandro?'' he asked incredulously.
"What do they have to do with anything?''

I tossed a hand in his face. "For all I know you've
been fucking both of them all along!''

And for the second time that evening I had someone
ask me, "Are you crazy?''

"Don't tell me you and Alessandro are 'just friends'!''
I taunted in a wretchedly plaintive voice. Clayton stared
at me.

"You're drunk, Luca,'' he said finally, more calmly.

"Oh, sure, I'm drunk. And now the truth comes out.
You'd rather be with Alessandro than me. You'd rather fuck
with him than me! Say it! Say it's true! And Claudia too!''
I was hysterical.

After a pause to allow me to collect myself — though
I still paced the floor madly — Clayton said with controlled emotion, "They are my friends. I don't say *just*
friends because they are important to me. *You* are important to me. I can't be with all the important people in my
life at the exact same time.''

"And that's why you get rid of me to be with them,''
I huffed (caustically sardonic, I did not doubt).

"I've never 'gotten rid' of you. You've been asked; you've said no." He studied me silently for a few seconds. "And to be honest, the time came when I thought it best not to mix these particular friendships. Obviously I was right."

"No, you wouldn't dare do that. Then I'd know about them, and everyone would know about you and me — what we do together!" I stopped directly in front of him. I was positive he couldn't deny this. I was sure he shared my sense of the "illicitness" of our affair. "You're afraid they'll know you're a *finocchio. A finnochio!*" I shrieked. *"Frocio! Recchione!"*

Clayton surprised me with a smile, his first genuine smile of the evening. "What makes you think they don't know? Certainly Alessandro and Claudia know what my sexual preferences are. Everyone *must* know about us. You're the only one who's been too afraid to admit the truth to himself — much less to anybody else."

"Are you saying . . . ." *they know?* I was thinking. But I could not speak. I was destroyed, I stood dumbly looking at Clayton, sympathy coming back into his face. That others could know — and treat us no differently — had never occurred to me. Had our love been such common knowledge? "You're lying," I said weakly.

"Ask Claudia."

"You're just saying that because you know I wanted to be with Marie tonight."

Some of the coldness returned to his face. "Then why aren't you with her?"

I stomped to the door. I hesitated, my hand on the doorknob. But this time Clayton did not take me in his arms and soothe me. I stalked out without saying another word.

I went home. Not to fuck Marie, but to meditate, in desolation, upon Clayton's paralyzing bombshell. I knew that I loved Clayton, and had always told myself that nothing could sway me from my love — even if the whole world knew. But now that the whole world did seem to know, I felt . . . betrayed. What *had* people been saying behind my back? In my paranoia, the spring had seemed spent in hiding. I had been slick, I thought, in keeping our affair beyond public scrutiny, and it was more the shame from this evidently pointless farce than from my sexual desires themselves that subdued my hubris that night. And now, just as I felt some kind of open proclamation was expected of me, Clayton and I had never been so distant from each other.

The next day Marie left for Venice. I was relieved to see her go; her presence was a disagreeable reminder of my callousness. I had little else in the way of comfort in the following days. I did not see Clayton and he made no attempt to see me. He knew, as he would later cite, that I had to work it all out for myself. I was miserable. Claudia said nothing about my unhappy face or the vagrant melancholy that rambled about the house with it. If she had known about me and Clayton, then she would also know that we had broken up. Was she pleased? Had she been disgusted by the entire affair? I could not bring myself to ask her these questions.

I was straining to come to terms with my sexual identity. It was like groping for a moon with which to light the labyrinth of night all around me. Was I gay? Was I bisexual? What did those words I had shouted at Clayton mean to *me: finocchio, frocio, recchione?* Queer, pansy, faggot. I have written that my love for Clayton obscured any guilt I might have had over my sexual desires. It is also true that Italian men are generally more pansexual than many other nationalities. But we are also men with a certain proud, even arrogant masculine image of ourselves — and the countless little doubts and critical chinks that this sometimes "hypermasculine" image is subject to are as easily assimilated into the neurotic whole as they are suffered. We are so strong, we think, it hurts. I now realized that that strength and the harm it bolstered itself against were more curiously entwined. I had no choice but to inflict upon myself the kind of penetrating self-examination that probes frenetically for all the lies one tells oneself. I was preoccupied in this task, in fact, for some years, but most painfully in those few days.

How strange, it struck me even then, to hope to extricate "truth" from such a treacherous creation as a human heart. Nor can I pretend that I have, since, solved the dark maze in which life traps us all. Who has ever thought through to all the logical cul-de-sacs and open passages of his life (though the one exit is clear enough)? Surely the most pathetic lie one can perpetuate is that one sees through all the lies. But at that time I had *one* man on whom to focus my sexual attraction to all men, and I realized that the worst lie I could have told myself then, the most monstrous self-deception I could have indulged, was to believe that Clayton was not important to me. He was — his body as much as his mind and soul. If I had any pride at all, I could not separate it from that fact.

Equipped with that fact, I decided that a talk, at least, was in order. There was, before anything else could be settled, one crucial detail that had to be dealt with.

I went to Clayton's one morning to ask him out for coffee. He met me downstairs. I had never seen him look so worn out. His face was haggard and unshaven, and his beautiful eyes were tired and smileless. He did smile with his lips, with a charming sort of world-weary bravery. Had *I* made him look so sickly?

At first we had trouble finding anything to say to each other besides the prerequisite and mutually inoffensive *ciao.* Even "how are you?" seemed fraught with hazardous significance. Greetings done with, we walked silently to the bar. Faced with each other in the bar, we spoke, but in a distracted manner, stiffly, still fumbling for something innocuous to say. . .the desultory conversation of people with more important things to discuss. At last I told him Marie had asked me to spend the summer with her in Paris.

He took this philosophically and said, "That would be good for your French. Are you going?"

"I don't know," I said glumly. "But I figure you'll be gone anyway, back to the States, and what's the use of staying around Trento in the summer?"

It was the first serious mention ever made between us of Clayton's impending departure; June would be his sixth and final month in Italy. He winced faintly, but did not speak. The affection implicit in my statement was obliterated by the issue it raised. I saw how heavily it weighed on his mind.

We said nothing for several minutes. Our stark futures lay dishearteningly ahead of us. Suddenly, and it really was suddenly for I had not planned to speak of any such thing, I began to tell him, "There is a boy here in Trento, a young man really, my age. His name is Francesco. We used to be best friends. We went to the same high school together. We did everything together."

I paused, tugging out the frankest words I could: "We used to play around together. You know, masturbating each other, that kind of thing. He's a very handsome boy and in those days he was my closest friend in the world. We even put our mouths on each other's cock. He let me come in his mouth. Then one day, in the throes of our teenage passion, he tried to kiss me. I was horrified. I told him only *finocchi* did such things — so he must be a *finocchio*. It seems funny now, I guess. Anyway, our friendship was never the same after that. I see him once in a while in the street now, but we hardly even say hi to each other."

The story, in the telling, seemed sweetly erotic to me, which it had never seemed before. "He never, in bitterness, told stories about me. *I* never said anything out of shame, but he may have had other reasons.''

Clayton had listened closely to everything I said. Now he looked at me quizzically.

''I don't know that there's a moral to the story,'' I said, flushing, ''but I've always felt bad because I wasn't honest with myself.''

Again neither of us spoke for a long while — we both just looked down at the table where my hands fidgeted helplessly.

Clayton never lost his power to amaze me. ''If I stay,'' he said, ''if I *can* stay — I'm not sure how I'd manage it — but *if* I stay, will you live with me?''

Even after so many conditional introductions, the proposal was totally unexpected. As much as I wanted him to stay, a myriad insurmountable obstacles loomed into perspective. ''How can I, Clayton?''

He just shook his head, finished his cappuccino and said, ''I don't know, Luca,'' his voice having forgone the optimistic familiarity he had let creep into it. He stood and started out of the bar. I caught up and followed him in the direction of his apartment, both of us sulking.

At the intersection where I normally turned off to go to my house, I told him I had to go home. He said he would see me before he left town, and sadly waved good-bye. I walked on a bit, my mind a flutter of conflicting ideas and impulses.

All at once I swung around and ran back towards his place as fast as I could. He heard my rapidly approaching footfalls and turned.

I hugged him desperately. ''Don't leave, Clayton!'' I gasped, ''please, don't leave!''

He held me tenderly in his arms as passersby eyed us with an idly speculative disinterest.

V   *Ciao,* Summer! *Ciao!*

I would like to write that I immediately went home, packed my bags and told my mother I was moving in with the man I loved. Even had this been the wisest course of action, or if not the wisest, the most imperative, I was to be spared making such a bold and dramatic break from home by a development both unfortunate and terribly lucky. Stripped of histrionics, my gradual departure from my mother's house was driven by heartfelt devotion all the same.

That afternoon Clayton and I had gone up to his apartment to talk over what we were going to do. We were almost high with the realization that we were together again, really together. And whatever our options, abandoning each other was not one of them. I was committed to doing anything I had to in order to keep him with me in Trento, and he was equally resolute in his desire to stay with me. We spoke about his finances and he indicated that he could possibly borrow some money from his father. He would have to contact the person he had sublet his apartment to in San Francisco to see if there was any problem in his remaining longer in Italy. He had originally promised to be back by the first of July. The apartment was special enough to Clayton, besides warehousing most of his possessions, that he did not want to risk losing it. And he was in no position to pay rent in San Francisco as well as in Trento.

At any rate, he said, the novel was as yet incomplete (still lagging a poor second to the priority I had clinched) and some more months in Trento would be ideal from that point of view. I think he said this not to diminish my importance to him, but to absolve me of any culpability should things not work out.

About my own situation I had only the gravest misgivings. I could not see how I could tell my family and friends that I was moving to an apartment a few blocks away without making it clear to all of them that our relationship was much deeper than a roommateship. And even roommateship, in Italy, was something just not commonly entered into at that time. My mother, in particular, I knew would think the whole arrangement preposterous. I was not at all sure that I could face her with the facts. However much Claudia knew (and accepted?), my mother was still unquestionably in the dark. The bald-faced absurdity of the proposition would not be hurdled without offering her an incontestable argument that would make it less absurd, if no more palatable. Although I spent many nights away from home, I was still an unmarried son in her eyes and my place was in her home. The short distance between her home and Clayton's would render my relocation not more easily lived with, only more indefensible.

At the same time I was exhilarated by anticipation. Love, the reality of which I had felt but which as an abstraction only sex had seemed to make concrete, was to be *lived*.

I agreed to bring more of my clothes and books over

to Clayton's and to settle in a bit. I was thinking that I could tell my mother I needed absolute peace in which to study for my upcoming final exams. Our initial steps together decided, we went out that evening for pizza. Afterwards I called my mother to tell her that I would be out late with Clayton. This had become by then a not unusual procedure. We had a lot of lost time to make up for.

But when we got back to the apartment, Clayton was already running a fever. He had a mild headache and said his body ached all over. I put him to bed, unmolested. He wanted me to go home, or, if I insisted on staying, to sleep in the living room so as to avoid contracting whatever it was he had. I was adamant.

"Unless you really don't want to sleep with me at all?" I had deviously delivered the ultimatum as a self-abasing question.

"No," he relented, taking my hand in his and holding it to his hot face. "I want you to stay. But don't say I didn't warn you."

I found myself intermittently hugged throughout the night for warmth when a clammy chill would sweep over him, or pushed gently away when the fever blazed. He did not sleep much that night and in his restlessness kept me awake too. In the morning the sheets were soaked with sweat.

Clayton's own theory on the subject of psychosomatic illnesses was that they often manifest themselves only *after* an emotional crisis has passed. As he expounded upon it later, the body seems to apportion its energy judiciously, and can summon the needed strength to get through any contingency, even the loss of love. But once it feels that the danger is over, it readily collapses from the strain. It is as though poisonous stores of mental stress are at last diffused through the body and dissipated in illness. I cannot vouch for the validity of this hypothesis, but I *have* always supposed that the apparent end of our affair was what tipped Clayton into sickness. His bout with the flu certainly followed upon a major turning point in our relationship, and marked its growth as a ring in a tree trunk records yet another year of experience and change, another season of life. That the precise manner of this metamorphosis afforded me the opportunity to skirt controversy is less meaningful to me now than the harmony it presaged, but just then I was only too glad to "look on the bright side": I had an easy out with my mother.

I was finally able to doze off for about an hour that morning. I awoke, however, to discover Clayton practically insensible from the fever. There was no aspirin in the apartment and, as it was Sunday, I thought it best to simply get some from home. My mother was alone at home and when I told her that Clayton was sick she rushed back with me, and the aspirin and a thermometer, to Clayton's. If she was putting two and two together, she did not volunteer the sum, but seemed only concerned with Clayton's health. I will never forget the touching look of compassion on her face when she first saw Clayton's red, bleary-eyed face on the drenched pillow. In that instant I exulted in my heart. Our need to help him is the same! We love him together!

She wiped his face with a cold washcloth and he whispered thank you with closed eyes. After taking the aspirin he looked at her as if for the first time and asked in Italian why she had come.

"You're very sick, hon," she answered in Italian (I trust no one will find fault with my translation of *caro* into "hon" instead of the less homey and intimate, if more correct, "dear"). She patted his hand and said, "Don't worry. We'll take care of you." Again, I almost cried to hear my mother's genuine care for the man I had pledged myself to.

My mother went home to make some soup for him

and told me to stay and check his temperature. If it went
up we would take him to the hospital. I sat with him all day,
and when the fever came down a little I held one of his
hands in both of mine and we talked. I stroked his hair off
his face and he told me, mustering what meager laugh he
could, that he hadn't felt so ill since he was a child. He
lightheartedly digressed into stories about his family. His
mother and father lived in a small town on the coast near
New Orleans. They were all fishermen and shrimpers; his
brothers had each had his own boat. But the oldest brother
had been killed in an accident on his motorcycle one rainy
night. The next brother had disappeared with his boat in
a sudden squall in the Gulf. The youngest brother had died
only two years before in a small town in Texas he had
been passing through. He had only been arrested for drunk
driving, but the next morning he was found dead in his
cell. The local police said he had hung himself, but nobody
ever believed that. Bobby had always been a crazy kid,
Clayton said, mixed up in all kinds of trouble, but not one
to go and kill himself in some backwater jailhouse in Texas.
His parents had hired a private investigator, but nothing had
ever come of it.

Clayton did not embellish this history with any
premeditated pathos; these were simply facts his feverish
mind had let surface. How improbably merciless fate had
been to one family. I had never heard any of this — me, who
had become almost proud of the tragedy in his life, as though
it were a badge of honor. After Clayton at last fell off to sleep,
I continued holding his hand, afraid to let go of what all
at once seemed so fragile and transitory.

Many years later I was to remember this moment in
a breathless pang of déjà vu.

When I went to fetch the soup from my mother's
house, I also packed a small bag of clothes and toiletries.
I also took my notebooks and school texts with me. I told

my mother someone had to watch him, and that I was the most logical candidate.

"But why so many things?" she asked, perplexed by the bag that perhaps did not seem so small to her. "You can come back home to change and wash."

"Who knows how long he'll be sick. Besides, I can study while he rests." Then, with somewhat more courage, I said, "I don't want him to wake up and find that I'm not there."

She let me go without further questioning. I never went back to sleep in my bedroom as long as Clayton was in Trento. By spending as much of my free time as possible at home, I was able to make this setup seem a natural and unthreatening ramification of a friendship welded more tightly by misfortune. What could be more unremarkable, and inevitable, than a friendship made fast by the need of one nursed, literally, by the other? My mother would understand this and perhaps had already begun to see our relationship in this light. As much as she had decried my absences from home, she had never seriously censured me for the time I had spent with Clayton since my father's death; she must have sensed that there was something good for me there. And now I told her that Clayton had *permitted* me to share the apartment with him because we were "buddies"; that it was my idea; that I wanted to have a place that was more my own. I told her I was old enough to demonstrate a little independence. And she did not argue, thinking maybe it *was* all just a boyish experiment. But even she could not have been utterly oblivious to the hard evidence, whether she wished to judge the case or not. She never commanded me to come home, but I would sometimes see in her eyes, or hear in the ironic turn of a phrase, a grievance for which she had neither explanation nor hope of redress. No other allusions, however oblique, to the true definition of our relationship were ever registered. We cared about each other, and that seemed enough of a label for her. She prayed, as always, for my happiness, and told herself, I'm sure, that summer and the American would soon be gone.

Clayton was very ill for several days. He would sometimes be strong enough to rise and walk about and even eat a normal meal, but within hours of such exertion he would be back in bed. Each relapse was less severe than the one before, and from that we took heart. The abdominal cramps and muscle soreness that plagued him were the worst of his flu, and when these symptoms subsided he was almost cheerful. The fever came and went many times, and he simply endeavored to ignore it.

In the time I was not tending to Clayton, whose forbearance was selfless to the point of masochism, and who only complained or asked for assistance in his most extreme distress, I did in fact study tirelessly. Clayton's toughness seemed like a goal I had to attain myself. Classes had been suspended for the summer, but I had two finals yet to take, geography and accounting. (Geography, a standard course in Italian universities, might more properly be termed social studies, combining as it does geography, sociology, political science, anthropology and demographics; it is not merely a matter of memorizing the capitals of African nations.) My marathon studying helped not only prepare me for the oral tests, but also relieved me of some of the useless anxiety over Clayton. It was even with a real measure of contentment that I sat at the table where I had taken my English lessons and pored over texts virtually enjoyable in what little claim they truly had on me. I was moved to think, This is *our* living room, this is *our* apartment. And at night I fell into bed with Clayton, reassured to know he was there for me and that I had not forsaken him.

Such are the facile, mindless joys of first love.

While Clayton was still in bed, but more comfortable

than in the beginning, he began to receive visitors. Usually people would just drop by to say hello and leave a book or magazine or some bland little sweet. Without my having to think it out consciously, I found that my furtive sensuality had freed itself. Our sexual relationship, I knew, suffused the house as palpably as genital odors (though we of course had not had sex for many days). I made no excuses to any of his guests for the unconcealed fact that we were sleeping in the same bed, or that I took more care with Clayton than should have been expected of a roommate or friend. I spoke directly, lovingly to Clayton and did not hesitate to touch him in their presence. And if I stood by the head of the bed for a moment and Clayton took my hand or wrapped his forearm affectionately around my thigh, I did not even think to watch for the visitors' reactions.

There were two exceptions to this general rule of relaxed intimacy. When Alessandro came to visit, I would nervously tense with undisguised hostility. We were perfunctory with one another; not even worry for our valued mutual friend could induce us to like each other. His visits were always long ones. Unlike with the others, I never lingered in the bedroom, but went into the living room to study instead, discreetly closing the door behind me. I was still unsure what to think about their relationship and did not want to tempt the precarious peace I had come to in my own mind by eavesdropping. I did not want to hear anything that might upset me in its warmth or familiarity. I had had enough of acrimony with Clayton over such trifles. And when I could not help but hear them laugh, I told myself I was thankful that there was someone to bring laughter to Clayton.

In his last visit during Clayton's illness, Alessandro also brought a bottle of Amaretto. Clayton was getting about the house with some of his old agility then and showed Alessandro into the living room. I, accordingly, pretended

I had something to do in the bedroom. When shortly I heard the usual laughter emanating from the *salotto*, I was not at all ready to hear my name called as well.

"Luca!" Clayton called. "Come on in here for a second, will you?"

I went in and was surprised to see Clayton pouring out Amaretto into three aperitif glasses (which, like everything else, had come with the furnished apartment).

"*Un brindisi,*" he said. "A toast. To better health, to better days."

"To better friends!" Alessandro said facetiously. Not facetiously enough.

"Are you sure you should?" I asked, refusing even to look at Alessandro.

"Aw, come on," Clayton said, pulling me down onto the sofa. "You've worked so hard to keep me alive. You've got to take in a little of the rewards. God knows you'll reap the penalties."

The three of us clinked our glasses together. Alessandro was sitting in the lounge chair opposite the sofa.

"Actually, I brought it for after his recovery — his complete recovery — but he insisted." Alessandro was ostensibly explaining this to me, but his eyes were on Clayton and he seemed only vaguely aware that I was in the room at all. I wondered if he had a girlfriend these days. He then looked appraisingly around the room and said, "Oh, well, if this does you in, I know a friend who would like to take over the apartment anyway."

Clayton laughed. "Dead or alive, my body comes with it."

This made me laugh, nervously, and Clayton, mistakenly thinking perhaps that I had let down some of my barriers with Alessandro, put a hand around my neck, pulled me into his shoulder, and sank back into the corner of the couch. Sprawled suggestively across the sofa, I looked into his eyes and thought, Yes, he *is* well again. He kissed my forehead and left an arm about my shoulders. My arm lay across his lap, and when I finally pulled together the guts to look at Alessandro, for I felt very self-conscious in this position, I saw with some satisfaction an uneasy expression of thwarted affections on his face. And for the first time I thought, Do I see something that Clayton doesn't?

Alessandro did not stay long that day, and though Clayton was as expansive and friendly as ever with him, I know that he, too, was glad to see him go. Not for my sake, but because for the first time in more than a week he was horny, and well enough to have sex. It was almost two weeks since we had fucked, counting the days of Marie's visit. Frustrated desire thus made up for any weakness on Clayton's part, and our romp in bed that afternoon was spectacularly energetic. We in fact cavorted about the entire house in a delectable sexual frenzy that required some housecleaning afterwards. That evening at dinner it was also good to see his hunger return with the same ravenous delight as his sexual appetite. At night we drifted into sounder sleep than times of late had bequeathed to either of us. Our slumber was a luxurious void.

The following day Clayton had to tender payment for his rambunctious frolic. He was late in rising and did so only with a force of will. He was tired and lethargic most of the day, and meandered sluggishly from room to room in a feverish haze. Still, it was a very minor falter in his general progress and it proved, in fact, to be the last day he was to feel in any way sick. (Over the years I was to learn exactly how anomalous illness was for Clayton, whose health seemed always robust and unflagging; he was not even much susceptible to colds.) At that stage the most vexing symptom was his grumpiness. Having been so well behaved through the worst of it, he was now disposed to an irritability with the smallest things. This was not directed at me specifically, but was simply a consequence of his long sickness. He was bored and annoyed by the whole business, was fed up with lying around the house all day, was cranky and thrivingly bent on flourishing snappy little orders to the accompaniment of a pervasive dissatisfaction with everything that was done for him — a situation as demoralizing for him as it was for me. It was a good thing he was getting better.

As things had not started out well that morning, I had to be especially cautious in collecting his laundry. Since his illness I had been secretly slipping his dirty clothes in with mine and taking them back to my mother's for her to wash. He had not yet caught on to this ruse. My mother never minded doing this small favor for me, but I knew Clayton would have been angry with me for making more work for her instead of being self-sufficient. His attitude was mind-boggling to me. I certainly had no intention of washing my own clothes even if Clayton persisted in such folly. Today I see that, while his standard of self-sufficiency was perhaps too stringent, his intentions were better placed than my own. The only product of my mother's labor that he would accept graciously was the soup or other food she would send over to us even after his recovery. He would have hit the ceiling had he known I was already plotting with my mother to have her come in at the first chance (whenever I could get Clayton out of the house) to give the apartment a thorough cleaning.

Because the slight relapse had put him on edge that day, I waited for a visitor to arrive and provide cover for my changing the sheets. The sheets were the only items he did not really object to my doing at my mother's; he admitted that it was a cumbersome chore to wash them by hand in the bathtub, and was willing to see me take care of them as long as *I* took care of them. So when I returned from my mother's with them I had to smile brightly and lie, "Yes, I didn't even ask her to push the buttons on the washing machine for me." But that morning his gaze seemed particularly wary and to elude it I had to await a guest to distract him while I worked to present the fait accompli of clean sheets on the bed — and, unadvertised, stuffed all his dirty clothes into my laundry bag.

The one guest I had not reckoned on was Claudia. She provided the second exception to that rule of relaxed intimacy Clayton and I had established in the company of others. I don't know why her visit so surprised — and unnerved — me. She was his closest friend in Trento after Alessandro (I did not then include myself in that "narrow" category), and she had not as yet visited him during his illness. It may have been her failure to appear up to then (for reasons unknown to me) that had convinced me I would not have to deal with her and Clayton in the same room. I had kept her abreast of his condition at home, and presumed that that would suffice for her. I had forgotten that, school being out, she would be leaving the next day for England to spend the summer with David. She had come that afternoon to say good-bye to Clayton.

Upon her arrival I immediately became flustered and felt myself grow clumsy and awkward around her and Clayton. My face felt like it was simultaneously blushing and blanching. I almost forgot that I had sheets to change. After I changed them and gathered the other clothes, I found her and Clayton seated out on the balcony. Summer was at last upon us with its full blast of heat and languor, and they sat sipping beers in the afternoon shade offered by the balcony's eastern exposure. As I approached they were speaking so softly, so solemnly it seemed to me, that I felt like an intruder and turned back into the apartment. Claudia soon left. Clayton sat quietly out on the balcony for a long while. I joined him briefly before taking the laundry to my mother's. He had me lean down for a tender kiss on the lips, but said nothing of their conversation.

I said my own good-bye to Claudia the next morning at the station. I watched her board the train with mixed feelings, and even now I cannot quite describe this ambivalence. In spite of my discomfort with her and Clayton, and some vestigial rivalry, my moving in with him had instantaneously resolved most of our domestic squabbles. And there was still a very special rapport between us. I was very sorry to see her go, and yet at the same time I had to think it was for the best, for her and for me. It was time to lead our own separate lives. There would be other times for being together.

Many things had to be tended to upon Clayton's recovery. He called the person subletting in San Francisco and after making sure that there was no problem on that end (he told the man that he might be staying in Italy indefinitely), he then telephoned his father in Louisiana. I did not know then how much Clayton hated asking his father for the loan. I don't think he feared being turned down, but I have since observed that many Americans are loath to rely to any great extent upon their parents. Standing beside him in the telephone booth at the SIP, the central telephone office, I could only guess at his anxiety by the way he unconsciously pressed his body against mine and fiddled with my hand. Friends squeezed into phone booths were an ordinary sight in the SIP, and I stayed with him throughout the long phone call to give him whatever spiritual support I could.

We left the SIP confident that the grimmest job at hand was done with. Clayton's father would be wiring him the money. We then stopped by the swimming pool where I worked and took a swim. I was on a short hiatus before my summer sessions of instruction would begin, but I knew Clayton would, after his long confinement, enjoy seeing some of the local boys in their swimming briefs. I was of course self-congratulatory about this generous act, which, surely, *had* to be a sign of my maturing love. Clayton, however, seemed to have eyes only for me. And though he had lost some weight while he was sick, in his bathing suit he was still beautiful and easily the sexiest man in the pool. I had to keep in the water most of the afternoon to hide my arousal.

Afterwards we went to the gym next door. Through a puzzling arrangement I could never quite figure out, this privately owned establishment had been persuaded by the city to make its facilities available to certain city employees and officials at no charge. I, being a public swimming instructor, was one of these privileged employees, and had often taken advantage of this added compensation for an otherwise poorly paid position. Now, with a little haggling, I was able to coax the owner into giving Clayton a discounted membership too. We both became regular patrons that summer. Clayton's debility following the flu was soon worked away. The exercises with free weights, indeed, restored him to a fitness and beauty I had not seen before — though *improvement* as such was impossible in my eyes. I, meanwhile, not only maintained my good body tone, but even began filling out with firm new muscles.

Another order of business to be seen to was Clayton's residency papers. Strictly speaking he was on a tourist visa, and it was expiring in June. It was actually his second visa to expire. The authorities in the local Ufficio Straniero (Foreign Office) of the Questura had made him renew his visa at the end of the first three months as well. There was some discretion at the local level as to the kind of visa extended to a foreign visitor, and in Trento the officials were not inclined to be magnanimous. They could have given Clayton a six-month visa in the first place. Moreover, as Clayton showed me on his papers, they had a habit of marking the date of expiration as a date earlier than the full three months.

Alessandro had helped Clayton with his first application and renewal. Clayton had been smart not to trust to his own Italian in trying to unravel the red tape. I now took the duty on, proudly, eagerly — unacquainted as I was with the malfeasance mandatory in all bureaucracies.

On the morning I went to the Questura with Clayton I had smugly noted the name of the man we were to see: Salvatore Andreini. Salvatore is a name that *reeks* of Southern Italy. I told Clayton in my provincial bigotry, and began to explain that the main reason the *carabinieri* and the other personnel of the Questura were the butt of so many jokes (hinging primarily on their stupidity) was that most of them came from Sicily and Calabria and Puglia and Campania. Everything south of Florence for us was the "Deep South," a land inhabited by poor, ignorant *terrone* out to steal employment in the North just so they could needle us with their hapless southern idiocies. It is, I reiterate, an ethnicism I have had to leave behind me in seeking a more cosmopolitan view of the world, but at that time these ideas were securely ensconced among my beliefs.

Naively bumptious, I assumed a proprietary air in the Ufficio Straniero, and was instantly crushed when Signor Andreini started addressing me as a child, that is, using the familiar form of the pronoun *tu* (you) and its attendant verb endings with me, instead of the more formal and polite pronoun *Lei* (you). Clayton could never understand my outrage at this impertinence, which was somewhat aggravated at that age, I suppose, by every young man's arrogance. Not having this grammatical distinction in English — a language in which every "you" is the same as any other, especially in the American dialect, so casual as to be crude at times — he could not or would not perceive the condescending and sometimes denigrating usage of *tu.* To him it was just plain friendly, and cut away any "class" distinctions. But then Clayton, in his linguistic confusion, would often switch back and forth between formal and informal pronouns and verbs in the course of a single sentence addressed to the same person.

To expedite proceedings, Clayton had consented to let me do all the talking. Trying to recoup some of my shattered poise after Signor Andreini's forwardness, I sat and exchanged a few pertinent remarks in English with Clayton. Signor Andreini looked at Clayton's file and then turned to me and said icily in Italian, "It says here your friend came here to learn Italian. Don't you think, then, you should be speaking Italian with him."

I explained that my friend did not yet speak Italian fluently, and then, still smiling innocently, muttered to Clayton, "The bloody asshole." My English vocabulary was forever expanding.

When Clayton was asked to write and sign a declaration as to the details of his stay in Italy, he had some trouble in composing the Italian. Finally the Italian official drily said to me, "You'd better do it or we'll be here till tomorrow morning." Clayton laughed at this sarcasm. Signor Andreini regarded him suspiciously as I wrote out the declaration.

My one moral victory of the day came during a discussion of Clayton's finances. They were particularly concerned with this aspect of his sojourn in the country, Signor Andreini said, because only the day before the Questura had had to pay for a young foreigner's air ticket back to Canada.

"But, Signore," I said snobbishly, regaining my aplomb and indicating Clayton's well-groomed respectability, "there are foreigners, and there are foreigners." He could not dispute that.

Clayton was given another three-month visa. Three

months less nine days to be more accurate — an accuracy the Ufficio Straniero could not be bothered with.

I took my geography and accounting exams a few days later and, having done well, finally felt liberated for the summer. My "liberation" was not dampened but enlivened by responsibility, which was becoming more and more a part of my life. By spreading the word, I was able to obtain for Clayton several more paying English students who were in need of tutoring before the fall term and its exams. I screened these people of any young men too captivating in their charms or whose handsome faces might plausibly, and dangerously, be construed as irresistible. A sign of my still immature love. Clayton was not averse to complimenting good looks, exorbitantly, when he saw them, but he had never given me, it was only then beginning to dawn on me, any real cause for jealousy.

I taught as many prospective swimmers as I could enroll, and even began to save a little money. Since my father's death I had also received a small allowance from the estate administered by my mother. (Or, rather, this is what she had told me when she began distributing the sum monthly.) Clayton and I shared the expenses of living together, though he would let me pay nothing towards the rent. He claimed that as his responsibility alone for having chosen to stay.

Under his tutelage I even became something of a cook. Well, a cook — I would not have starved . . . not right away. Clayton himself was a good cook, despite his dis-concerting (for me) proclivity for mixing too many different kinds of food in one dish. Used to a "purer" cuisine, I was often put off by a review of the varied ingredients in one of his concoctions, or simply by the dismaying jumble of food on my plate. Exotic as these dishes were to me, they were based, Clayton insisted, on honored culinary traditions and recipes. I appreciated the taste of much that he prepared only with closed eyes. And though I learned from him, I approached his formidable cunning in the kitchen with some trepidation.

(The love of combining flavors in cooking, no matter how outlandish, is perhaps an unfortunate trait in all Americans, accustomed as they are to eating everything off one plate. We Italians of course prefer our meals served in courses. Later it would be with something like horror that I first witnessed the ghastly slopfest that is an American Thanksgiving dinner.)

Housecleaning and laundry were recurring topics of disagreement, though in these disagreements neither of us had recourse to any conduct more vile than simple exasperation. Upon finding his clothes cleaned, ironed, and folded in the drawers, he would sigh wearily, "Luca, please don't make your mother do these." But it was not until I caught him washing out some of *my* underwear by hand, along with his, that I was shamed into mending my ways. At least after that when I took the dirty clothes to my mother's house, I actually did them myself without asking her for any help. (She did have to show me how to operate the washing machine.) I put the clothes in the machine; I took them out; I hung them out to dry. My mother was astounded, and maybe a little hurt. I deliberately crumpled the dry clothes so that Clayton could unmistakably detect my mishandling of them. He thereafter seemed content that I was not making a slave of my mother.

Not in the cause of clean clothes at any rate. I could not think of any good reason for Clayton to be saddled with housekeeping — especially since he performed it so inadequately, and more especially since my mother was all too willing to step in. The first time I had her come over to clean the apartment, I had to shunt her out of the way only minutes before Clayton came home from an afternoon at Alessandro's. I told him I had been busy *all* day with the housework. He looked skeptically around the apartment, but then thanked me with a quick kiss on the cheek. I became careless after a while, though, and gave my mother the keys to get in and out of the apartment when Clayton and I were out together. Returning home once and finding a sparkling kitchen floor where an hour before tumbleweeds of dust had scattered, he blew up and feistily declared that he would rather live in a pigsty than force my mother to be his housemaid. Subsequently I reduced her stealthy housecleaning forays to once a week.

My mother was as baffled by Clayton's temper in this matter as I was. Nor did she ever link her efforts to the unexplained little gifts of pastries or flowers that he always brought with him to her house.

What she thought, if in fact she ventured to think anything of our sleeping arrangement at that time, I can only guess at, for in all these years I have never asked her. Perhaps on my next visit I will broach the subject. Old people often become exceedingly candid about such things, and my mother, in particular, has brandished glints of an openness and liberal-minded laissez faire inconceivable of her in those days. It has never been unusual in Italy, in any event, for friends of the same sex to sleep in the same bed. And I was always meticulous in tidying up any telltale remnants of an intercourse more active than sleep. Most probably she had already decided not to ask herself questions about the circumstances of our living together. I like to think that it was her enduring fondness for Clayton that never permitted her to say an unkind word about him or our relationship. But what *did* she think? . . .

Physical affection between males openly expressed in public has, in general, always been more accepted in Italy than in America. Today it is still not peculiar to see men strolling arm in arm through the streets or young men huddled seductively close in conversation. These are not necessarily displays of homoerotic attachment; more often they simply reflect a physically intimate sociability more freely practiced by Italians. Clayton and I availed ourselves of this freedom, and often walked about Trento perpetually touching each other, as lovers do, or with one of our arms resting on the shoulders of the other.

Nevertheless, I was rather leery the first time I went out with Clayton in a company of friends. He had invited me along after telling me that Alessandro, Stefano, Michela, and others were getting together at a bar that evening. I vacilated, but when Clayton said that he really wanted me there, I assented.

Italian bars are not like American bars. They might more appropriately be called cafes. They are well-lit, well-furnished, often stylishly decorated places dedicated more to the drinking of coffees than alcohol. The smaller ones are just a place to stand and have an espresso. There was a new bar, one of the very nicest ones, just opened in Corso Tre Novembre that was popular with Alessandro's crowd. We sat around that evening on the plushly upholstered chairs and drank beer and wine. Everyone was getting a little tipsy, and the topics under discussion became more and more personal. But my fear that our physical closeness would be embarrassing to someone in the bar, far from being realized, had to lie sulkily in the back of my mind as Clayton, seated next to me, remained totally engrossed in the convivial goings-on. I watched Alessandro, opposite Clayton, with deceptive idleness and felt old, venomous sentiments I thought I had dismissed rise from the murky waters of my seeming isolation. He was so transparent, I grumbled to myself, reveling as he was in Clayton's irrepressible laughter, absorbing his complete attention — and gloating over my relative ostracism. Everyone was older than I was and, I had to confess even then, apparently more experienced and sophisticated.

I learned for the first time that night that Clayton and Alessandro had an oral catalogue of local luminaries, *trentini* characters notable for a physical feature or personal quirk. Their running joke had disseminated itself through the group, till a single epithet came to represent a whole series of associations and one word could send the entire group into gales of laughter. There were *il Carciofo, la Mela, la Gatta, la Nana, il Gnocco,* and *la Topolina.* The Artichoke, The Apple, The Cat, The Dwarf, The Potato-Pasta Dumpling and the Little She-Mouse. "Predolin," the name of a popular TV game-show host, was anyone with a phony smile; "Kokoschka" was a certain friend of Michela's who had done her German thesis on the obscure Austrian painter and who never let anyone forget it; "La Bella" was a notoriously ugly and charmless waitress in a Trento pizzeria who was often startlingly discourteous to her customers. "La Loren" was the raggedy, schizophrenic woman who loitered about the Piazzo Duomo talking to herself or dancing whimsically across the stones. The cliquish humor of these sobriquets did little to assuage my emotional dislocation. I began to wonder if my nickname would be *il Muto,* the mute, or simply *l'Altro* — the other one.

As inhibited as I felt in this rapacious company, I was sufficiently relaxed to laugh with the others when Michela took the floor to recount a story and Stefano, drunk, abruptly interrupted her to tell her, "Michela, your head doesn't fit your body."

"*Che cazzo dici!*" she squawked. What the fuck are you saying! She turned to us indignantly, imploringly. "No one has *ever* said this about me. What does he mean!"

Michela, Claudia's oldest friend, in fact did have a head that did not fit her body. Her delicate, pretty face was much too small to be perched on top of her long, gangly body, which towered above my own by several inches. Being tall and thin, and fascinated with high fashion, a typical Italian obsession, she always looked elegant. But with her arms and legs stretching out from her torso, there was also something in her oddly proportioned appearance that defied aesthetics. Alessandro had once said she looked like Olive Oyl, and for once at least the appelation was on the mark. Her too-small head was always jerking about in an exaggerated, puppetlike animation. Her hands were never in repose, but flew about her like frantic birds tethered to her body by the two sticks of her arms. Her personality was at times outgoing and gregarious; at times coolly reserved, demanding and hypercritical. She was a little "dizzy." But she was also intelligent, sharp, expressive, vivacious, funny — the best of all the Italian liveliness so often badly parodied by others.

"Where was I?" she resumed, returning the conversation to a monologue. Michela liked to talk and did not suffer interruptions faintly; Stefano's interjection had been the more objectionable on this basis. "Yes, the last week of school." She taught Italian in a German elementary school in Bolzano, a city north of Trento which, while technically within the borders of Italy, has never relinquished its Southern Tyrolean identity. Austrians and Germans seem less alien there than Italians. "We were supposed to take the students on an outing to a park. A picnic. They said it was walking distance from the school, but when I had gotten my group about a kilometer down the road we came to a hill. I say a hill — it was a *mountain*. Like *this*!" and her hand made a diagonal slash to indicate the steep grade. "I can't walk this, I told them. I *can't*. And I was carrying my bag — the big one. Well, I started up. The park was at the very top of the hill. You could see it in the distance like the sun rising over a mountain range a hundred kilometers away. And I'm walking and walking — but I *couldn't*. I just *couldn't*. I finally had to leave the students and hitchhike. I got a lift right away and told the children I'd meet them at the top."

The vision this conjured of a fastidiously elegant and supercilious Michela dumping her students to bum a ride from a stranger tickled Clayton wildly. He fell back against me laughing. When all the laughter had died down, Stefano asked, "Who picked you up?"

"A *baccano* of course!" she answered, which was to say *what else?* with discouraged conclusiveness. *Baccano* is a Trentino word of derision for the truly provincial mountain folk of the region, and for anyone who shared their rustic ethos. In the Trentino dialect it is the equivalent of Rome's *burino*, the South's *cafone*, or standard Italian's *contadino*. "Redneck" or "hick" or "peasant" might be the best translation, though "boor" or "country bumpkin" would do as nicely. It was a word Michela used with splendid fervor. But then she used all her words fervently. "And he was short!" she said, adding the ultimate insult in a Trentina's repertoire. This familiar prejudice was always comical to Clayton. We traded amused glances. I was a little more at ease.

Soon ribald stories commenced going around the circle about memorable, and risible, sexual encounters. Alessandro told about the time his girlfriend had in the delirious bliss of orgasm called out another man's name. Without skipping a beat, Alessandro had breezily replied, "But, my dear, you're in the wrong bed. This is Alessandro." I could believe it of Alessandro. This kind of trenchant, ready wit we called *peperino*, and no one could deny Alessandro possessed it. Loathing smoldered in my chest.

Luciana related how her boyfriend, in a pique of frustration with an uncooperative condom, had thrown it against the bedroom door — where it stuck. Michela, as usual, had the funniest anecdote. During sex she had once fallen asleep. "I was just *too* tired." The laughter roared through the bar.

"But didn't he even bother to wake you up when he came?" Alessandro quipped.

Clayton's turn came. He told a story I had never heard.

"When I was much younger, maybe Luca's age," he said, "I was madly in love with this older man, an Italian-American in fact. One day I went to his house where I was supposed to fix dinner while he visited a friend in the hospital — or so he said. Anyway, I got to his place, where I was used to sleeping all the time, but where I had not slept the previous night, and discovered — how can I say? — conspicuous and incontrovertible 'evidence' that my friend had had another person in bed with him. I told myself I could handle it, not to get jealous. I told myself I was more mature than to let a little sex interfere with a truly loving relationship. I told myself I was more sophisticated than to be bothered by an instance of what was surely only fleeting glandular secretions. No real harm done. While I told myself how well I was coping, I went to start dinner — and promptly set his kitchen on fire! The fire department had to be called and everything. It was an accident, I mean, of course it was an accident, but, you see, I was actually repressing all this terrible anger inside. I *did* start the fire. The embarrassing thing was that the man understood my suppressed jealousy better than I did."

Somebody chortled. Michela turned to me and said, "You've been forewarned. So when the house catches fire — eh?" and shook her hand in benediction. There were laughs and I felt my face redden. Just then Clayton leaned his face close to mine, his arm on the chair behind my back, and whispered urgently, "Never again, Luca. *Honesty,* even if it hurts."

"Never," I repeated aloud to the others. "Why do you think I have my mother come in to make the bed?"

This got a round of laughter, and even a tolerant smile from Clayton. He clapped a hand on my knee and fondled my ear with the hand behind my back. It was precisely the gesture of affection I needed at that moment. And by then I did not care who was offended to see it.

The banter rolled entertainingly along. I started to feel like a part of the group. Still, I was grateful when the evening came to an end. Nor did I fancy reprising it another night; it all felt disconcertingly like an oral examination at the university — the examiners deceptively benign. Luckily summer was throbbing and humming all about us, and its arrival always signaled the departure of friends and family.

Doubly lucky for me, most of Clayton's friends were teachers. Students and teachers were always the first to depart. Within the week even Alessandro tore himself away from his best friend to embark on his vacation to England and a two-month course at Oxford.

The summer was for Clayton and me an epiphany. A serenity had come with the heat, and in this tranquil, sultry wave changes washed gently over our life together. Scintillating romantic ecstasy gave way to a communion of souls. We spoke as if communicating in the same language for the first time. And in our empathy each word breathed love. We still quarreled, of course, but the doubt that we would not be together forever alighted in neither of our hearts. Sure of our love, the choice to trust each other bespoke no bravery.

Our sex was as exciting as ever; our caresses now offered something more: acceptance for what we were, and what we hoped to be. We could talk softly in the dark and know that the other understood, or would be valiant in endeavoring to understand. The dream of love had become a day-to-day reality. Dante's face was, after all, only a mountain — but a uniquely beautiful and solid rock of a mountain. And in all this there was a new romance.

In August there was no one remaining in Trento, it seemed, other than the occasional tourist en route to someplace else. August is everyone's vacation month in Italy, and like newly hatched turtles they flock to the beaches with single-minded zeal. My mother had gone to stay with a cousin in Santa Margherita Ligure. I had the use of the car and Clayton and I decided to go to the seaside resort of Rovinja for a week. We had little in the way of extra cash, but Yugoslavia is cheap and we wanted to celebrate. Clayton had finished the first draft of his novel.

We got back to Trento on my twenty-third birthday, August 31. We hardly had time to drop our stuff off at the apartment before heading over to my mother's for a small family party. We excused ourselves early, though, and went alone to an outdoor cafe in the Piazza. Drinking past midnight in the warm night air, we talked and whispered and howled at the moon, and got happily, happily drunk. We stopped the car on the way home and necked like teenagers in a dark lane under the Valsugana railway.

Back at the apartment Clayton pulled out his birthday present to me, a gift-wrapped object that could only be a tennis racket. He had splurged and charged the new racket to his seldom used American Express card. And somehow he had kept it hidden from me. I began bouncing about the apartment, joyfully swinging the still wrapped racket. A backhand across the bedroom. A forehand lob in the living room. An overhead smash on the balcony.

"Clayton, we've got to play in the morning!" I shouted to him, at last ripping off the paper. "Clayton? Clayton?"

Clayton was reading a postcard taken from the stack of mail he had only had time to toss on the kitchen table earlier before going to my mother's. The card had the toothless, smiling face of an ancient Peruvian Indian on the picture side.

"What's wrong, Clayton?" I asked apprehensively. From the look on his face I was sure someone had died.

Writers write figuratively of such things, but I swear to this day that Clayton sobered instantly. By what intricate and abstruse biochemistry I do not know, but I heard him say to me with frightening sobriety, "I have to go back to San Francisco, Luca."

He clutched me to his side and lowered his head onto my trembling shoulder. Across the vast barren and frigid ice floe my mind had in seconds eroded into, there flashed the lament: Good-bye, Summer. It seems like only yesterday we had said hello. Hello! Good-bye, Summer. Good-bye.

VI   By Grace of Neptune

The name Trento comes from the Latin *tridentum.* Three teeth. The three teeth are supposed to be the three hills upon which Trento was originally founded. Or at least this is the most credible theory as to the etymology of the town's name, its unknowable beginnings lying lost in antiquity. The city has since grown up on the floor of the valley around the three teeth, and I doubt that many citizens of Trento could tell you which three hills the city's name refers to. Indeed, for many *trentini* the word simply means trident, and in fact the three-pronged spear has become the official symbol of Trento. (The English word "tridentine" does double service here, Tridentine being the correct adjective for someone or something of Trento.) The trident being a symbol of Neptune, the god of the sea has also become associated with little landlocked Trento. There is a fountain of Neptune in the main square, and his name or visage, or his trident, shows up with friendly regularity about the town.

On one of the last warm days of summer before Clayton left Trento, he and I sat beneath Neptune's fountain in Piazza Duomo saying very little to each other. Suddenly Clayton turned to me with a heart-melting smile and said, "Look on the bright side, Luca. Neptune's been very kind to us. He's granted us something under his stern dominion not frequently bestowed upon his subjects. He's speared both of us at the same time on that fork of his. Right through the heart. We're both hooked for good — and you have to admit there's something sweetly, if painfully, special in our impalement on that trident of love. The hook won't be easily dislodged." This shed more sadness than warmth and light, and we went back to saying nothing.

And in spite of this eloquent sop, "Pig God" was more on Clayton's lips in those days than the grace of Neptune.

I could not help asking myself if ours was, after all, nothing more than a tourist's affair. Were we, in reality, to be humbly gratified by the rapture of summer, while, regardless of what was said, letting our feelings fade into wispy, pleasurable memories of a passionate fling long ago and far away? Clayton must have asked himself these questions too, but the answer in his eyes, in our hearts, was always *no.* There was something more substantial to our relationship. Clayton's commitment to me was irrefutable every time he looked at me. Every touch between us was infused with unyielding affection. And as much as I owed Clayton, my allegiance to him was not a duty — what I felt was not a debt to be repaid, not a commodity to be transferred to someone else, not a condition, like infatuation, to be subscribed to lightly and then just as lightly repudiated. *No,* our love could never be like that. *No,* we were bound by ties proscribed by a mere "affair." Our love had a strength and tenacity forbidden to the flimsy tendrils of "summer romance."

The card had been from Clayton's friend Ken in San Francisco. Tersely he had woven a tale of woe: "Your sublessee has defaulted on the August rent and absconded to Hawaii with some of your things — including the TV. Do airlines let you take such things on board? Maybe he hocked it for the air ticket. Anyway, your landlady has meanwhile come down with a bad case of epilepsy and each day promises a new grand mal. She insists the only antidote for her malady is the confiscation and selling of all your furniture. I have, instead, reduced these seizures to petit mals by covering the August rent. I can do so again only for September. I regretfully suggest that these matters require your immediate and personal attention. The cat did *not* die."

Clayton had to explain to me that the tag line was a feeble attempt to leaven this dismal picture with humor. Clayton owned no cat.

Further explication was in order to make me understand what Clayton had so quickly and effectively been resigned to: his finances were in worse shape than I had been willing to consider. Even if his apartment could somehow be saved without his returning to the States, he was without the resources to continue as we had been going along. Most of the loan from his father would soon be gone, and now he had to worry not only about paying that back, but paying Ken back as well. Tutoring English was not going to make these ends meet. The one positive strand to be extracted from this entangled web (spun not in deceit but in hope) was the forthcoming conclusion to Clayton's first major literary effort. A final typed draft of the novel and publishing prospects would be more easily followed up in the States.

Clayton was set on staying at least through September, even though this would be stretching his money reserves very thinly. In that last month he began using his one credit card, American Express, constantly, always moaning slightly under his breath when he pulled it out. He had to explain yet one more thing to me: the card was more like writing a check than employing real credit. When the bills arrived in a month or two they would all have to be paid at once. He was "floating" the card, he said. He had left his bank account in Ken's charge, to take care of just such expenses in his absence, but the funds in his account, he assured me, would be totally exhausted by now.

I had up to then viewed a credit card as *the* passport to riches, and dreamed that wealth was incumbent upon the possessor of the card. Clayton told me he had gotten his employer to lie to help him get the card, and that he assumed half the people with American Express had done the same.

Clayton had at first even offered to buy me a ticket to San Francisco on his credit card, but when I was apprised of the actual situation I could not let him do it. I spoke of my studies and proudly asserted that I could not just fly off to San Francisco to be someone's "kept boy" — though Clayton of course was in no position to "keep" anyone. We would have to have a more secure material foundation on which to build our lives together. There was some truth in this, but I would still probably have left everything to be with Clayton had our finances looked any healthier. Anemic as they were, I could not expect to wrench a whole new life from them. Money cannot buy happiness, but it *can* stave off so much unhappiness. No amount of existential despair can erase the fact that the miseries of the world are sometimes surprisingly mundane. In this case, a little surplus cash would have provided the difference between the contentment of being with someone I loved and suffering the torments, at once sublime and banal, that mere physical parting can cause.

My savings had gone toward our Yugoslavian vacation, so I naturally turned to my mother in hopes of financial aid. She informed me of the true state of our family finances and I was shocked to hear how badly off we really were. My "small" allowance was in fact the larger part of my father's pension, which my mother had thought best to give me with a certain ostentatious generosity, as though there were plenty more where that came from. She did not want me to feel impoverished or insecure. Now, knowing how desperate I was to go with Clayton, she had to tell me the truth. Our family debts were more monumental than I had been led to believe, and were being paid off at an alarmingly slow rate. While not destitute, our status was not much better; we were solvent in reputation only. My mother's job and her deft skill at juggling creditors were the only things keeping us above water — along with that portion of Claudia's salary as a teacher that had not gone for her summer in England with David. Claudia had just returned from her vacation and she, I learned, had possessed from the beginning a clearer understanding of our money problems. My mother had trusted to my sister's pragmatism, while coddling my own illusions. My belated education in the family budget, indeed, heralded a period in which I began to feel that I was learning too much too quickly about everything.

Dazed by all these discoveries, I was too distraught to be of much use to Clayton. Instead, he now had not only his own sorrows to manage, but my dispirited grief as well. After his initial depression, he summoned what element of cheer he had left in himself to tell me comfortingly that it would be a short and temporary separation: that he would send for me as soon as he had the money, or would come back to Trento. Working as a waiter he could make enough money to pay off his debts and buy a plane ticket within a few months. And, who knew? — maybe his novel would make him a little money too. Gradually, reluctantly, I was reconciled to his leaving.

Once we had both accepted the fact, a strange kind

of melancholy descended upon us. There was nothing lugubrious in our dejection. It was just that everything suddenly seemed both terribly frivolous and urgently important at the same time. We went through the paces of our daily life knowing it was all we had left of each other. Calmly exchanging words in the kitchen, Clayton might wrap his arms around my waist from behind, kiss my neck, and then go back to cooking dinner as though this step had been only one more step, however essential, in the preparation of a more inscrutable recipe. Our amorous play in bed, embedded now in a deeper context, drained all our emotions from us, and afterwards we would lie together very still and a little sad; it was the one feeling, after love, that we were never able to empty ourselves of that September. And in a wistful moment either of us might choke on a word in the other's arms and silently cry.

It was September, too, that I first met Fabio. He was a new swimming instructor, about my age, at the pool where I worked. Torn between spending all of Clayton's remaining time with him and the need to feel productive (though in my wildest fantasies I never deluded myself that this money was getting me to America), my presence at the pool became rather sporadic. Fabio helped cover a lot of my missed hours at the pool. Besides being so obliging, he was also quite attractive, although his lithesome good looks were not enough to distract me from my more pressing concerns. But I had noticed in our first meeting in the lockers a look in his eyes, intense yet evasive, that I might have been tempted to describe as prurient had I thought much about it then. I did not deem his interest unwarranted as much as I felt it was utterly unworthy of *my* interest. Clayton was on my mind, not this pretty boy, and it was without any effort at all that I dismissed his attentions as merely friendly curiosity.

I had rudely accommodated at last the idea that

An Italian Elegy

Clayton had to leave, but I had not given up completely the idea of joining him in San Francisco — if not immediately, then soon. I knew this would be up to me to arrange. I could not depend on Clayton's vanishing assets to fulfill my dream. It would be, if I were successful, a tribute to the power of my love. I contemplated quitting the university and getting a real job. I had insisted on reducing my mother's allowance to me to the barest minimum and felt it now behooved me to start bringing in money to the family. A good job would do this and even let me dream of going to America.

The one little snag in all this was that I had no training for a good job, and the kind of job that might have paid me well for knowing nothing was disappearing with the summer. It would be winter before the resorts started hiring young, unskilled labor again. Only a university degree would help me attain the income level I needed and desired. And my graduation was two years off. In the chronic national unemployment crisis, I could not hope to obtain any of my goals in the forseeable future. The conundrum I found myself trapped inside of acquired an added measure of frustration.

My mother, needless to say, would have been taken aback to see me leave the university, and Trento, to run off to live with an American man. She was already anxious about the plans Claudia and David were presumed to be making. Still, she was not selfish in that way, and I know she would have given me the money if she'd had it. Because college education was not subsidized by the state, it was not uncommon for Italian students to flutter in and out of courses over a sometimes seemingly endless epoch of years. Staying in the university would certainly have been the conscientious thing to do, but leaving it was not, on this account, a more worrisome matter for me or my mother. My graduation, and the lucrative future it implied, was in any event not so imminent that it could not be prudently pushed back a term or two — *if* I had had a worthwhile alternative for me and Clayton. As it was, there was really nothing to substitute for my classes, no viable option for the sake of which I could postpone my schooling. My time at the university seemed all at once singularly obtrusive, absolutely necessary, agonizingly inadequate and dishearteningly irreplacable.

Claudia had returned from England in a more wholesome frame of mind than I had seen her since our father's death. A profound joy now seemed to imbue the very way she moved across a room. And to this happiness I had contributed, albeit unconsciously, a pleasant surprise. She had returned to Trento to find me a changed young man. Gone was the fractious, indolent little brother she had said good-bye to three months before. In his place was a mature, or at least more mature, person of some character and responsibility. At our apartment she was undisguisably impressed to see me regularly cooking and cleaning, washing dishes, and even wringing out a few small items of clothes by hand. Living with Clayton had worn away some of the rough, adolescent edges to my personality. I had tasted compromise and it was not fatal. Though still independent, and even stubborn at times, I was not so brash or impudent as I had been. I was inclined now to deal with people more patiently and in a reasonably adult manner. I had lost some of my swagger, and in the loss I felt I had gained a new respect for other people's feelings.

I do not want to make it sound like I had become a saint overnight. In forty years I have never risked canonization. But I certainly *felt* more sensitive, and a bit wiser. The good times had made me want to share my love, and whatever virtues it had given birth to in me, with the world; the bad times had seared into my being the immutable primacy of that love. The lesson, however, was more than wisdom for the pain. It was pain for the wisdom, too. I was learning too much, too quickly.

An Italian Elegy

Maybe it was because of something new Claudia saw in me, which merited her confidence and assistance, that she proposed one day that Clayton and I go visit crazy Uncle Ugo before Clayton left. She had casually made the suggestion with such subtle import that it took some reflection on my part to realize that the idea was not as casual as it had seemed.

Crazy Uncle Ugo, my father's brother, had been the one to maintain that our father had been kidnapped, all evidence to the contrary notwithstanding. He also happened to own a profitable little vineyard near his home in Folgaria. He was, unfortunately, clinically mad, and this aspect of his personality, in some imprecise relation to his excessive drinking, made him an unpredictable and volatile creature. He could be exceptionally kind, or crafty in his cruelty. Claudia knew that if I caught him on the right day, in the right mood, he would gladly give me the money with which to go to America.

The afternoon Clayton and I drove up through the mountains to Folgaria it was ostensibly for him to say good-bye to my many relatives there. I say ostensibly; it was the only reason as far as Clayton was concerned. I had kept him unaware of my real motive. I figured that if Uncle Ugo was in good spirits, I could carelessly drop the information that I too would be going to San Francisco if not for my family's misfortune. He would pick up the hint (or not — one cannot trust to the acumen of eccentrics — in which case I would have to be more indelicate) and then perhaps, depending on his affability that day, thrust the money into my hands with a gruff laugh and a slap on the back.

We had already paid our respects to my other relatives in the area when we got to Uncle Ugo's house. We were both amazed to see that an elaborate table of freshly made pastries and treats had been laid out for us. They were honored, as so many had been, to have the American as their guest. This

119

augured well for my quest. And things did proceed favorably for a while. We were even secretly entertained by my cousin Franco's outrageous flirting with Clayton.

I liked Franco, but we had never been close. I felt I hardly knew him. So I was somewhat astonished — also kindly amused, as it so happened — to see him making the most flagrant passes at Clayton. He was a year younger than me and very handsome, though something of a mess. His greasy hair was always combed with pitiless exactness; his clothes were an ill-fitting pile of dirty laundry, his personal hygiene questionable. That his beauty shone from under all these bushels makes it all the more memorable. But he was not a bright boy, and was only capable of making up for his dullness with an erotically supple appeal. Poor Cousin Franco.

Around the table were seated my uncle, his wife Aunt Irene, Franco, his younger brother and two sisters, and Clayton and I. Over wine and snacks Franco would lean close to Clayton to say something, an ordinary intimacy with Italians, but not so ordinary when Franco's sensuous lips and beaming eyes were saying at the same time something more intimate yet. From time to time he would lean back in his chair and when Clayton's eyes fell on him he would tug briefly, suggestively, at his crotch. Italian men are infamous for touching themselves in public, but Franco's gesture was bereft of the customary unconsciousness that normally renders such touches innocent. No one else at the table seemed to notice except Clayton and me, and we did not mind in the least. We smiled at each other conspiratorially. Our relationship had progressed sufficiently in trust that Clayton could even be mischievous about it. After one of Franco's overtures Clayton would reiterate an invitation to him, blandly delivered: he should come and visit us one day before Clayton left town. And then Clayton would artfully dodge Franco's excited eyes by smiling at me.

I suspect Franco would have shown up at the apartment eventually had Clayton not been leaving so soon. Poor, sweet Cousin Franco.

The conversation was relaxed and friendly, but I was having trouble finding just the right words with which to get my message across to Uncle Ugo. Uncle Ugo appeared to be in one of his saner states of mind, and cordial, but his talk loped disjointedly, if amiably, from one subject to the next. He also persisted in speaking Trentino, so that I was busier translating for Clayton than usual. Clayton himself was taking the entire afternoon in his stride, as he always did with my family affairs, and was even speaking Italian as well as he ever spoke it.

Then Clayton made a mistake. It was a small mistake, really, but a peculiarly fateful one. During a lull at the table Clayton had meant to ask my uncle, *"Avete mai sofferto una secca?"* Have you ever suffered a drought? A perfectly logical question to ask a grapegrower. But this is not what Clayton actually said. Phonetically, he had haphazardly voiced the last velar stop and not doubled it. The question came out, *"Avete mai sofferto una sega?"* Have you ever suffered a hand-job? or, more sensibly, Have you ever been jacked off? This was a very different question.

I know that under other circumstances my Uncle Ugo would have merely laughed at this faux pas, seen it for what it was, a slip of the tongue, or even taken it as the occasion for some bawdy joke of his own. But that day, at that particular moment, it was the one remark to tip his teetering sanity into paranoia. His whole face seemed to retract. His eyes narrowed, the mouth tightened, pulling lips taut over broken little teeth, and he peered at Clayton with a scornful distrust.

"No, I'm not the kind of man who lets other people jack him off," he testily said in dialect.

Clayton immediately perceived the change in tone,

though not the reason for it. I expeditiously explained in English, being careful not to smile and hoping that Clayton would pick up on this cue not to make light of his mistake. I told him to forget about the drought.

"What are you saying!" my uncle demanded. "He speaks Italian, no? Let's hear it in Italian. A guest doesn't do his host the disfavor of whispering in foreign languages in his house!"

This was spoken so fast, so unclearly, with such a Trentino accent, that Clayton did not understand. He stared blankly at Uncle Ugo, and then at me.

"Oh, don't tell me he doesn't understand," my uncle continued disparagingly. "I can see he understands everything I say. He's just playing stupid. Both of you."

(The suspicion of uneducated people that, because you speak a little of their language, you can understand everything they say, no matter how fast or lazily they pronounce it, or how idiomatically they express themselves, was an attitude I would often meet with later myself. Such people prefer to believe that the foreigner is simply being obstinately difficult, if not downright subversive.)

By then everyone was trying to brush aside Uncle Ugo's distemper. Aunt Irene brought out something else to eat, while her daughters chattered nervously about this and that. Even Franco, in his witless way, tried to help keep the conversation out of his father's reach.

Undeterred, Uncle Ugo abruptly turned to me and said, reproachfully, "Your mother tells me you and this American share an apartment together. You've got a home of your own. Isn't it good enough for you?"

His look was full of not-so-thinly-veiled contempt. I started to repeat, rather tangentially, that Clayton and I were giving up the apartment and that Clayton was going back to San Francisco; that I might have joined him, but I didn't have the money. Dauntless, I squeezed every ounce of significance that I could from this cicumlocution.

"It's like you were married or something!" my uncle exclaimed. He was not about to take any hints about a loan — though not for want of acuity: He turned to his wife. "They even talk to each other like they were married! A goddam married couple!"

No amount of gentle cajoling could coax my uncle to his senses. My aunt and cousins sat looking helplessly about the table as my uncle's interrogation became more aggressive. Clayton and I were politely unspecific in our answers. When we had endured as much of his cantankerous abuse as good manners dictated, we left.

Aunt Irene said good-bye to us at the door, tearfully, kissing us and apologizing for her husband. We thanked her, told her we had had a nice time, and smiled unconvincingly.

On the drive back to Trento I was glumly silent. Clayton thought it was because of the overall unsettling effect of the scene at Uncle Ugo's. He tried to tell me that it did not matter, that all in all it had been a colorful day. I could not tell him the real reason for my mood — that my last hope to join him in America had just been dashed to pieces. As I drove I held his hand in my lap.

I have perhaps up to now given the impression that all the linguistic fouls were Clayton's. Such was certainly not the case, though I tended to be more cautious and deliberate in my use of English. Because it was Clayton's language, I endeavored to think before speaking, at least with him and at least in the beginning. My pronunciation was fairly good, too, so that I did not make the kind of egregious errors comparable to Clayton's in Italian. I was forever making mistakes, of course, but my mistakes were more often due to misunderstood usage rather than carelessness.

I had, for instance, confused for many years the words "bitch" and "whore," which I had first encountered in speech in England. I thought they were interchangeable and that, if anything, "bitch" was the preferred vulgar slang for either a prostitute or any woman of "loose morals." I had used the word "bitch" many times with this meaning and Clayton never said anything to me about it. If he had insisted on rectifying all my mistakes in those days, I am sure we would never have made it through a single conversation.

One afternoon, however, in making a *giretto* about the town, we had come across an old acquaintance of mine. She was in fact a girl I had had sex with in high school, as had most the student body. After we parted in the street I told Clayton this and said that she was something of a "bitch."

Clayton thought for a moment and then said, "In American usage [he was always pedagoguishly careful not to lump American usage in with British usage] you can't really say bitch to mean whore. Whore is a prostitute, or anyone who prostitutes themselves, or a woman who likes sex, usually with lots of different partners, and sometimes the word is also used for men in this sense. There is nothing particularly bad, I think you'll agree, in liking sex, or even in being a prostitute, and there's nothing particularly wrong, *I* think, with the word, though it's generally considered obscene. Bitch, on the other hand, is almost always a term of opprobrium [Clayton often chose Latinate words with me, which, while uncolloquial in English, hence, making him sound a bit like a dictionary, were familiar in Italian] and refers to a woman one simply doesn't like, though maybe more especially because she's hard . . . not a very nice person. Think *rompepalle* — ball-breaker. It's also used sometimes by men, for men — gay men at least — to slightly different effect. If you must say 'bitch,' use it only in anger. Or in humor. 'Bitch' and 'whore' can be funny. But I have some better advice for you," he said seriously. "Don't use either one. There's no reason for *you* to. And they have sort of a sexist ring to them."

To this day I use these words only when speaking of men, or in the verbs "to whore around" and "to bitch." I do not know that this was the purpose of his admonition. Certainly there is still something sexist in my usage. His advice not to use the words at all was a trifle pompous, but I did take his counsel to heart in my own wry way. My misguidedly functional interpretation has, idiosyncratically, fossilized through force of habit: The only "bitches" and "whores" I seem to know are all male.

Another word that often misfired in my English was "sleazy." Having defined the word for me, Clayton must have regretted, even in his amusement, hearing me use it so often and in so many unlikely situations. Sleazy became my favorite adjective for anything or anyone I found unpleasing. I overused it much as I had overused the Italian word *schifoso* (disgusting). Bad pizza was sleazy, the muggy weather was sleazy, unfashionable clothes were sleazy, and I even felt sleazy myself from time to time, meaning vaguely out of sorts. Once an attractive older lady in an expensive fur and sporting inexpertly bleached hair whizzed by us in line at the supermarket, and I blurted out to Clayton, "What a sleaze-bucket!" Clayton laughed uncontrollably, uninterested in the fact that the woman had cut in line in front of us.

And whenever Clayton told me he was preoccupied about something, meaning only distracted, I would ask him with solicitous sympathy, "What's wrong?" I was repeatedly misled by the Italian cognate *preoccupato,* which means worried or troubled.

The most endearing misuse of English for Clayton was not mine, but Michela's. Her first foreign language was German and whenever she found herself stumped in English for lack of the right word, she often fell back on her German vocabulary. The one English word that seemed always to elude her was the very simple word "fat." Thus, she would speak of a *dick* woman or a *dick* man, or her *dick* students. Even I had to laugh. Long after Clayton had informed her that the word meant *cazzo* in English, she would still use it to describe a person, apparently incapable of breaking her old pattern. Towards the end of his stay in Trento, Clayton had taken to using the word in this way also, and we would both collapse into laughter over someone's "dick" sister or the "dick" clerk at the Upim department store.

Why do I remember Clayton and I laughing together so much that September? I do, but I am not sure why this particular image bursts through my memory of the melancholy of that period with such vividness. Yes, there may have been something desperate or even hysterical about our laughter, but it was not — how could it be? — disconsolate. Maybe it was only, as they say, to keep us from crying. I prefer to think that it was our way of taking care of all the humorless months to come.

We exited a beer hall one afternoon around the middle of September and were drawn to a man who sat sketching on the sidewalk with colored chalks. These sidewalk artists are all over Rome and Florence and Milan, and are often very accomplished. This man had his hat out on the pavement to collect money from any appreciative passersby. When we came closer we were both appalled to see how really awful his artwork was. His drawings were little more than a child's doodles: a few pathetic flowers, a tragically executed mountainscape, a blotch of pastels that, judging by something that looked like a crown of thorns, was supposed to have been the face of Jesus Christ. We tossed some coins into his hat and went chuckling infectiously down the street — erupting into full-blown laughter every few steps. People must have thought we were the most carefree couple in town.

In Clayton's last week we went to Rovereto to see a wonderfully daffy Italian production of Tennessee William's *Cat on a Hot Tin Roof (La Gatta sul Tetto che Scotta).* Clayton knew the play well and I had seen the movie with Paul Newman and Elizabeth Taylor at a revival movie house in London. We were both curious to see how a story so inherently "Southern" (American) could be adapted to the Italian stage.

We had been waiting in anticipation for months for the touring company to come to Trentino, and not even our shortage of cash could stop us from attending the play. (I bought the tickets with the last of my allowance for September.) Throughout the play, though, we had to stifle our giggles at the cavalier style with which Maggie and Brick and Big Daddy and Sister Woman had all been transplanted to Sicily and given "Southern" (Italian) accents. On the way home we laughed and laughed remembering such musically Sicilian lines as *"quei mostriciattoli senza colli da Palermo"* in place of "those little no-neck monsters from Memphis."

The prevalence of dubbed movies, which Clayton had railed against since coming to Italy, made the cinema an infrequent night out for us. Clayton was not chauvinist about it, I must admit; he would, indeed, only go to see Italian movies in Trento. It was not the English he missed in an American or British movie, but the integral texture, the "feel", that sound gave to a film. Performances, he fumed, were oblitrated by dubbing. Italians are not much disturbed by this "ravaging" of the original soundtrack.

When at last an English-language film with Italian subtitles was offered by the local film society, Clayton dragged me to it. It was Lindsay Anderson's *If. . .* Put off by the mangling English accents (Clayton had ruined my ear for British speech), I followed the subtitles instead. What was funny was the couple near us who took turns reading the subtitles aloud. Normally this would have infuriated Clayton. But he only laughed, and we left the theater cracking up in each other's arms. That was Clayton's last weekend in Trento.

All of Clayton's friends had returned from their summer vacations by the end of September. His last night in Trento we threw a big going-away party at my mother's house. There was nothing very festive about it. Clayton drank a lot and was therefore able to feign some merriment for our sakes. But it was a sad evening for all of us. Sadness and laughter. That had been September.

As we finally headed back to our apartment in the early morning hours Clayton called out to Alessandro, "Say farewell for me to La Nana and la Bella and il Carciofo and la Loren . . . ."

Walking into our apartment together for the last time, I was already beginning to feel nostalgic about it. I still remember the rich redolence of garlic and butter that invariably permeated the kitchen, suffusing the entire apartment with the smell of "home." Clayton had refined my taste for garlic, a food more popular in the South than in the North. I remember the old furniture that Clayton thought charmingly antiquish, and that I thought of as junk. I remember lounging in the huge bathtub watching Clayton, naked, shave in front of the bathroom mirror. I remember mornings on the balcony studying, while Clayton wrote at the table in the living room he used as his desk. We would look up now and again from our respective work and be comforted by the presence of the other on the other side of the picture window. I remember a bedroom of moonlight, of gasps and whispers.

We talked in bed for a long time that last night. Then we made love. We talked on afterward, striving to say everything that had to be said before it was too late.

Clayton's open return air ticket was from Milan. The next morning I drove him to the Malpensa Airport. A considerable distance from Trento, the drive never seemed so short. In the terminal I pulled out a ring I had bought him. It was a plain gold band that I had gotten at a discount in a shop where an aunt of mine worked. Even then I had had to borrow the money from Claudia. She had not asked me what it was for. I gave the ring to Clayton. It was a silly, sentimental, old-fashioned thing I had done. But that is the privilege of a young man in love.

I had had engraved on the inside of the ring a tiny trident, and "Love, Luca."

Clayton, who never wore any jewelry, put the ring on. We stood embracing in a corner of the gate area until his flight was called. He murmered how much he would miss me, that he would call in a few days, and at least once a week after that, and that he would write as well. He said he would either be back in a few months or send for me when he had the money. I wanted to tell him I would do everything I could to get to San Francisco. I wanted to tell him how much I was going to miss him. But I was physically unable to speak.

The weary drive home was complicated by the blur of tears in my eyes. Several times I thought panic would have me running the car off the road, or head-on into another car.

In Trento I packed my things and left the apartment that evening for the last time. Clayton had settled everything with the landlord; I would return the keys the next day. I went back to my mother's house and my old bedroom. I was devastated. None of my ramshackle affairs before Clayton — not even my father's suicide — had prepared me for this shattering feeling of lost love.

I felt Claudia staring at my dispondent face as I unpacked my things.

"It's just that I'm going to miss him," I said with tremulous understatement. *Sentirò la mancanza di lui.*

"I know," she said, and hugged me.

And because she did know, I hugged her back fiercely. I did not know then that she and David had already set a wedding date in December. I would be glad when I learned it. There were other things, less welcome, awaiting me in the coming months, feelings of heart-rending loneliness and frustration, which I wish I could have remained ignorant of. But I was to know all of it. I was learning too much, too quickly.

VII   *Un Voto di Castità*

Submerged in a state of shock, the first few days after Clayton's departure elapsed unmarked by me. What I said or did did not seem to matter. Then, upon reentering the university, the panic that had been inchoate during the drive back from Milan broke over me with the ferocity of a hurricane. I could concentrate on nothing. My speech and movements took on an unnatatural cadence, jumbling together hurriedly and then stopping abruptly. The nerve-wracking feeling of being *trapped* became the toxin that infected those months of my life, the implacable anxiety killing any hope of a return to the routine of my life before Clayton. There was nothing I could do to stem the almost nauseating yearnings that beset me. My days were a mine-field of memories. At night my sleep was ripped into restless fragments by dreams of Clayton. Usually I could see him or hear him, but I could not reach him; his touch was unreal, ghostly. Sometimes old nightmares of my father's disappearance seeped back into my sleep, and sometimes the distended, water-exacerbated flesh I identified was not his, but Clayton's.

Or worse, I would dream of holding Clayton in my arms, feel his kisses on my face, his body against mine, touch his warm, heaving chest with such solid immediacy that I would awake crying. And continue crying.

Within a few days I had come to know all that Claudia had suffered in her many months away from David and in the breathless vacuum in which my father's death had trapped *her.* Now I suffocated in the rarified atmosphere of love. Seething with need, I was sealed tightly away from all that nurtured me, from all that made me feel strong and free. I cast about forlornly, desperate to be unshackled from a burden I had taken on unknowingly, in heedless youth, pleading not with words, but with eyes that only Claudia understood.

My relationship with Claudia assumed its most enduring form then. There had been times when we had felt like enemies, but now we were allies in a war against life, or the cruelty with which we felt life had mockingly usurped love from us. In love, we decided, we could not compromise any further than we had both already done. To give "reality" one more inch of our territory, to forfeit even the weakest frontier in the name of a peace of mind at once practical and heartless, was unconscionable capitulation. We reinforced each·other's fortitude, steeped in the conviction that we had declared one inviolable boundary of affection that the attritions of time and anxiety would never win from us, even in madness. We became true and lasting *friends.* And when Claudia informed me that David would be taking his doctorate in November and that they planned to marry soon after, it was vindication of my own beleaguered hope.

And yet, while commending myself for an intractable

love, I am not sure I would not have traded some of my love had I really perceived the pain ahead of me, had I really been able to know how complete my desperation would be. Having survived it all as much by sheer luck — and a little bluff — as by determination, I cannot honestly weigh what strength of character or adaptability I wrested from this peculiar torture against the raw pain it inflicted. Suffering is not a science, durability is sometimes scant balm, and no one looks covetously upon misery. Surely, who does not want to be able to yield swiftly and painlessly to the torturer's threats, rather than become acquainted with his skill. I have known deeper, sharper sorrows, but those months were the most *excruciating* of my life. However unconscious I had been at first in submitting to the full horror of our separation, I was pitifully conscious throughout; the process was infinitely ingenious, relentlessly thorough. I cannot remember that autumn and winter without their connotation of anguish. The wound, like the love, was piercing.

Clayton telephoned me less than a week after his leaving, and that alleviated some of my helpless panic. We talked for a long time, though I cannot remember much of what was said. We must have repeated how much we missed each other over and over. Clayton told me he had already written a letter and mailed it his second day back. I had sent a letter off to him as well. (Delivery time was about two weeks in those days.) We may have said trite things; we may have paused for long silences so as to hear the other breathing. The telephone conversation, insufficient and forgettable as it may have been, at least made us tangible to each other. I did not want to hang up and neither did he. But when I felt myself about to choke, I told him I did not want to waste his money for the next phone call and we said our good-byes: "I love you." "I love you."

That first phone call reassured me that Clayton would

not forget. . .could not forget. I was able to begin studying, if with unreliable diligence. I seemed to live from
letter to letter, phone call to phone call. At the end of a
period without word from him — never more than four
or five days — I was like a laborer who had impulsively
squandered his paycheck before the week was out, scroung-
ing frenziedly about for the wherewithal to get through to
the next payday. And always the letter came, the phone rang,
and my panic was again deferred for a day or two. Sometimes
for only a couple of hours.

In addition to my ongoing sessions at the swimming pool, I had gotten a position as night clerk in a hotel
in Trento. I was not paid much, but I felt fortunate to have
landed the job at all as I knew no German, a virtual necessity
in a hotel in my region of Italy. Through the nepotism of
a cousin of my mother who knew the owner, however, I
was hired in October. This is the usual course of employment in Italy: one knows someone who knows someone.
In the civil service this practice has risen to a kind of
code of ethics, making it difficult for orphans and the more
shunned breed of outlaw to enter into it.

Between classes, the pool and the hotel, my schedule
did not allow many hours for sleep. But then I was not sleeping well anyway. I was unable to save any money. I was no
closer to America. Unabated, the despair flickered only upon
receiving the latest word from Clayton. As I had had to
"choose" to stay in Trento and attend the university, so I
was now constrained to keep jobs that promised me little
more than diversion. My job at the hotel did not require
much in the way of work, so at least I was able to use the
time to study.

The main reason I could not save any money was the
laughably paltry amount of my pay. Another reason was my
phone bill. As soon as I had gotten the job at the hotel I
had called Clayton and talked for an hour. Thereafter we

took turns calling each other on a more frequent basis. But with my calls to San Francisco and Claudia's calls to England, our phone bill became the marvel of the Trento telephone company — and a full-fledged atrocity in our mother's eyes. I was not, however, about to give up my telephone time with Clayton.

One evening I advised my mother that I was going to be phoning Clayton and unexpectedly set her off into a tirade about the costs I was profligately incurring and the evident confusion as to my true identity: "Excuse me, I didn't realize Dino de Laurentis had moved into the house. If I had known, I would have had them put in a separate phone for you — a nice gold phone with a direct line to California. Or maybe you should just move back to Hollywood!"

As I was at the end of one of those periods during which I had not heard Clayton's voice, I was on edge and primed for just such a skirmish. "*I* pay for *my* calls," I said abrasively, "but if you like, I *will* move!"

One thing led to another and finally, when she screamed at me something to the effect that didn't I think maybe it was time to start dating girls again, thinking about a family maybe, I slammed my way out of the house, yelling back at her that her example of motherhood had certainly not made family life an inviting prospect.

I made my phone call at the SIP. Clayton was of course aware of my tone of voice, more morose than usual, and asked what was wrong. I did not want him to worry. *I* was worried he might insist on making all the phone calls himself, to his own pecuniary detriment. Poverty is less galling when shared equitably. I told him that it was simply that I missed him so much. It was a short call.

At home I discovered that my disgruntled mother was not speaking to me. Among the three of us the tables now seemed rather askew, if not perfectly turned, and

Claudia and I had to smile at each other about this. Claudia was going over to a friend's for dinner that night and when she left my mother made it ridiculously obvious, by steering clear of the kitchen, that she was not fixing me dinner. I jokingly asked her if I could at least have a crumb of bread. She did not smile. I told her airily that I was not as good a cook as she, but that I would not starve. I made myself *spaghetti alla carbonara.* My mother did not speak to me or cook for three days. When I still would not apologize, her will weakened and eventually we found ourselves chatting amicably over a big lunch she had prepared for us.

I remember that during that time when she was not speaking to me, I had a very strange visit from my cousin Franco. My mother and sister were at work; I was studying. As I have said, Franco and I were never close and the visit had me puzzled from the beginning. He started pacing nervously about the kitchen while I made coffee for him. He was going on inanely about nothing in particular, as he was wont to do, when suddenly he commenced splurting out a long and convoluted story about some boy he had seduced and was in love with. The boy was eighteen and lived in a miniscule moutain village called Nosellari, not far from Folgaria. Having fucked the boy three times, gotten him to administer fellatio on Franco twice and jerk him off once (here Franco used vividly corresponding hand gestures), he had presuaded himself that what was involved was more than lust.

I did not mind that he was presuming a liberty with me based solely on his conjectures, however accurate, about my relationship with Clayton. I was even pleased that Franco trusted me with this information. But I did not know exactly what he expected of me. His predicament did not strike me as a very serious one. As soon as he finished exhaustively, albeit inarticulately, extolling the beauty of his mountain Adonis, I set the cup of coffee down on the kitchen table in front of him and asked him how much sugar he wanted.

"But what am I going to do, Luca!" he brayed.

"Fuck the boy a few more times and see what comes of it," I said placidly. This seemed to satisfy Franco and he sat down to drink his coffee. I was glad to have done my part for *someone's* peace of mind. I never heard anything further of the affair. Poor Cousin Franco.

It was also around that time that Clayton's beauty began assiduously haunting my dreams. I would arrive home from the hotel about four in the morning and, as tired as I was, dread going to bed. I conscientiously took to masturbating every morning just before falling to sleep, not because I was horny, but in hopes that my dreams — even more "real" than my daytime longing — and my increasingly precious sleep would not be interrupted by sexual desires I could not enjoy.

The days were sapping life from me. With little sleep, a full load of studies, swimming classes, and an evening at the hotel hovering over me all day, I was looking older, worn and defeated. Claudia tried to keep my spirits up, more faithfully than I had undertaken to do for her, but my face, I'm afraid, never lost its preyed-upon expression. I continued going to the gym when I could, driven by a compulsive vanity that whispered, "He'll be back — tomorrow, next week, next year — but he'll be back!" It was just as well that my days were churned free of any extra time. I was interested in nothing, aroused by nothing, moved to feel *nothing*. My love for Clayton had wilted whatever other emotion attempted to spring forth from the arid soil of my heart. Unhappiness was the only other sentiment that managed to grow there. Any extra time would merely have been blighted by more unhappy thoughts.

I came home from the university one afternoon.

Another letter from Clayton was waiting for me. It was really little more than a card, the cover of which was a black and white photograph of a rumpled, empty bed. For a writer, his letters were always mysteriously laconic. He wrote that he was back working at the restaurant, though he could only wheedle four shifts out of them for the time being. He was just about done with the final draft of the novel and "on the prowl for publishers." Then he closed with the three words that always chilled me: "I want you."

    I want you, Luca. I want you so much I'm
going crazy. I want you, Luca. I want you.

    I kept the card with me the whole afternoon. If I got up from my desk where I was studying, I would take it with me, clutching it as a psychologically damaged child might cling to a certain toy, trauma transforming the trivial into something essential. When Claudia and my mother asked me what I was holding, I did not answer, but simply shrugged and waved it once in front of them, as though it were all so clear. As though it were all so painfully clear.

    How painfully clear, indeed — and repellent — the onslaught of those months seem to me even now. I thought after all these years that writing it all down on paper would mitigate some of the sharpness. I envisioned that the mental effort of organizing these memories would deny them their old lacerating force, would dull the jagged, cutting shards. But I feel the anxiety with the same intensity. And the worst was yet to come for me. I cannot dwell on these sensations. I cannot spew them out with rational objectivity. The pain, regurgitated in even so cautious a fashion, is still *real*.

    In light of the adverse changes I had gone through physically, I am surprised that Fabio saw anything in me at all. But, then, I cannot flatter myself that Fabio was ever the most discriminating of suitors. Fabio was the swimming instructor who had eyed me so salaciously since coming to work at the pool. By November, though, we had become good friends. I did not see him socially outside the pool, but he made my time there more bearable. Besides being likably intelligent and alert, he had a winning sense of humor that had me laughing through most of our duties together — not a negligible feat in those days considering my state of mind.

Wednesdays and Thursday were my nights off from the hotel, so one Thursday I consented to pick up another instructor's students for the evening. That every lira counted was something I had to constantly remind myself. As the pool was closing that night I noticed that Fabio and I were the only ones left in the changing room. We had just come in and were pulling off our swimming briefs. I was not watching him, so when he went by me under the pretext of getting another towel, I was jolted to feel him brush his penis against my bare buttocks. I turned and looked down as he went back to stand at his locker, two up from mine.

Fabio had one of those enormous penises that, even in extreme sexual excitement, as it appeared to be now, engorged with blood to the size his body deemed safest for its other parts, still hung down at a forty-five degree angle. He acted as though nothing untoward had happened. He looked me in the eye and asked what I was doing after leaving the pool.

''Going home,'' I said.

He looked down at his erection — or the penis as erect as it would ever get — trying to draw my own eyes to it. I could see that he had the imperious attitude, common to some men with large cocks, that this physical attribute entitled him to unlimited access to any number of doors.

''I thought you and I could get together and . . . .'' For the first time his eyes unbashfully went over the length of my body, while he jutted his cock into the air with a subtle motion of his hips. One of his hands played seductively over his chest as the other pretended to scratch his balls distractedly.

I was not sure if he was joking or not. "Oh, stop this stupid game and say what you mean," I said with brittle severity, not sure to what extent I myself was joking. He laughed and I laughed. But he continued to stare at me hungrily.

"Come on," he said, shaking his cock again with a pump of his hips, hands now on his thighs. "Don't tell me you wouldn't like to play a few games yourself."

"Anything you play with that," I said, indicating his penis, "is going to be a pretty rough game."

He laughed again. Taking my lack of offense to be something more (though, as I was naked, it should have been plain that I was not interested,) he finally took his cock in his hand and raised it toward me, pulling back the foreskin to reveal the glistening head. "*Dai, ciuccialo*" he said low, Come on, suck it, he said low. "You can suck mine and I'll suck yours."

"Fabio," I at last said to him humorlessly, "leave me alone!" I then turned away from him and finished dressing. When I turned back again I was relieved to see that he, too, was dressing.

I must explain that although I was initially jarred by his approach, I was not really riled — and certainly not disgusted. On the contrary, I rather admired his uninhibited audacity. Fabio was an attractive young man and at another time I might have succumbed to his charms, physical and moral. I knew he found me attractive also, and maybe this had shaped some small part of our friendship.

In Clayton's absence I had never forsworn sex with other men or women. My heart had taken its own vow of chastity. *un voto di castità*. And it was a chastity that had nothing to do with the activities of my genitals, per se. My passion for Clayton had siphoned from my libido anything I might have spared Fabio or anyone else just then. Emotionally I was barely subsisting from day to day. I had not conceived of sex as the answer to any of my prayers. That masturbation was to be supplanted on occasion, passionlessly, did not unburden me of my loneliness in Trento, but, rather, invested sex with an indelible hue of mourning.

Possibly my liberal sexual stance, after so much petty jealousy, now impresses the more righteous reader as expedient and self-serving. Such a view would be predicated on the naive premise that a person's foolishness is uniform, the primeval darkness unblemished by glimmers of insight or sparks of sagacity. The fact was that I had a not-so-precocious acceptance of sex as not only an expression of love, but also as a necessary function engaged in by human beings for fun. I did not have to have a philosophy about sex — it simply *was.* My ill-manufactured jealousies with Clayton were invariably *emotional* first, and sexual only by association. And though later I was to realize precisely how foolish it is to try to punctiliously divide the physical from the emotional in the confluence of love and sex, at that time I did not deceive myself that I had a right to infringe upon Clayton's choices of sexual release in my absence — anymore than he had a right to dictate mine. Yet I know I would have told him all or even forsaken all other outlets had he commanded it. But he was too understanding and generous for that. He was not so mean or cowardly as to expect such a thing of me. Once our love had been firmly secured in each other's heart, the "extramarital" orgasms — at least in the absence of the other — seemed literally immaterial to our feelings for one another. A time would come when we would have to grapple with this issue again, but while apart from each other our trust went beyond sexual fidelity.

Sometimes I called Clayton in the morning in Italy, it being late at night in San Francisco. He was always thrilled to hear my voice regardless of the hour. I would ask him if he had been sleeping, and if he said yes, I would feel the urge to ask him, "With whom?" Clayton would have been honest enough to tell me the truth, though he did not want to hurt me. And that would have hurt him. So I never asked. It would have hurt me; I admit it. One of the first lessons of caring, though, is learning not to provoke needless hurt. I did not want to hear meaningless, yet insidious paeans to erotic adventure, and neither, I'm sure, did Clayton. The longing that had imprisoned our souls had taught our souls, if not our bodies, one chorus, one verse: "I miss you. I want you. I love you."

I went over to Fabio and asked him out for a drink. I did not want him to think my spurning of his, after all, abundant offer was a more serious rejection than it was. Perhaps I was thinking of my old friend Francesco. He quickly checked my crotch to see if my other head had changed its mind, smiled dubiously, and then laughingly agreed to repair with me to a nearby bar. I truly liked Fabio.

On the way to the bar I explained to Fabio that I could get into sucking cock, or having mine sucked, and that he was certainly handsome enough to tempt anyone. But I was not in the mood to have sex with him, and probably never would be. Then I told him about Clayton. It was good to talk so openly to someone about him. Fabio listened somewhat spellbound, I have to say, to my confession of love. I tried not to bore him, as Franco had bored me. He kindly gave me his full and sober attention, hanging on each word I used to briefly detail our relationship. And when I was silent, afraid to say anything for the dryness in my throat, Fabio put his arm around me and said, in a voice both awestruck and fraternal, "I'm sorry. I didn't know."

In the bar, in a hushed tone, Fabio returned the envious wonder I had inspired in him with his own amazing tale. There is a small recruitment center and military base in Trento. This *distretto* is in fact very near my mother's house, and not far from Fabio's. As a teenager he had discovered a certain dark, deserted driveway of gravel bordered by trees and bushes where some of the young men in service might pass on their way back to the *caserma* in the evenings. There, if one knew what one was doing, one could get a fast *pompino* before the boys returned to the barracks, or give one, however one was inclined.

Fabio had done a lot of both, and later when he had the use of a car, he would often take one of the youths back to it for more intricate coupling. These experiences, of course, had not only whetted his appetite for cock, but also given him an exaggerated sense of the importance of his own hefty organ. The irony was that he preferred to suck cock himself, or be fucked.

I had never heard of any of these secret highlights of the night life in Trento. I listened as raptly to Fabio as he had to me. My mouth must have been agape with disbelief most of the time. The pinnacle of sexual achievement for him was to have a group of the young servicemen over to his house. His manner a model of guileless innocence, he would herd them into his room, lock the door, and while his family watched TV in the living room, they would experiment with a raunchy variety of lewd combinations.

Upon leaving the bar Fabio said, half-seriously, "If you ever change your mind . . . ." I nodded and thanked him, and watched as he went off in the direction of the *distretto* adjusting the bulge in his pants.

Fabio and I continued to socialize throughout the rest of the year. He became my best friend, after Claudia. I had stopped seeing most of my old friends when I moved in with Clayton, and after Clayton left I had no desire to rekindle friendships that had come to seem stale to me. And when at last I too was slipped into his bedroom as a guest, with no soldiers to watch us, I was gladdened to feel myself comfortably stirred enough to have sex with him. Impelled by Fabio's enthusiasm, our relaxed, playful groping rapidly escalated until what had been initiated in jest could not be turned off. I ended up mounting and fucking him. It made him happy, while my own sexual pleasure was overshadowed by a sense of having perfomed a small favor for someone who had given me understanding friendship when I most needed it.

It was an act seldom indulged again, but never without real affection.

I have not been too shy, it is clear, to mention sex. And here, after so pointedly refraining from discussion of the more specific physical nature of sex with Clayton, I find myself unable to go on without resorting to some unabashedly explicit comments in order to present an important psychological factor.

Clayton and I did everything together, but, while he was not averse to anal stimulation himself, he was more especially fond of fucking me. It was a joy I had come to crave from him too. He was the only man who could ever bring me to orgasm just by his rhythmic thrusts in me — not that I have been intent on permitting everyone a stab at this distinct success. These spontaneous ejaculations of mine were, in fact, a regular feature of our sex together. My explosive rapture was more than a testament to superior technique, however; it was indicative of how wholeheartedly I gave myself to him in our most intimate moments.

Conversely, I confined my sexual activity with other partners to fucking *them*. This reflected natural predilections as well as a keener truth: never, in the time Clayton and I were lovers, did sexual desire *lure* me into being fucked by anyone other than Clayton. It was, quite simply, a fantasy never imagined. Flipping my penis into someone else and working it around, though, was a role I acceded to time and again without compunction, or indeed much thought of any consequence. Fucking someone can be so. . .detached, so *easy* a maneuver that one can almost, even in pleasure, have a kind of objective sex. This fit my somber mood in those months. I proffer it as additional corroboration for the uncomplicated and cold appeal sex had for me then — when it was able to penetrate my lonely disintegration at all.

Later the often mechanical "detachment" of fucking someone was to have a more profound significance for me.

Until I could feel Clayton inside me again, I had to content myself with the letters and phone calls. The only thing to get me through those days seemed at times to be the promise of his voice, after days of impatient anticipation, over the telephone. Then I would hear the deep, soothing sound of his words, calm and passionate in the same breath, and feel his face close to mine, closer. . .so close. I would shut my eyes and listen for that certain sonorous timbre, a quality of intimacy in his voice, that told me he was here, in the same room, right next to me. And with each call I had another chance to tell him I loved him, I missed him, I wanted him. We would at last say good-bye and afterwards I could feel a little freer of the pressure in my chest, the stress of having him not with me — until the anxiety built again into panic before the next phone call. My life continued to plod along vacuously, unwinding, as it were, into nothing, bracketed only by these tenuous contacts with the man I loved.

I knew that Clayton's birthday was November 12, so a couple of weeks before that date I went into town to buy him a birthday gift. I did not have much money, of course, but I had to get him something. I decided on a pair of gym shorts, along with a T-shirt. I had noticed the outfit he usually worked out in had been getting frayed and discolored. I had to guess at his size.

On the way home I ran into Alessandro in the Piazza Fiera, just outside the walls of the historic center. He was in a rush, but stopped to tell me excitedly that he was going to America. He had won a *concorso* (a scholarship/grant competition) to study abroad. The *concorso* actually paid for part of the trip; his grandfather had agreed to give him a large grant of his own with which to defray the expenses. Alessandro was to be at the University of California at Berkeley for a year. And, best of all, he would be staying with Clayton across the bay till he found his own apartment.

My envy was hydrochloric. It burned through my stomach, into my liver, and menaced my entire cardiopulminary cavity with combustion. Yes, Clayton had said something once about some such offer to Alessandro, but it had all seemed so vague and indefinite. Alessandro added that he was not even waiting until the end of the term at his *liceo*, but was leaving in the middle of the school year to fly off to San Francisco in a few days. He left me in the piazza with the hurried effrontery, "I'll say hi to Clayton for you."

I went home and slunk into bed, too crushed by Alessandro's news to utter a syllable, too shaken to move. I did not eat that night. I did not speak to my mother or sister. I skipped my classes the next morning and instead lingered in bed, my mind replaying again and again words I had heard before — where, I could not recall: "Why! Why! Why!" In my impotent rage I beat the wall above my bed, till the plaster cracked. Then I slumped under the covers and cried as shamelessly as a baby.

Claudia came home from work to find me still huddled in bed. My incontinent grieving veering into neurasthenia, she held me until I could speak. I told her everything. It all seemed to come out of me in one long torrent of a sentence. And as always she understood — as only *she* could. She said very little, but her look was loving, encouraging.

I arose at last to wrap and mail Clayton's gift. I was able to go on, somehow, and get through to Clayton's next phone call, when he nursed my latest wound with a gut-wrenching sob: "I wish it were you, Luca — I wish it were you arriving on that goddam plane!"

Claudia married in the first week of December. She too was leaving her teaching post in the middle of the school year, to live with David in England. He had garnered a prized membership among a team of post-graduate researchers at Oxford. His career would always be an academic one. My mother was heartbroken, and my sister and David consented to a church wedding only in hopes of mollifying her disappointment that they were choosing to live in England. Claudia vowed that she would be back often, starting with a Christmas visit following their honeymoon in Spain.

They did return often, but their home was to remain in England. They do have a house near Lake Garda today, to which they retreat with the children in the summer. My mother has subsequently reconciled herself to the situation quite nicely, having a rather full and independent life out-side of her children's.

During the wedding, though, I began to speculate unhappily on how she would react should I ever manage to leave Trento as well.

I was sincerely happy for Claudia, but I did not savor staying in Trento without her. She had been my one unchallengeable support throughout my deepening crisis. I could not have wanted — or lost — a better friend. Seeing our lives together come to its final end, I was about as impassive as my mother.

I remember at the church being stunned by Claudia's prettiness. Her radiant, earthy attractiveness was new to me, her eyes far lovlier than I had ever supposed them. All our strife had not disfigured her tranquil beauty after all. Or our love. By the conclusion of the ceremony I had tears in my eyes, and for once they were not tears of despair, or at least my despair in losing her was matched by the happiness I knew she was entering upon. With the last of her many kisses that day she whispered to me, "I know it will work out for you too, Luca."

"*Ti voglio bene,*" I whispered back. I love you.

The holiday season descended upon us with unseasonably warm weather that year. Fabio was able, against much gloomy resistance, to talk me into going up to Monte Bondone to sun. It turned into a pleasant drive, and once in the sun at the top of the mountain I was grateful to him for having persevered. The mountain was crowded with sun-bathers. It was warm enough that we could strip down to our swim suits. Lying in the sun together, Fabio regaled me with stories of his wanton escapades in the dark near the *distretto*. None too wise a preoccupation, I thought, considering the skimpiness of his attire — and his easily aroused, hardly concealable barometer of sexual excitement. No one seemed to notice or care.

Someone suddenly called my name. I opened my eyes and saw Antonella, my old girlfriend, standing over me. I had not seen her since the summer. With her was an older man, about forty, tall, balding, plump, and with a slightly sinister babyface. A friendly greeting exchanged, she introduced him to Fabio and me.

"This is my uncle, Maurizio," she said, smiling at him demurely. "He's visiting from Milan."

"A pleasure to meet you, gentlemen," he said formally, removing sunglasses and shaking our hands.

His fulsome smile, formed with tiny, tobacco-stained

teeth, was instantly identifiable, his manner professionally unctuous as he told us how lucky we were to have such good weather so late in the year. Alessandro and Clayton would have called him "Predolin." He had kept his eyes fixed on ours, but after he put his sunglasses back on I could not help feeling he was examining the rest of us.

Antonella asked why she never saw me anymore. I explained that it was due to my studies and the two part-time jobs I held. I could still sense her uncle scrutinizing our bodies. As neither of them was dressed for the heat, they soon went into the shade of the bar with her other relatives to have something cold to drink. Maurizio pulled off his glasses again, shook our hands again, and smiled his Predolin smile as he withdrew with his niece.

"Get that guy," Fabio said deprecatingly. "Let him off his chain and he'd have his head buried up our asses right here and now."

I said nothing.

"I thought for sure he was going to smile at the girl and politely excuse himself, saying, 'Please, I have to give the gentlemen a couple of quick blow-jobs.' And then dive into our crotches."

"You're one to talk," I teased. "If you didn't carry that 'weapon' around like an extra leg all the time. . . ."

"Me!" he raised his voice defensively. "It was *you* he was drooling over."

"Come on," I said, "half the people here could hide behind your dick and still not have any toes or elbows showing."

"You'd be surprised how many guys aren't interested in a big cock," he said, his tone full of disillusioned amazement. "Anyway, if you weren't so busy mooning over your American friend, you'd realize you're one of the sexiest men in this stupid town."

He had never said anything so complimentary to

149

me and I was sure it was just a silly ploy to try and cheer me up. I looked at him as though he were a child I had just caught in some far-fetched lie, and scolded him mildly with raised eyebrows, "Fabio. . . ."

"It's true. Hey, don't turn around, but *lo stronzo* keeps looking this way." I had no intention of turning around. "Yeah, he has his eyes glued on you like he hasn't had a meal in six months and you were a plate of *ravioli alla bolognese.*"

I said nothing, but closed my eyes and went back to relaxing in the sun. After several minutes Fabio nudged me and whispered, "*Guarda, ecco lo stronzo.*" Look, here comes the turd.

"Excuse me, I don't mean to disturb you." The man was hulking obsequiously over me like some great, predatory cherub. "I couldn't help but admire your physique. And your face is striking too." He handed me a business card. "We're always on the lookout for new talent. Please come and see me in Milan after Christmas and I'll see if we can use you. If you're interested."

I blinked into the grinning, gargantuan baby's face roosting above me. The cherub, its eyes obscured by the smoky, curved lenses, seemed more and more vulturous. Was it hungry, or merely intrigued? I took the card.

"I'm an executive for a modeling agency in the city," he added, sweat beginning to bead on his fat little neck. He lowered his glasses and scanned me one last time with unmistakable sexual intensity. And then he trotted off to the ski lift that would take him and his group to the bottom of the slopes. I looked at the card: Maurizio Corsentino. Vice-President (like that, in English). And the name of the agency.

Fabio urged me to pursue the proposition at once, even if it meant what it so clearly did mean. "So you pop it in, pop it out, wipe off the shit, and take your money. You aren't going to get to America teaching the backstroke or checking old German tourists into that hotel." When he saw that this was *not* the tack to take with me, he said, more calculatedly, "Listen, you should at least check it out to see if it's legitimate. I hear those models make a lot of money. And, who knows, maybe you'll get some free clothes out of it, too."

He left off there and went over to introduce himself to a handsome young man sunning nearby who *had* noticed Fabio's barometer.

During the Christmas holidays I debated with myself whether to follow up the lead or not. I mentioned it to Claudia when she visited us and she said I would be a fool not to call on the man in Milan; I certainly had the body for a model. But then she had not seen Maurizio or his hyperthyroidal leer.

In January I took the train to Milan and did call on Signor Corsentino. I was shown into his large, modern office and received warmly. Then, having delivered a pretentiously solemn lecture on how hard a model's life really was — though of course I had the looks — with long, tiring hours of posing, and on how unglamourous the work behind the scenes would be, awfully boring normally, and on how much training I would require before any assignment could be entrusted to me — *then* he made a graceless lunge for my pants and began unfastening them. I violently pushed him away and angrily left the office without saying a word. Hopelessly downcast, I sat waiting dolefully on the railway platform for two hours for the next train to Verona to connect to Trento.

At home there was another letter from Clayton. Again, it was only a card with a short note.:

Luca,

I am at last saving a little money. The novel is ready for publishing — all I need is a publisher. Alessandro has gotten himself a very charming little

apartment in the city near a BART station (our Tube), so
he gets back and forth to Berkeley quite easily. I'm
really sorry I missed Claudia's wedding. No one deserves
happiness more than she does after what she's been
through. Give her my love the next time you speak to
her. (Please let me know her and David's address in
England!)

Feeling blue. The days go so painfully slow. The
nights are wretched without you. I don't know which is
worse. It's all hell. Sometimes I think of forgetting about
the book and selling everything I own to buy a one-way
ticket to Italy — and *you*! But the loans aren't even paid
off and I can't rest till something comes of the book.
I'm not convinced, though, that any of it is worth the
trouble without you. I want you till it hurts, Luca. I
want you tonight. I want you *now*. Can any of this make
it easier for you? No, I know it doesn't. But, you see,
I'm in love with this beautiful young man in Trento, and
my love for him doesn't let me sleep at night. Forgive
me.

Talk to you soon. Love to your mother. I love you
so much, Luca.

My life, as always,
Clayton

Maybe it does not seem like much of a love letter. I
could not read it without my throat tightening in spasms,
my eyes flooding with pain. I wept uncontrollably,
childishly, and this time Claudia was not there to console me.

I had sunk to the lowest, most depressing depths
of my lonely deprivation. The desperate feeling of being
trapped had never seemed so viselike. The very floor I
walked on was a trap, binding me to a reality I could not
escape. The rooms and furnishings of my mother's house
were a shrinking cage. In all those anxious nights, in all those
anxious months, I did not suffer more than I did that one

night. I told myself I could not go back to Milan — knowing all the time I had to. The clammy pit I was trapped in had only one way out, a light far above me, as far from me as San Francisco. No decision had been placed in my hands; I had to get to Clayton, or perish.

That evening I called Maurizio. I had gotten his home phone number from Antonella. I told him I had been nervous, rash. I apologized as humbly as I could for my haste, my thoughtlessness, my precipitant bungling of what I knew was a rare "opportunity" for a young man of my inexperience. I asked if there was not some way I could see him again and make up for my rudeness.

The next afternoon, as he was locking the door to his office, snatching, so to speak, at some immediate proof of my good faith, he said, "I don't mind really. I rather like it in fact. A little skittishness is tantalizing. I prefer you straight boys. It's more exciting." And as his mouth gulped in my cock, I thought: I cannot tell him he is repugnant for purer reasons; I cannot tell him I am not here for a career, or fame, or stupendous wealth; I cannot tell him I am not here for anything but my life; I am not here — until I had to think of something else.

I did get assignments as a model and I did make money. Not many assignments and not a lot of money. But I was getting farther than by any other means at my disposal. I had become ruthless about money, not for its own sake, as I had greedily yearned for it before, but because it was the one and only way to end the nightmare I was living. It was the only way to Clayton.

Sadly, Maurizio's lechery was not the only lechery I had to satiate in order to get the work I did. There was a seemingly endless succession of ad men, photographers, fashion executives, and even designers themselves, all of whom demanded some offering in return for which there was sometimes only the faint hope of another show, another photo session, another layout for a magazine. They were almost all men. One woman from one of the more prominent fashion houses of Milan held out the bait of a feature in *L'Uomo*. It did not materialize. An executive from a public relations firm promised me an "in" with Armani. I never saw him or any of his clothes. Nonetheless, in supplication, I fucked them all. (If they liked, they could give me a blow-job.) I had to work fast. I did not have time to wait to be adored, or to lay my bets judiciously. My only talents were my looks and my desperation. In two months I had made enough money to think that in a few weeks I would be able to dispense with the shit and buy a ticket to San Francisco.

And if I ever asked myself why I did not just take my body down to that bar in Via Monviso in Milan and sell it to the highest bidder along with the other hustlers, it was a question endowed with no moral force. My plight had inured me to doubt, made me impervious to the nicer delineations of proper and improper conduct. All my self-rebuke had been drowned in need. I was doing what I had to do.

Only once did I come close to being violated without my complicity. In a three-way with another girl model and a male photographer. I was fucking the girl when the photographer tried to enter me. I had had no idea just how painful this could be. I had to tell him as tactfully as possible in my delicate position *not* to do that. Fortunately, he complied with my request.

Thus it can be seen that my ultimate abasement was, after all, at least partially voluntary. The horrendous dilemma *had* coerced a decision from me. I could not pretend that I was not the willing protagonist of the plot: I was the butch stud. I was the ambitious model out to get all he could get from them. I let them think I was dumb. I affected a surly, quiet persona, cultivated a hardened exterior, wore a cocky sneer on my face that told them I *was* just another hustler who thought he was hot shit. I explained nothing to anyone. I let my sullen presence speak for itself. I let them think that I thought it was a simple and effective "attitude," a pose to ingratiate myself into their world and make off with as much as I could. And they were right. But for motives they would never have guessed. I was not going to enlighten them: Love had reduced me to a shambles, and only *then* had I chosen to be a whore.

I will not say that I did not enjoy some of it. I did sometimes feel adored. Some of the sex was pleasurable. But the sex never left me satisfied. Mystics say that the orgasm is symbolic of death, and without Clayton I learned the full scope of that relationship. I wanted Clayton. He knew me and I knew him. They only person I fucked in all those months that I even *liked* had been Fabio.

But I cannot regret what I did.

I was never riddled with fears for my commitment to Clayton. The whole sordid, shabby business attested to my steadfast love for him. My disgrace and degradation were a confirmation of the one unbreakable thread of decency left in me. Whatever I had done for love, the love itself was undefiled. Heartsickening loneliness was still the only companion I counted on.

Returning from Milan after a long weekend of drumming up trade, I had looked at Clayton's Valentine card with such bitter shame that I could not even cry. When he called to tell me he had picked up a copy of a Milan newspaper in San Francisco and seen my picture in an ad, I told him merely that I had lucked into a job through a friend . . . and changed the subject, guiltily aware that my voice had become empty, distant, guiltless.

If I have sped through this account with a certain cynical alacrity, know that it is a nuance born of self-hatred. There was no room left in my cage for pride or self-respect.

I do not want to imply that my experiences represent the unprincipled essence of the fashion industry and
modeling in Italy. I worked for one small, not very
prestigious agency. I am sure the majority of models and
agencies are legitimate. But when one works on the
periphery of such a business, one must work feverishly
to get toward center stage, especially in a fashion capital
like Milan.

Nor do I wish to overstate my own minor exploits.
I was not unique. There were many more beautiful men and
women with more snarled, Machiavellian and lurid histories
in the business than mine. My own story, however, was
undeniably. . .sleazy.

Just when I had decided a few more weeks of
"modeling" would suffice for my plans, winter slapped
me with memories of the preceding winter and my father's
disappearance. It had also been the winter I had met Clayton.
Gnawing reminiscences of how his presence had helped me
through that trial made my task both more difficult and more
imperative. Perhaps because of these memories, I found
myself in an even blacker mood than usual.

Maurizio was hounding me then to attend a social
function that he insisted was too important to forgo. A
party was being held in Milan that weekend. Actually, it was
being given in a villa outside Milan by a very famous
designer. There were to be other luminaries from the fashion
world attending, some with the kind of clout that could
get my mission more quickly, if no more pleasantly, accomplished. I did not want to go, but with single-minded
pluck I forced myself to be there, immersing my dread of
the evening in my general ill humor.

The villa was a sprawling, expensively decorated
home above a small wooded lake. The guests were all
cosmopolitan, elegant and beautiful — at least in the social
sense of the word. It was the sort of affluent, refined milieu

I was not yet quite used to, but in which I was expected to participate with unreserved delight — *not* as though I had always been a member of its elite ranks, but as though I was positively apoplectic to have been asked to join them.

I spoke to no one. I was fortunate in having established a public personality that did not allow me to fawn over anyone. My image was more insolent. I was conscious of being cruised by several important-looking people, but I did not know who anybody was, and with this excuse to myself withdrew into my perpetual depression.

Shortly people began to leave the large salon that was the hub of the party. I wandered through the house and discovered that several rooms were serving as orgy chambers. Group sex, which I have never liked in spite of my dalliances with three-ways and four-ways, would also have been a tactically flawed strategy in the type of campaign I was waging. I launched myself back into the salon.

A small cluster of people stood around the bar. An older, impeccably and femininely groomed queen was entertaining them with his witty repartee. Queens, a species I had only recently come to know, are by some mysterious, subcultural alchemy precisely the same throughout the world. Identical humor (by turns campy and corrosive), identical gestures, identical bitchiness. My own disposition towards them depended at that time on whether or not I was expected to fuck them. This one I thought amusing, and stayed near the circle of friends to listen.

I was incensed to feel Maurizio suddenly sidle up to me and whisper, "I think there are some people upstairs you should be meeting." His smooth, fat face was perspiring, his clothes were in disarray. He was drunk and clumsily put his hand on my crotch.

It was such a small act, really — hardly even an insult after all I had made myself endure. But one drop, we say in Italian, will bring the cup to overflowing. I shoved him away and yelled, "Keep your filthy hands off me, *stronzo!*"

Everyone was looking at us. My outburst had utterly confounded Maurizio. He stood staring dumbly at me. I glared back. In that instant I saw in him everything I had grown to despise in that merciless winter, in myself. With three months' store of malice, I spit in his face — something I have never done before or since to anyone.

The spittle had landed oddly enough, for I had not propelled it with this aim, on his nose. The thick mucousy sputum dangled preposterously from the end of his nose and over the infantile mouth.

"My dear," the queen gleefully exclaimed, flapping a frilly handkerchief, "*here,* take this — you've got *coitus interruptus* all over your face."

Everyone laughed, except Maurizio and I, and this remark along with my swift exit probably saved us all from a nastier imbroglio. Maurizio did eventually come running after me shouting ugly, angry things — some of them true, some of them not: "*Figlio di troia!* [Son of a slut!... Untrue.] *Credi di essere cosi furbo! Cosi furbo! Non sei che una puttana, tu!* [You think you're so smart, so cunning, You're nothing but a whore!...True.]"

"You'll never work in this business again, anyplace in Italy!" he blustered. I left him to his roaring, at times astute, fulminations.

On the train to Trento I thought, What would Clayton say, even in his good-natured generosity, if he knew that I had prostituted himself as I had? Would *he* revile me as a whore? No, but he would be hurt. That would be worse than vilification. I pushed this masochistic reverie out of my head.

Although Maurizio surely did not have the power to blacklist me single-handedly as a "model," I figured it was best if I believed he did. My rickety career would have to be cut short. I could not go on like this. I had just enough money for the cheapest possible air ticket, a model's portfolio, and experience (oh, I had the experience all right!) in one of the fashion centers of the world. It was not the cushion I had hoped to arrive in San Francisco on, but it was adequate.

Clayton's voice on the telephone was concerned.

"Luca, I didn't expect to hear from you today. I was just leaving for work. Is there anything wrong?"

"If you still want me, I'm coming to San Francisco. Right away." Why *If you still want me?* He had always wanted me. It was my own guilt-ridden self-contempt, an insecure plea for validation.

His affirmation was ecstatic.

"Want you? If you don't come here, I'm coming there! I was going to call you in the morning. The book's being published!"

VIII   Take These Memories with You

"**P**orta questi ricordi con te," Fabio said to me at the Trento train station, handing me a small gift-wrapped box. "These memories" included, as I was to discover upon opening the box on the train, a package of *confetti* (the Italian candy commonly given before weddings, not the American "confetti"); a photograph of Fabio and me that we had taken months before in the automatic photo booth in the rail station; a photograph of Fabio alone, on the back of which was written his address and phone number, and an identical print with the same information, and a note: "If you meet any rich Americans with big dicks coming to Italy, give them this"; a set of keys to his family's home and to his bedroom door with the injunction that if I ever returned to Trento late at night, I was to quietly sneak in and sleep with him; his authentic Swiss army knife, an object Fabio cherished with boyish veneration, although he did not give it to me in the juvenile belief that I, too, wanted such a knife (he was not an unintelligent man) but because he knew I knew how much it meant to him, and would remember him for it; and a condom which had been stretched over his tumescent organ and inscribed in oil crayon with: "*L'amicizia è. . . .*" — "Friendship is. . . ." (this was a reference to a rather pompous and primly shallow tract on friendship by an Italian author then popular in Italy).

I did not recognize the wadded-up rubber at first, and when I held it up out of the box I was embarrassed to see the matronly woman across from me in the compartment ogling it with a surprise not easily discernible as disgust or admiration. I blushed and put everything back in the box.

The scene at the train station had been blessedly brief. My entire family was there to see me off of course. My grandmother and aunt took turns showering me in cloudbursts of tears, but my mother was remarkably restrained. None of us knew when I would be back, I least of all, and the large, overstuffed suitcase I was taking reassured no one. But with a worldly grace that, in truth, startled me, my mother hugged me warmly, shed a few touchingly heartfelt though decorous tears, told me to give her love to Clayton, and was able to maintain a relatively stolid demeanor even as she begged me not to forget her. After all the tears I had cried that horrible winter, it was a physiological miracle that I had the ones left in me that I did.

Fabio embraced me, and as I waved to them all from the departing train, he called out, also begging me not to forget him.

I was taking the train to Frankfurt, from where I was then catching a charter flight to San Francisco. It had, upon consultation with a travel agent, presented itself as the least expensive way to get there. My air ticket was issued for a return three months hence, but it could be changed to anytime up to a year. I figured I would either come back with Clayton, or. . .I was not sure what I would do in any other case.

Emigration to the States, I knew, was virtually impossible without compelling reasons, such as being married to an American or having extraordinary professional credentials. I had had enough trouble just getting my visa from the U.S. Embassy in Milan. They had been brusque, impertinent, uncooperative, and at times thoroughly obnoxious. (I was reminded of my visit with Clayton to the Questura, the fact now dawning on me that bureaucrats are the same incompetent martinets everywhere regardless of nationality.) I would of course try to stay in San Francisco and find work if Clayton and I decided to live in the States. My studies had already foundered during my career as a "model," so I had even less worry about leaving the university than I had before. I could continue my education later, maybe even attend a university in America eventually. I did not fool myself, however, that there were not practical, and problematic, considerations to be faced. But they seemed then puny problems. The important thing was to get to San Francisco, to get to Clayton.

As for Trento, I was prepared to leave it all behind. I would miss my mother, of course, and Fabio, as I was already missing Claudia. But I could not conjure in my mind or heart a picture of Trento unpolluted by the acrid stench of the months I had just trudged through there. Something noxious and unremitting had entered my memories of my hometown, and my attachment to it, for all the joyous memories I still possess, had atrophied, decomposed to some irreversible degree in the putrid processes of those months.

I was dead tired when I arrived at the San Francisco airport. The long overnight train and then the long flight, during all of which I had been unable to sleep, had undone me physically and mentally. I felt totally wasted. I began to fret, with punch-drunk nervousness, about my appearance, wondering if my exhaustion showed, if Clayton would find my looks, after all these months of longing, a frightful disappointment.

But his face evinced nothing but delirious happiness when I saw him outside the customs area. He swept me up in his arms and held me so tightly I could hardly breathe. I squeezed him back just as hard. My energy was immediately resuscitated. I felt like I would never sleep again as long as I could hold Clayton and be aware of his body next to mine. The only thing we said in those first moments was each other's name. We just stood hugging one another for a while, afraid to let go.

Clayton pulled back at last to look at my face. His eyes were moist. "Don't ever let me run off and leave us alone like that again, Luca."

We swore to each other that we would never again sentence ourselves to such a prolonged and indefinite separation.

He grabbed my bag and with his arm around me we walked through the airport. My heart was beating so chaotically in my chest I thought I would pass out. My legs were unsteady and my vision a mist. If anything had been worth all my suffering, it was this moment, this embrace, this touch. All the heartache had been washed away in an instant.

Clayton walked us toward a smiling man standing in the concourse of the central terminal. It was Ken. He looked about my age (I found out later he was actually thirty), was about the same height as Clayton, slim, black, and with a handsome, relaxed face set off by gently confiding brown eyes. We were introduced, greeting each other with a handshake, and then Ken took my bag so as to free Clayton's attentions.

"I waited out here," Ken explained, a playful gleam

in his eyes, "because I hate long good-byes — and I *hate* long hellos."

"Ken drove me out to the airport," Clayton said as we walked toward the garage. "I don't have a car and though I could've just borrowed his I didn't trust myself, in my excitement, to get me safely here — much less get us safely home."

"The truth is," Ken said, "I finagled my way into coming along. I wasn't about to miss this for anything in the world. It's one of my perks for having nursed him in your absence — not to mention the rent I paid! And the *landlady*!"

I did not understand all of Ken's English. I did not care. Clayton and I were looking at each other, talking softly, searching for something to say that would express our happiness. When we realized that our eyes were saying it all, we just shut up and stared.

The first thing that impressed me in the garage was the size of the cars. It looked like a battlefield of tanks. Even the cars that Clayton and Ken insisted were subcompacts struck me as larger than the average Fiat. We got to Ken's car, a "modest" orange-red Honda wagon, and put my bag in back.

"This is Darlene," Ken said. "But when she's acting up I'm tempted to change her name to Karen Ann Quinlan. Let's hope she starts."

Again I did not understand everything.

"You don't mind, do you, Ken?" Clayton asked, getting into the back seat with me.

"Yassuh, yassuh, anything you say, boss," Ken replied, drolly changing his voice, "I's just the chauffeur. I can see the grits and corn pone is *cookin'*. Ya figure this here parkin' lot takes MassahCard?" I seemed to be understanding less and less. I began to wonder if I had forgotten American so fast. Ken started the car. "That's a good girl. The urn of bolts on the mantelpiece is still a few years off."

In the back seat of the car I put my arm around Clayton's shoulders and he leaned me back to give me a long, deep kiss. It was the kind of kiss I had neither received nor given since he had left Trento. My famished mouth satisfied itself and, in turn, my hunger for sincere, fiery affection. Our hands ran over each other's body in passionate clutches.

"You're not going to need these," Clayton said, breaking off to indicate my heavy layer of clothes. It was still March and I had worn my warmest clothes. I did not know then that winter clothing is needed in San Francisco only during the summer.

I do not remember my first drive into San Francisco. That is to say, I do not remember anything outside the back seat of Ken's car. I do remember at one point seeing Ken glimpse us in the rearview mirror. We were only embracing, but thinking that perhaps we were intent on something more he said, "Don't mind me. I've wormed my way into the act as far as I go. I'm just proud to see Clayton's taste in men is as irreproachable as ever." And then, more to himself, "Mmm-mmm! Ain't love grand!"

Ken left us at Clayton's place. It was early evening and he said he had other plans — "Unless of course you really *want* me to stay." Clayton gave him a menacing look. Ken shrugged and turned to me. "It's all up to you to take care of him now, Luke," (This was an apocopation that was going to stick with many of my American friends.) He wagged a reprimanding finger at me and said jocularly, "You've had that poor man ranting and raving about some kind of 'Pig God'!"

"I will take care of him," I said meekly, and Ken drove away honking.

I was to learn later that Clayton and Ken had been

lovers some years before. They had since remained good friends, a peculiar convention among Americans. Or Californians.

Clayton's apartment was actually a little two-story cottage tucked behind the houses that fronted the street. The neighborhood, I was told, was called Noe Valley. We had to go through a long, narrow alley to get to the cottage. There were two rooms downstairs, a living room and a study, and upstairs were the kitchen, dining room, and bedroom. All the rooms except the bedroom were tiny. I did not think it especially well-furnished or decorated (Clayton, whatever his taste in men, did not have a gifted eye in other matters). I thought, in fact, that his apartment in Trento had been more comfortable. But I sensed at once a certain charming, homey quality, something that was Clayton, in the appealing, well-kept cottage. I could see how he would not have wanted to lose it. The faint scent of garlic butter hung in the kitchen air.

The picture of me in the clothes ad from the Milan newspaper was framed and sitting on the bedroom dresser.

"Compravo riviste e giornali italiani per mantenere il mio italiano." He spoke to me for the first time in Italian. *"Non mi aspettavo di trovarci un uomo così bello."* I was buying Italian newspapers and magazines in order to keep up my Italian. I didn't expect to find such a beautiful man in them.

I tried to look at the photograph without thinking of everything that had gone into it.

We made love. I was shocked to realize how even in my extremity my idealization of him and his prowess had been a pale shadow of the real power of his lovemaking. Passion seemed to burst anew into wildly exquisite blossoms of pleasure for both of us. But we had more than six months of sexual frustration to make up for: we had a seething, incalculable love to unleash, a love that would never be expended. And lying in his sheltering grasp afterwards, for the second time in my life I thought, If I must die, let it be *now*, in his arms.

Our ardent rejoicing was incendiary. We closeted ourselves in Clayton's cottage for the next couple of days, reveling in every burning second. He was still working as a waiter at the restaurant, but he had arranged before I arrived to have the days off. He had foreseen the fires that would engulf us.

The check he was to receive from the publisher, covering a flat payment for the novel as well as an advance on sales of the book, was due any day, but it would not be so vast an amount as to allow Clayton to quit his job. Notwithstanding the meager sum, he had been all set to fly back to Italy as soon as it came in, if only to pick me up and bring me back with him. We would have both been broke in that event. As it was, penury threatened only me. I had enough cash to eat, abstemiously, for a few weeks and that was it.

The check arrived about a week after I had. Clayton promptly went on a jubilant buying rampage. I told him to save his money, but within a few days he — *we* — had hectically but neatly spent several hundred dollars, not counting the debts he had paid off. He took me to the best restaurants, bought himself and me some new clothes, rented a car and drove us down to Big Sur, and then back to the most deluxe hotel in Carmel for an erotic evening overlooking the Pacific. And, not least of all, he bought me a simple gold band engraved with a small trident and "Love, Clayton." It was a silly, sentimental and old-fashioned thing he had done. But that is the privilege of *anyone* in love. Having been denied admittance for so long, we were not about to loiter respectably about the entrance to heaven, but instead made a mad dash for the most flamboyant rewards.

I began to meet Clayton's friends. They were all nice people, in the casual light by which one cannot help but

judge new acquaintances. I genuinely liked Ken, and he
would often join us for dinner or the movies. He had no
steady boyfriend at the time and after our first selfish days
Clayton and I were both happy to have him along whenever
he was availalbe. He never treated me as less than a dear old
friend, and though I did not always understand his humor,
he often made me laugh.

It was 1972. Naturally, I was impressed with the
freedom men and women enjoyed in publicly displaying
affection towards their own sex in San Francisco. And yet,
unlike the easy intimacy of Italians, there *always* seemed
to be a sexual implication to an arm about a friend or a head
cocked closely to a companion's. There was a perpetual
charge in the air, a gamey, sweetly pungent electricity, as
though dangerous pheromones were being released into the
atmosphere. Indeed, one could not walk down certain streets
without feeling one's own pubic sweat involuntarily
stimulated. It was exciting, but a little unsettling. I missed
the nonpolitical, nonglandular affection Clayton and I
had enjoyed walking down a street in Trento, our bodies
pressed together.

Clayton seemed truly worried when he told me he
had known so many loverships to crash on the rocks of the
City's sensuality. I only smiled impatiently and kissed him.
How could I tell him that I had, in anguish, sacrificed too
much ever to abandon the love he gave me?

Of course I loved the City, too, but first because it
was Clayton's city. Its beauty was Clayton's beauty. Taking
me on a stroll through the Italian neighborhood in North
Beach, it was *his* neighborhood that enchanted me, not
mine. Sitting atop the stony crags above the beach, sunset
cocktails at the Cliff House were his magic, not nature's. His
company is what made the City dazzle for me; because it
was sacred to him, I worshipped at its shrines.

Clayton's love of the City turned antic for me

sometimes. I thought he was crazy for trying to fine-tune my appreciation for the circus-like arena at Market and Powell Streets, with its bible-thumpers, street musicians, souvenir hawkers, "street freaks," and general rabble of noise and scene makers. He also spent an inordinate amount of time trying to explain such enigmatic graffiti as "Flipper Died for Your Sins," "So Punish Me — Give Me a Bad Hairdo," "Hot Kitty Sizzles in Hell," or the parking space spray-painted with, "Reserved for Poopsie."

I did have some problems with the language. Not everyone spoke as clearly as Clayton. If Ken jokingly shifted into a very heavy black American accent, or, as he sometimes did, into a pseudo-Southern lilt, I would lose most of what he said. Other people spoke too rapidly or too indistinctly or merely slurred all their words into one long. . .meow. And because I spoke English with some fluency, they would never believe that I did not understand them.

Once I went to the corner grocery store to buy a few items and the man behind the cash register asked me something perfectly indecipherable. I prodded him with "Pardon?" five or six times, but still could not understand him. The man finally slammed my change peevishly down on the counter and walked away. "Get this joker," he said to the other clerk. "Thinks he's being cute." As I understood these remarks immediately, I was sure he had been pulling *my* leg all along.

Another time Clayton and I had a small argument after a tennis match. (I *had* been pleased to see him wear the shorts and T-shirt I had sent him for his birthday.) Upon my using a rather well-chosen Italian expletive, Clayton slyly quipped, "This is my country. In my country we speak *English*."

"You call this English?" I retorted. We both laughed.

What American I did understand always seemed excessively peppered with slang and vulgar words and expressions. As a consequence, I took to speaking with a bluntness I did not comprehend the effect of. "What racket are you in?" I might ask a stranger at Ken's house. Or I would say to one of Clayton's married neighbors, "Oh, so you like to fool around in your spare time?" Even to Ken, I found it a simple thing, too simple perhaps, to tell him the clothes he was wearing were "trash" or that as a driver he was "really lousy." Looking back, it may have been this loony laxness of mine with the American language that made us such fast friends. He thought I was a "hoot."

Sometimes, however, my English had me on the brink of real trouble. If an old lady on the bus started telling me her whole life story and its manifold miseries, something that happened to me with eerie frequency, I might say to her, "Oh, fuck it off, dear," meaning, I imagined, "Don't let it get you down." One of San Francisco's more tempestuous harridans would not hesitate to create a scene on the bus over such cheekiness.

When I saw Alessandro again, I was relieved to feel our old animosity unaroused. Maybe it was due to the fact that I was now a familiar and sturdy fixture in Clayton's life. Or maybe it was simply because we were kindred aliens in a world that did not speak our language. Indeed, at our first meeting in months we fell into speaking Italian with such velocity that Clayton had to ask for a translation. He must have been glad to see that his friends were no longer rivals for his affection. While Clayton was working one evening, Alessandro even escorted me about Berkeley, showing me the campus and taking me out to dine on Telegraph Avenue.

It would be years, though, before our friendship progressed to the point where Alessandro could confess to me, "I *was* jealous of you. Not because there was anything sexual between me and Clayton. [Nothing overtly sexual I would editorialize.] But here was this stupid, *spoiled* brat taking my best friend away from me."

The weeks passed swiftly, happily. I worried a little about money, but I appeased my conscience by telling myself I would register with one of the modeling agencies in San Francisco one of these days. This time I would attempt a legitimate career as a professional model. I had my portfolio, my looks...my experience. (I think Clayton, in his categorical enthusiasm for me, had contributed to my false sense of security regarding employment.) In the meantime, Clayton paid for almost everything, while I kept up a bubbly stream of postcards to my mother and Fabio, and to Claudia in England.

If Clayton was not working, either at the restaurant or on the new novel he was starting, we would play tennis, or go to the movies, or tour the city, or cook ourselves a big Italian meal at home...or fuck. When he was working, I explored the city on my own, or went to the gym (Clayton had paid for my membership), or visited Ken or Alessandro, or just lounged around the house, cleaning, sunning, watching TV.

One of Clayton's neighbors in the building facing back upon the cottage was a young woman, a remnant "hippie" it appeared from San Francisco days gone by, with a little six-year-old boy. Whenever she saw me she would say "*Ciao!*" and then tell her son, "Look, he's from Italy. *Italy.* All the way from Italy, a long way off. He's Italian," as though, in fact, I were some sort of circus freak. The boy would fix me with a horrified stare and step back one or two steps.

The week Clayton's book officially came out we threw a party at the house. I was so proud of him it never even occurred to me to read the book. My literary English was not very good then, and reading anything longer than a letter was a chore. As I have noted before, I had no inclinations toward literature in general, not even Italian literature, and Clayton's writing had never really interested me. I had never asked to read the novel in any of its versions in all those months. It was the one thing to comprise any sort of separate world of his own apart from me, and as important as it was to him, he seemed almost to respect me for not making a fuss over his literary ambitions. He knew I was proud to see his name on a book because he was *my* Clayton Hayes. No doubt he would have liked me to read the book and appreciate it, but he did not pressure me in any way to become a "fan." He had so much more from me than that. Before the party, though, I felt obliged to at least skim through the book, and did so with shameful haste and carelessness. Some of it may have been funny, some of it may have been erotic, some of it may even have been pro-found; after wading through what I could, any of these facts would have come as news to me.

I tried to tell him later that I thought it was great, but he smiled, pinched one of my tits, and said dubiously, "Oh, really?" I admitted I did not understand what the title, *Organ of Conceit,* meant. I thought it must have referred simply to the penis, since the story seemed to me to be an *endless* chronicle of the synchronous, ambisexual mis-adventures of a man and woman, friends since their childhoods in a swampy parish of Louisiana. "No," he said, "the 'organ' is the 'self,' a sexually egocentric view of reality. It's —" Then he looked at me, laughed, and implored me to stop him if he ever started going off like that again. "Don't worry about what it all means, Luca," he said. "It doesn't matter." Well, I thought, at least I have something to say now at the party if anyone asks me my opinion of the book.

The afternoon of the party Ken came over to help us make hors d'oeuvres. I had more fun setting up for the party than I was to have later at the party itself. As we cut up vegetables Ken asked me if I had met everyone who was coming. I thought so.

"And George?" he said with a wicked note of caution. I asked if he was an old lover of Clayton's. "Oh, no," he answered. "he's very. . ." and swiveled his hips spastically and made a jerky rotation of his forearms.

"Handicapped?" I asked, guessing at the meaning of this pantomine.

He burst into laughter. I was pleased to be able to repay some of the hilarity Ken had afforded me.

"No, Luke, I mean he's swishy," he said, catching his breath. I was still in the dark.

In light of my recent experiences, it was bizarrely discouraging how long it took him to make me understand that George was a queen.

"Just treat George like the *true* heiress to the throne and you'll be fine," was his last baffling word on the subject.

I did know most of the people at the party. Alessandro came with an American girlfriend I had not met before. Everyone was very kind to me and Clayton made an announcement early on to the effect that the party was really in my honor. He would trade any Nobels or Pulitzers, he said, for *me* any day of the week. My own devotion to Clayton was unquestionable, I hoped, in the quiet manner in which I helped make sure everyone was comfortable, returning every few minutes to Clayton to tell him how much I liked his friends.

I have always had smooth, clear skin, but by one of those strange little ironies of life, on the one day I was expected to host — and charm — all these people, a pimple had erupted on my neck. It was a large suppurating bruise of a pimple that was quite beyond being camouflaged. Once the party was under way I nervously went back and forth to the bathroom to dab alcohol on it. After one of these visits I emerged to see that George had arrived.

His carriage was stately, if not regal. He was about forty-five, thin except for his paunch, and with fastidiously coiffed graying hair. He moved with a slothful grace and elegance, as if his feeble metabolism could not possibly support a normal breath or hurried gesture. His voice had the density of warm honey. But as parsimonious as he was with his energies, his biting sarcasm, I quickly learned, was spryly and promiscuously dispensed.

"Eve! This must be Eve Harrington!" he said the second he set eyes on me. He turned to Ken. "Kenyatta, surely you know all about Eve. *You've* seen this act before." Then to Clayton, "Don't turn your back on her for one moment."

When no one laughed at any of this, or laughed, if at all, only in perplexity, he said with a sigh, "That's the problem. I *tried* going butch, but it just didn't . . . go. Now that I've gone back to being gay and campy, nobody understands my allusions. My *dear,* what is that thing on your neck?"

"It's a pimple, I'm afraid," I said, touching it.

"No, no, no, no, no, no, no. Models never have *pimples,*" he cooed. "Ingrown hairs, maybe, but never *pimples.*"

I had been prepared to like George. I had the feeling that this intended accommodation was not mutual.

"Luca, Luca, Luca." He seemed to be mulling over the name. "This name has confused me. I thought in the Romance languages 'o' was masculine and 'a' was feminine. Shouldn't 'Luca' be a girl's name?"

"There are some exceptions in Italian," I explained. "Luca is one. Andrea is a man's name too."

"Oh," he said with utter disinterest, his smile nakedly polite. He took a drink from Clayton. Clayton, sensing the perilous chemistry, hovered nearby.

"You can call me Luke if you like. A lot of my American friends do," I said diffidently.

He gazed at me with withering disdain. "Luca will do quite nicely, thank you."

"You can't expect George to use Luke," Ken said, trying to inject some less invidious humor, "when he's spent a lifetime making everybody's name sound *more* feminine."

"You got it, girl," George said, smacking his gin-moistened lips. "Oh, Kenyatta, the old ways die hard," he moaned. "What's to become of all the young men these days when they've all forgotten their girlish ways?"

I suddenly looked upon George as a challenge. I knew that if I could handle the responsibility of dealing congenially with this friend of Clayton, ableit this *queen*, I could only gain in his estimation.

I began asking George how long he had known Clayton and where they had met. George had befriended Clayton when he had first come to the City. He had helped him get his first job and find an apartment.

"Unfortunately," he sighed, glass to lips, eyes survey-ing the room, "I'm probably the only one here who's never slept with him. You don't have to tell me how you and Clayton met. I know Clayton. I know his style: 'I've got a dick, you've got a dick . . . .' " He seemed to have a momen-tary spurt of energy. "What kind of creams *do* you use? Your skin is really quite lovely — except of course for your. . .unlovely *thing*. Beautiful, really. What do you use?"

"Nothing," I said, and paused. "Soap."

"Nonsense, my dear, you've got to start using creams and lotions *now*. If you start too late, you only end up with oily wrinkles. How old are you?"

"Twenty-three."

"And you've got to start lying about your age. You can't just start telling people you're twenty-nine when you turn thirty-five. People remember these things. Believe me, *I know*. Maintaining an international standard of glamour is *not* easy. Vanity can't be left to chance."

Alessandro commented at once: "*Lui t'ha lasciato*

abbastanza di merda?" Has he left you feeling enough like shit, or what? While definitely *peperino*, this rhetorical question perhaps seems a bit ambiguous on paper. I assure you the tone was in my defense, and totally welcome. By me at least.

Interpreting Alessandro's Italian as an insult, George petulantly addressed me again. "Well, at least you don't smell. So many Italians do, you know. Garlic, garlic, garlic. If not worse. The garlic, mind you, even seeps into their perspiration."

"The only one who smells of garlic around here, George," Clayton interrupted, "is me, I'm afraid. Luca is as sweet as rosemary — *even* his perspiration."

"Oh, do use that in your next book, Clayton," George dryly replied.

George was winning. I was beginning to feel pricklingly self-conscious. The reference to body smells, especially, was to stay with me. I had, under Clayton's influence and in the absence of a bidet, grown accustomed to showering daily. But I was now aware of a general reputation of Italians for dirtiness, and it intimidated me. The next time I went into the kitchen I smelled my skin.

"Of course, I don't say they aren't beautiful," George went on. "We have our young friend here to remind us of that." He opened a flowerlike hand in my direction, making his exclusion of the other Italian in the room, Alessandro, as blatant as possible. "I went on a Mediterranean cruise once aboard an Italian ship. Yes, they did stink, but the Italian staff was *inspiring*."

Apparently merely inquiring upon a point of idiomatic usage, Alessandro said to Clayton, "Is that what you call hitting the nail on the head?"

As if on cue, Clayton rejoined, "Or doing *something* on the head. . .of the Italian staff." The others laughed.

George smiled the thinnest smile I had ever seen. "I

176

leave the floor to those more knowledgeable about these things," he mumbled into his glass, and thirstily downed his drink.

Then, donning a fragile mask of goodwill, he asked me, "What do you want to be when you grow up, Luca?"

Ken again rushed in to my aid. "George wanted to be a girl detective when he was a kid — you know, like Nancy Drew. He got half his wish. Now if only he could tell the difference between a magnifying glass and a loaded gun."

"Oh, no, Kenyatta," George purred, "I know the difference. . .and I've still got my girlish ways."

I decided it was time to fend for myself. Determined not to come off as flip, I said, "I hope to get work soon as a model here in San Francisco."

"Ah, such a bright. . .secure future."

"Well, of course, it's only temporary until — "

"Oh, well, we can't all have futures. Tomorrow doesn't have room for all of us." All at once his eyes balefully lit up. "Is it true all models sleep their way to the top?"

"George!" Clayton barked with barely controlled anger, "the inquisition is *over*!"

At which point someone in the crowd devised a diversion and piped up, with irony that escaped me at the time, "Is this where someone turns to us all and says, 'You are all *eating* Sebastian Venable!'?"

Equally merciful, another person deadpanned, "Or, as our British cousins might say, the poof is in the pudding."

And for the moment the diversion worked as the tension in the room was dispersed by unanimous laughter. But something in the fierce way George's question had been repulsed by Clayton made me think that maybe Clayton himself had inferred that my past in the fashion industry had not been exemplary, or if exemplary for a model, not characteristic of the paragon of decency one might desire as a lover. He never asked me in depth about those months, maybe because of my evident reluctance to offer anything more than a few vague remarks about my "career." I had, in this one realm, been cagey with Clayton instead of candid. But he did not care; he did not care except insofar as he cared not to see me hurt by painful, prying questions.

Later, as Clayton was pissing in the bathroom, I took the opportunity to step in and ask him, as nonchalantly as I could, and in words less provocative, why he had hung on to this disaster of a friend. Buttoning up his jeans he philosophically, wearily answered, "He makes me laugh sometimes — and laughter can redeem even the most rancid of friendships. I guess everyone has to have one friend who nobody else could ever remotely be expected to tolerate. And he *was* very kind to me when I first came to the City. He wasn't so bitter then."

The talk at last turned to Clayton's book. Everyone was excited for him and encouragingly adulatory. We were all so proud of him. Those who had read the book were full of praise. They were saying — and why not? — exactly the kind of things one has friends for. Not that their evaluations of the novel's qualities were disingenuous; it just was not a night for serious literary analysis. We were celebrating the end of a long and arduous project. Some of them asked Clayton to sign their copies of the book. When someone asked me what I thought of the novel, I responded with the intellectually foggy, "I think it transcends the orthodox dimensions of storytelling with a sexually egocentric self-awareness of reality. I think it's a very important book." Clayton looked at me with a cockeyed smile half-reproving, half-amused.

"I enjoyed almost every page of it," George said with typical truculence. I bristled. *Ci risiamo.* Here we go again. "My own literary legacy is a verse I composed in my untamed and faithless youth: 'Perfidy and lice — could be better, but nothing nice.' Now I am faithful, unshakably faithful, to my cynicism if nothing else. I have no choice. Life is like bad sex: One can't be ungrateful, but one *can* be dissatisfied. Until you can only ask yourself, 'Why bother?' '' There was something so mournful about this little monologue that I almost began longing for the catty George and his affected, mordantly urbane badinage. He did not keep me waiting. "You have my permission to use that soliloquy in your next novel, Clayton." Then, more to the others, "You know, my family crest is a pair of bleary eyes rampant on a field of cigarettes and coffee. The family motto? *Why bother?*" He finally faced me again. "But of course you wouldn't understand. Life has been little more for you than romance and . . . romance. Oh, I don't doubt you've cried a few baby tears, the tears of an infant who hasn't gotten exactly what he wanted exactly when he wanted it. But let's face it. *Parliamoci chiaro.*" His Italian stunned me: Let's speak frankly. "You've been *lucky.*"

"But *I'm* the lucky sonovabitch," Clayton protested, his temper again on the verge of flaring.

"The catamite is lucky," George said serenely. "The sugar daddy is merely. . .grateful."

Clayton was so irate he could not speak. George took advantage of the storm's lull. He spoke each word slowly, with myriad diverse implications, a multitude of insinuations: "I, too, would have plied my. . .craft with book dedications to such cunningly beautiful *boys.*"

"What?" I asked, stirred awake by the mention of the book's dedication. I had been musing over all that George had said before he spoke in Italian; the realization that they had been the words of an emotionally bankrupt queen did not sweeten their message for me. Now, not quite sure what this term meant but sensing its importance, I looked around me for some explanation.

"Didn't you know?" Ken said, too cheerfully,

anxious to change the tone of the discussion, if not the topic. He handed me an open copy of the book. "Here. . .you must be kidding."

I stared at the page, blank save for the words "For Luca." My genuine surprise surprised everyone.

"I didn't know," I said haltingly. "You didn't tell me, Clayton."

"I didn't think I had to. You've seen the book." His anger was gone. We looked at each other for several seconds, till his smile, at its warmest and most intimate, made me smile and blush.

George peered somberly into his glass of gin, like a gypsy unhappy with the crystal ball's forecast.

After everyone had left and we had cleaned up, I sat by myself out on the patio in the night chill. Clayton, detecting my need to be alone, had let me wander outside without following. I was pondering all that I had heard that evening, as well as the voice of dissent that had raised itself inside me, and that I had so scrupulously ignored.

We all feel we have something of beauty to offer the world, morally or physically. Only when this self-image is exhausted and one's own value seems illusory, artificial, if even that, does one end up at the bottom of a river. I had proved to the world, I bragged to myself, that I had physical beauty — though the cost of the evidence had been dear. But had I purchased anything really? What personal worth had been established by my "beauty"? Where would I be when it was gone? What was I to boast of when I was no longer young and handsome? Did I have anything more lasting to offer Clayton? Did I have anything more lasting to offer *myself*? Was love, pure and blinding, really enough to build a life upon? Could love ever exist in a vacuum? Love had justified all my suffering, but had my suffering been no more than the vanity of a stupid, lovesick boy?

I began to wonder if I *could* be more to Clayton than

a "kept boy," a pretty catamite, a whore to Clayton's sugar daddy. Yes, Clayton loved me and I loved him with a need that still ached, but was there anyplace to go from there? Did I really care about nothing except my love for Clayton? These were ugly, thorny questions I put to myself. But then my dignity and integrity had come to seem such ephemeral things, my pride an absurd hallucination. Love, in all its intransigence, had seemed to prove only my weakness after all, my moral infirmity, my lack of character, my complete emptiness as a person. *I* was nothing, a meaningless cipher in an equation that I had believed from the beginning *must* be love.

For the first time since leaving it, I thought of Trento with homesickness. Trento, which circumstance had made synonymous with unhappiness, now evoked in me something nostalgic and bittersweet. I looked back to the time before my father's death, before Clayton, before I had learned so much so quickly. Had it all been a mistake? Shouldn't I still be that foolish boy who wanted to do nothing but make money and fuck girls.

Clayton came out of the house. He stood behind the deck chair I was sitting in and put his hands on my shoulders.

"Let's have breakfast at Hopwell's tomorrow," he said. Hopwell's was the homey little cafe around the corner on Twenty-fourth Street. I had become very fond of big American breakfasts. "We deserve a nice, long, relaxing morning."

I knew that with this inconsequential suggestion Clayton had hoped to lighten my pensive mood. I nodded. I interlocked the fingers of one of his hands with mine. With his other hand Clayton lifted my chin and leaned down to kiss my lips.

What had I besides a kiss, an embrace, my body, to give him? With what else could I proclaim to the world *my* dedication: "For Clayton"?

IX Andrea Sapetti

The success of Clayton's first novel was mysterious, both as to the reasons for its popularity as well as the mode of its ascent in sales. The publishers, adept — as Clayton modestly put it — at pandering to the baser tastes of the marketplace, had committed themselves with a rather far-reaching but unspectacular campaign to distribute the book. The only reviews it got initially were the kind of insignificant promotional reviews any halfway skillful publisher can arrange. Sales were not tremendous in those first six months, and, indeed, the book was never destined to make anyone's best-seller list. And yet it sold, steadily and continually. It seemed especially popular among college students, and no one was more surprised than Clayton when he received his first invitations to speak at various campuses. Because success crept up on him so slowly, it was almost as though it never arrived.

At the end of the first six months, however, it was

clear that Clayton Hayes was here to stay. With sales going respectably well for a first novel and an advance from the publisher for the new novel Clayton was working on, he quit his job at the restaurant once and for all. By the end of the first year as a published author he would be enjoying a measure of fame and fortune — solid dollops of each.

In those days we used to go quite often to Fanny's restaurant in the Castro (now long gone) to have dinner and, afterwards, to listen to Faye Carol sing in the small bar downstairs. Faye, a jazz vocalist, has always been one of my favorite singers in the Bay Area, and even today I will go out of my way to see her. I had fallen in love with her the first time Clayton took me to hear her. (I had in fact gotten thoroughly drunk that first night and made an awful scene jumping up and down, clapping my hands thunderously, stomping my feet, and shouting, *"Brava! Brava! Bravissima!*!! Faye took it all graciously and ended her set with an appreciative bow in my direction.)

One night at Fanny's we were startled to have our waiter come up to the table with a copy of *Organ of Conceit* and ask Clayton to sign it. It was the first time a stranger had asked for his autograph, or even, I think, recognized him in public. Clayton said to me while signing the book, "I used to be a nobody. Now I'm a nobody with a name." Shortly after that the first interviews with Clayton began to appear in the local press.

Clayton never attempted to explain the success of the book. In a way, he did not have to. Its sales had been so stealthy, its popularity so largely a product of word-of-mouth, that no one came up to him and asked, "How does it feel to be an overnight success, Mr. Hayes?" He never made any claims for the book that could have been interpreted by anyone to mean that *he* thought it was "great literature." But he was altogether convinced, with more than adequate evidence, that it was entertaining, especially to those younger, college-age readers. His own deeper perspective on the novel, elucidated to no one else and which perhaps I alone knew he had, was not imposed on interviewers or fans.

Critics of course eventually caught up with the success of the book — that is, they could no longer ignore a book so much discussed. As so often with such reviews, which follow upon a general and positive familiarity with a book among the public, the critics were almost uniformly negative. They seemed as a body to resent the popular success of a work so "barely distinguishable from trash" (as one critic wrote). In all fairness, for this is still the overall judgement of the critical establishment upon Clayton's work, these acidic critiques, tainted by vengeance as they were, were also earnestly sincere. They were not merely hasty reprisals for a success that had taken them unawares. Many people, even some who had bought the book and enjoyed it, would have argued that it was simply not very well written.

One of the most eminent, and cruelest, critics of the day had written with memorable sadism at the end of his scathing review: "If you should, however, find yourself unable to make your way this far through the book, take heart, gentle reader. As Mr. Poe once observed in another context, we can assure you that it is in infinite mercy that the book does not permit itself to be read." Another pundit for one of the national magazines eruditely hinted that not only was this travesty of literature not the greatest artistic achievement since *The Brothers Karamazov,* but that there was something morally reprehensible in the fact that the work of Clayton Hayes might appear in the same bookstores in proximity to any work by Dostoyevsky.

Clayton's forbearance in the face of all the belated barrages of criticism against his book was stoic, and even good-humored. He was fond of telling friends, and even interviewers, "Anytime I've written something clever or witty, I assume that I've stolen it." More seriously, he would explain that he was simply doing something he enjoyed doing, and lucky to be getting paid to do it. But despite the fact that he liked to stick the most unrestrainedly hateful reviews on the refrigerator door, I know that this assault on his literary aspirations pained him. I know that under all the wisecracks and self-deprecating humor he was hurt to have to acknowledge that his novel had not been accepted as art, and that so many critics had labored so hard to furnish a refutation of his credibility as an artist. It was a disappointment that not even his popularity could atone for, a rejection his growing audience could not absolve him of.

And the more barbarous the criticism became, the more clamorous his success seemed. He did have his defenders of course, not even counting those unenthusiastic critics who had, in "kindness," described his work as "crafts-manlike." But the reviewers who liked the book inevitably wrote with unbelievable hyperbole. It was indicative of how peculiarly intense, hot or cold, reactions to the book ran. "A monumental book of our times," one woman had deliriously written, "as important to the conscience of our society as *The Great Gatsby* was to its society fifty years ago." Clayton read this less as a comment on the artistic merits of the book than as a straightforward statement of its fashionable popularity among young adults. "Or possibly it's just symptomatic of the reviewer's own brand of demen-tia," he had humbly joked. Such drivel persuaded no one, explicated nothing — certainly not *why* so many people bought and read the book.

No doubt with this stinging lack of seriousness in the critical view of his first novel in mind, Clayton began to work manically on his second. He seemed forever distracted in that period, and for days at a time would only "come up to breathe" when he made love to me. He had bought a word processor and the perpetual clickety-tap of the keys composed an odd sort of score for the musical playing that season at Clayton's cottage: "Luca in Love with the Obsessed Writer." His long stretches at the keyboard, broken only by his desire for me, formed a counterpoint to the more moanful sounds of our fucking. These competing sounds, in fact, seem in my memory to be simultaneous concerts, and I have to remind myself of the impossibility of this audio memory. We never fucked while he typed.

I was never so happy to see him at last complete a work as I was that October. The whole thing had become a damn nuisance.

In reality Clayton's writing had become even more pernicious for me. The more grandly his career flourished, the smaller I seemed to shrink — in my own eyes, never Clayton's. I was proud of him and basked in the reflection of his brightening reputation (with noncritics), but there were shadows, sunspots, that fostered deeper and deeper misgivings about my own worth. And though I too masked this profound insecurity with humor, introducing myself occasionally as "Clayton Hayes' philistine lover," or "the famous writer's 'insignificant other,' " I could not eradicate my feelings of inferiority and worthlessness.

Clayton did what he could to bolster my sagging ego. He could see the blows landing. He never failed to introduce me to anyone of importance whom he met, treating me with almost servile ardor in front of them, and he conferred with me constantly about any decisions to be made. He let everyone know, in interviews, at parties, in private meetings, how vital I was to him. He also tried to keep me from brooding by enlisting my aid in making travel arrangements or in seeing to the details of a public engagement. I always accompanied him. He thought it would make me feel better, more wanted. In truth the benefit was all his. He wanted me there with him — though today I cannot see how I did not bore him terribly. But I never did. I still would have preferred, however, to stay away from the publicity functions that soon became obligatory. The sunspots grew darker, denser, obstructing what pleasure I might have had in our joint public appearances.

Finally, when both of us realized I had to do *something,* I went to register with the most prominent modeling agency in town. My portfolio in hand, I was sure I would impress the powers that be with my experience. But the woman I spoke to looked dully at my portfolio, listened uninterestedly to my resume, and took a few idle notes. She told me there was not much work available at the moment, and that they were having trouble as it was finding jobs for their "known quantities." She would do what she could and get back to me. I never heard from anyone at the agency. I went to several more agencies, all with the same depressing results. I did get one job modeling for a pathetic little affair at the Macy's in Modesto, but only because someone got ill at the last second.

I could not believe it, and neither could Clayton. He railed against their blind stupidity and promised he would speak to friends about getting me into some photo sessions. "They wouldn't know Apollo," he cracked, "if he drove up to their offices in a sun-drawn chariot." But the fact was that it was simply too competitive in San Francisco — and I surely was not about to resort to my old tricks of the trade. I slumped deeper into depression. My money was practically gone, though Clayton had never accepted such a division; he assumed I would not mind nor hesitate to use the joint checking account he had opened in our names. I was, nonetheless, cognizant to the penny of what was "my" money and what was "Clayton's." He could not understand my meticulous accounting in this regard even after I proclaimed it a matter of "moral rectitude" (a phrase I had heard Phil Donahue use on TV). We had a long and heated argument over my phone calls to my mother, Clayton *demanding* to pay for them himself. He won, as in so many such contests those first months. He had to win. I had nothing.

I began to wonder what even getting modeling work could mean to me. I would have money all my own, but would I really feel any better? Wouldn't I still feel like a "kept boy"? Was strutting on a runway going to make me feel I had accomplished anything? What a shriveled lump of "beauty" I seemed to be next to Clayton, who was doing something he considered important. He knew his value as a person, while I consigned myself to the junk heap of superficial charms that nobody truly valued. I felt like shit — pretty shit, but shit..

That Clayton loved me at all was the only thing that gave me courage in those days. What worth I had was the worth I saw refracted into a glowing warmth when he looked at me. Because *he* loved me, I could not hate myself totally.

One afternoon I left Clayton to his writing and went down to North Beach with Alessandro. We liked to sit in the Caffè Roma having cappuccino (I had learned to *sip* coffee in the American style) and watch the unlikely hordes swarm past the windows that faced Columbus Avenue. From this strategic, triangular vantage point one could study the cross section of creatures that paraded down the thoroughfare. The Financial District, Chinatown, the night clubs of Broadway, Fishermen's Wharf — all were within walking distance. There was always a motley selection of tourists, local Italian-Americans, Chinese-Americans, and assorted punkers, deadbeats and bikers to be remarked upon. In the restaurant itself we often had the chance to meet Italians visiting the States, though we never met anyone from Trento.

This particular afternoon Alessandro and I were making each other laugh by exchanging nonsensical bursts of heavily accented Southern Italian. As Americans do in

the States, Northern Italians find the southern pronunciation of their language ripe for comical mimicry. Alessandro's
humor, which I had once found insufferable, had come to
be relied upon by me for amusement.

"*Chi fu, coglioncini,*" he chanted in a Neapolitan
singsong. "*Vidi, vinsi, venni!*" He was lambasting both
Southern Italian grammar, which uses the simple past tense
conversationally (something we Northerners never do), as
well as Julius Caesar's famous line: I saw, I conquered, I
came. We use the verb "to come" with the same sexual connotation that English speakers do.

Suddenly a woman sitting next to us started speaking to us in an Italian strangely accented by both Sicilian
and American. Obviously not having comprehended that
we were making fun of southern dialect, she spoke quite
sincerely. She asked us where we were from and how long
we were staying in San Francisco.

"*Te prego!*" was Alessandro's immediate response.
These two little Trentino words cover a lot of ground; in
this case they meant something like, "Please! Who does she
think she is to butt in with her rotten Italian!"

I thought her appealing though, and carried on the
conversation without much assistance from Alessandro. It
turned out that she was American, a native San Franciscan.
But her family was Sicilian and she frequently went back
to Sicily to visit her not-so-distant relatives. Her Italian was
astonishingly incoherent — or rather, astonishingly coherent
for being such bad Italian. We soon lapsed into English. Her
name was Claire. She had been born Chiara de Cesco, but
Claire, with Americans' preference for French, had proven
the most manageable variant of her real name. She was
vibrant, talkative, and brutally funny. She was also very short
and dark, but for the first time these physical features
were virtually invisible to me. I think even then I must have
guessed that we would become best friends.

Getting up to leave the cafe to go back to work (she was a barber, with her own shop nearby), Claire mentioned that she was giving a little party at her home that weekend and invited both of us to attend. We said, yes, we would come, and she gave us her address.

"*Non tirare un bidone*," she said before turning away, using the wrong imperative form of the verb. Don't stand me up. Then she turned back towards us. "I knew you boys were Italian even before you said a word. The most beautiful men in the world are always Italian." We laughed and she winked at us as she breezed out the door.

I went to the party alone. Alessandro had never had any intention of going and Clayton wanted to work on some revisions. The party was a small, friendly gathering. No one, though, was anywhere near as delightful as Claire. I have met few people whom I liked so instantaneously — and so wholeheartedly. The sentiment was mutual. We spent most of the evening laughing together. When I told her, reluctantly, for his name had ceased being unintrusive, that my lover was Clayton Hayes, she asked me who he was. I am ashamed to say now that I felt like kissing her. Here, at last, a friendship of my own. Although I liked Ken and Alessandro, and others of Clayton's friends, they *were* Clayton's friends. I had had no one whose image of me had not been foreshadowed by Clayton.

That night going home from the party I was struck with my own unrepetent selfishness. I would have been exultant just a few months earlier to make points with new people through my relationship with the noted author. Now I cringed from the vaunt that the man I loved — and who loved me — was Clayton Hayes. My self-image was tarnished, and I resented having to gild it with another's glory. I had become closed and mean-spirited. And in this thought there *was* remorse.

Claire and Clayton met some weeks later when I had

her to the house for dinner. They liked each other, but there was not the special attraction between them that I had with each of them separately. Clayton, whose own heart never seemed mired in selfishness, was genuinely happy to see how joyously I flaunted this new friendship. And though Claire's affection for me may at first have been sexually tinged, an urge, I'm afraid, I never returned, that is not necessarily a bad thing in friendship — as I had learned with Fabio. Claire respected my relationship with Clayton, and has been perfectly content all these years to share my company with nothing more than platonic kisses and embraces to show for it. And, of course, my love.

Claire was responsible for getting me my first real job in San Francisco. She had an old, bisexual boyfriend who was leaving his position as a sales clerk at Wilkes Bashford, the men's clothing store, in order to move to Los Angeles. She had him put in a good word for me and I was hired. That was at a time when the question of a green working visa could be discreetly ignored by both employer and illegal alien. It was not a terrific "opportunity" for anything except making a little money of my own. But I did have some fun working there and I *did* know something about fashion. Once or twice I was even asked to model in the store. Showing off the clothes, though, no longer seemed any more glamorous or prestigious than selling them. The money might have been better, but I had begun to look upon modeling, and models, as a vapid, mentally inactive corps whose ranks I had no desire to reenter. There was really nothing in modeling for me but bad memories.

Being a sales clerk was as useful and useless as any other job would have been at the time. I was satisfied not to have to "sell" Luca Savelli to anyone. My unambitious inertia did not want to be disturbed. Or was it that there was no reason to disrupt my headlong rush into obscurity? I made enough money to feel self-sufficient, and for once was depositing money into our joint account instead of withdrawing it.

In November Alessandro married his American girlfriend. They had a small ceremony and reception in Berkeley. Her apartment was there and, as it was larger than Alessandro's, that was where they would be living. He was working part-time in a bar. His year as a graduate student was Tp, along with his visa. But if the sole purpose of the marriage was to keep him in the United States, they did not let on. Though they have long since divorced, in those first few years they seemed very much in love. That they have remained close friends tends to lend credence to this view.

Whether it was a scheme or just coincidental, Alessandro's solution to the problem of immigration reminded Clayton and me of my own uncertain situation. We had not made any long-range plans, but we both looked forward to living in San Francisco for at least a few more years. With Clayton's help I had gotten my tourist visa extended. My alien status, though, was an ongoing concern for me. Moreover, I still did not have a green card for working legally in the country.

For Clayton's birthday that year I made reservations at the St. Orres Inn in Mendocino County for the weekend. Clayton had bought a car in October and I knew he was eager to take it out for a good long drive in the country. Also, our sexual activities had slackened off a bit, due partly to Clayton's energies being drained by the novel, and partly due to my own anxieties. We had both been distracted by too much.

Nothing bedeviled either of us that weekend, and, unlike so many "loaded" festivities, delicate designs of overwrought hope and expectation, our weekend did not blow up in our faces — or at least not in any unpleasurable way. The scenic drive up the California coast was a magnificent start to a weekend that was one of the most romantic we were ever to have. At the inn we had one of those erotic marathons of ours that always did us both good. On the evening of his actual birthday, in the dining room of the lodge, I was like an infatuated schoolboy again, nervous with excitement as I handed him his birthday gift. It was the first really nice thing I had ever been able to buy him with my own money. I had carefully shopped for a watch that was as expensive looking as it was handsome.

His eyes looked up from the box to me, and I knew I had — for once, I sighed to myself — done something that truly moved him. I knew that he did not care for fine *things* at all, but he was sensitive enough to see what had gone into this particular gift. Murmuring gently emotional words of gratitude, he took his old watch off his wrist and put on the new one. We smiled and toasted to his birthday.

He put down his glass of champagne and laid his hand on mine. "I know it's my birthday, Luca, but I have a gift for you, too. If the object of my birthday is to make me happy, I hope you'll understand how happy you'll make me by accepting this."

He pulled some papers from the inside pocket of his jacket and handed them to me. I unfolded them and vainly endeavored to make sense of their English. Clayton finally had to explain that the papers represented my ownership of the cottage. He had made the down payment with the advance from his second novel and put it in my name.

"It doesn't resolve the problem with Immigration, but I'm working on that," he said. "In the meantime, I'm your beholden tenant. . . if you'll keep me."

Maybe I should have been angry that Clayton had not let my present to him shine by itself on his birthday. But I could not be mad at him. All I could think was how much Clayton loved me and how, in dejection, I had demeaned that love and myself with self-pity. My eyes brimmed with tears.

"If you don't promise to stay forever, I'm throwing all these papers into the ocean right now," I was able to croak.

Clayton looked at his wrist and smiled. "By the face on my beautiful new watch I see that it's time you were in bed, young man."

Kidnapping of a Modern Hero came out in February 1973, fast upon the success of *Organ of Conceit*. And in contrast to the first novel, *Kidnapping* was a huge and instant hit, far surpassing his first. It soon appeared on best-seller lists and "Clayton Hayes" became a name that even so hard-core a member of the *illiterati* as Claire would have recognized. Clayton had already started work on his third novel of course, work that was interrupted at an accelerating rate by interviews, promotional appearances around the country, and speaking engagements at universities.

But whereas the critics had had to snipe from the rear upon the advance of his first book, they had a ready store of ammunition for their frontal attack upon his second one. The critical bombardment of his work was tumultuous in a way his success had never been. The critics' virulence seemed inexhaustible, though Clayton took it all indomitably, with a smile. Any bitterness their vitriol engendered in him was borne with humor. The criticism, he said, guaranteed his humility.

On our refrigerator appeared a clipping from a newspaper that included this pungent observation, under-lined by Clayton: "That he has nothing new to say is perhaps common to every writer in the world. His dogged resistance to saying any of it in a manner the slightest bit interesting is singular and deserves some kind of notice." It ended snip-pily with, "Hayes' books have become, it would seem, a pabulum for the college set, who have yet to learn that pulp is an acquired dislike."

My own reading of the book was even sloppier than

my reading of the first had been. It is a complex story —
and, admittedly, rather fantastic. The story revolves around
a young Italian man who is "discovered" by an American
producer in Italy, taken to Hollywood, made a star, a citizen,
and is eventually dragged into the dim arena of international
politics. By playing upon his worldwide popularity, and by
projecting an image of childlike wisdom and determination
(he is the titular head of a movement to end hunger all over
the world), he shrewdly manuevers into a position to assert
power in both the political machinery of the States and in
certain international intrigues. But then he learns, too late,
that he is only a pawn in the hands of the group of American
businessmen who have in truth sponsored his career as a
"modern hero."

I do not want to spoil the book for anyone who has
not read it, but I must in pursuit of nonliterary aims. I have
a point, to be made shortly, about the ultimate effect this
book, or a part of it, had upon me, and I think a familiarity
with the story will facilitate this undertaking. For those who
have read the book, I am about to refresh your memories.

The cabal of businessmen eventually decides to have
their puppet kidnapped and martyred in the course of a
European tour for the hunger program. The Italian kidnap-
pers are ostensibly a radically leftist band of terrorists. The
Americans hope thereby to obtain even greater political
leverage with a name and image they will be free to
manipulate without having to deal with the actual person.
Throughout the novel, meanwhile, there has been a
homosexual love theme. At the beginning, while still a
teenager, the protagonist is lured to Hollywood by the
wealthy producer, who is also a notorious pederast. The
"hero" leaves behind in Italy his true lover, another Italian
youth named Andrea Sapetti. In America, of course, his
public image is strictly heterosexual; he even marries and
fathers several children in the service of this cynical ploy.

As a result of this betrayal, or at least as a result of this setup in the story's plot, it is of course Andrea who is the leader of the Italian terrorists. He is thus employed to wreak a personal revenge against his former lover by kidnapping him, but without knowing the real source of the bankroll. When he uncovers the truth, and learns that the American plutocrats have arranged to have them all murdered in a "rescue" by the Italian authorities, he is able to save the "hero's" life, but not his own.

I did not understand half of this upon my first reading. Indeed, the only reason I attempted to read it with any discipline at all was because Ken had told me that the character of Andrea Sapetti sounded suspiciously like me. I read the passages that introduced this character more closely than the rest of the book and realized, yes, physically he was me, and even some of his personality was mine. (If you have read the book, perhaps the scene after the kidnapping in which the "hero" tries to speak English to him and Andrea shouts at his old lover, "This is my country! In my country we speak Italian!" will now seem more piquant.)

But it was for the most part boring and tedious in the reading, and it was with something of a guilty conscience that I told Clayton it was even better than the first. Clayton only chuckled and mussed my hair, something I was beginning to notice he did whenever he did not quite take me seriously.

With the success of Clayton's second book came two attendant developments that were related in some, as yet, indistinct way.

The first was Clayton's new coterie of friends and admirers. This very personal acclaim had doubtlessly been spurred by the photograph of Clayton on the jacket of *Kidnapping*. He was, as people were forever telling him at booksigning parties in bookstores, too handsome to be a writer. He started receiving letters from all over the country, some simply complimenting his books, others proposing the most unliterary of encounters. In San Francisco he acquired an entourage of young readers, mostly male, who seemed to follow him from bookstore to bookstore, from campus auditorium to campus auditorium. The more persistent "groupies" would even track him down to our home.

Most of these admirers were no more than anonymous fans for Clayton. From time to time, however, a friendship would be sparked between him and one of the more intelligent members of his avid following, and I would find myself entertaining him or her in our home. I had never thought to be jealous of any of this as the whole business seemed so silly to me. They would talk about his books or literature in general. There was for me even something touchingly innocent in their infatuations with Clayton.

During one appearance at B. Dalton's (I had run down the street from Wilkes Bashford in the middle of the day more to say hi to Clayton than anything), I was introduced by Clayton to a "Robert." "You remember," he said, "he wrote me the letter I showed you. He's a student at USF." I remembered nothing and was aware only of how intently Robert was eyeing Clayton. My defenses were stirred by the unusual beauty of his face. He was about my age, and shorter than Clayton by an inch or so. He had black hair that seemed to fall flawlessly about a superbly chiseled face of unidentifiable ethnic origin: Asian maybe, or Mexican, or maybe both. Clayton, I could see, returned the interest. I thought, I will let him indulge this little attraction, and moved away as the two of them animatedly — and to my mind flirtatiously — chatted by the stacks of *Kidnapping*. Later, browsing through another section, I overheard Robert indicate me to a companion of his and whisper, "That's his lover." And when the companion commented upon my own good looks, Robert said, "Yes, but you know how it is. After a while you just take things like that for granted. Besides,

I'm sure they have an open relationship. The way Clayton was looking at me, they better have.''

I did not laugh this off, but I did not worry over it either. Only after Robert became a guest in our home did I even recall the exchange. At first his visits were sporadic and brief. Then, undiscouraged by Clayton, he began to telephone and drop by regularly. Clayton enjoyed his company and if I were doing something with Claire or Alessandro in the evening, he and Robert might go to the movies or out to dinner together. I did begin to experience minor twinges of jealous paranoia, but I told myself that Clayton and I were long past such destructive games. He was entitled to a little flirtation and I was glad Robert could provide the diversion for him.

The second development threw a whole new color upon the situation. Sexual relations between Clayton and me took another and more conspicuous dip — due this time primarily to Clayton's own apparent lack of interest. Despite my promptings, he was in the mood to fuck only once or twice a week. This was a starvation diet for me, having had my appetite whetted by epicurean excess for a year now. Clayton apologized, saying he was just tired and that it was only temporary. But my hunger for him mounted unappeased till I became demanding. He would relent under pressure, but his lovemaking was without its old athletic vim — while I felt more and more often as though I had raped him.

One morning I awoke in an especially foul temper. The night before I had (and literally) unsuccessfully begged Clayton for sex — always a humiliating role. Ken had spent the night at our place because the floors in his apartment were being redone. He looked at me in the kitchen that morning, seeing the stylish pair of balloon trousers and gray boots I was wearing to work, and said, as if searching for just the right compliment, "Don't we look...*très* homosexual this morning. Oh, well, maybe the Quentin Crisp look is making a comeback.'' The scowl on my face must have made it clear that it was not a morning for joking. I was thinking, unkindly, not all queens are swishy. He squeaked a ''sorry'' and timidly went back downstairs with his cup of coffee.

That day at work I saw Clayton's old friend George step in off Sutter Street and look casually about the shop. It all seemed so accidental that it had to have been planned. I had not seen him since the party months before. Anyone could have told him where I worked. I went up and said hello as friendly as I could and asked if he was looking for anything in particular. He was not at all surprised to see me.

''Well, as I live and breathe. Fancy meeting you here.'' Then, letting his eyes wander a moment, he mumbled, ''Just looking . . . just looking.'' Taking the sleeve of a sweater in hand, he pretended to examine it, saying, ''Such a pretty boy I see Clayton with these days. Robert, that's his name, isn't it? But then Clayton has so many pretty friends.'' He drifted over to a display of woolen pants. His movements were even slower than usual. I tried, none too hard, to hide my impatience.

He looked into my eyes as if waiting for me to say something, and then pranced in slow motion to a tie rack. Without looking up from the ties he was handling, he at last said in a low voice, ''Of course, there are those who say a hole's a hole, it doesn't matter. And even if a hole aspires to something more, you can't really fuck a beautiful pair of eyes or an enchanting face. Only a hole. And Lord knows, you *can't* fuck a friend.''

His words always had an insinuating intimacy to them, as though he knew everything about me. They sounded like irrelevant, random thoughts at first hearing, but were weighted with much more meaning than one could grasp at once. At that moment, in fact, I was rather tangentially thinking, Had Fabio, who I liked, really been, in the act, only a hole? No.

George's hand traced a gossamer film of insouciance through the air; his smile seemed to divulge some awful secret; his sentences, couched in immaculate enunciation, threatened some imminent cathartic revelation. "These clothes are for the young. But, no, youth *is* only a fashion. It appeals to some. It doesn't matter *who* wears it." And with that he floated out of the shop into the hazy sunlight. I stood staring as he put on a pair of dark glasses, looked back at me, and then turned in the direction whence he had come.

The overall impact of this visitation was unequivocal, even if all the innuendoes had not been. The security I felt with Clayton had been completely undermined. I returned home that evening even more crabby than I had left it. Clayton, seeing my mood, trod lightly (but not guiltily) about it. Ken had gone back to sleep at his apartment and we ate our dinner in sober silence. Clayton finally asked me what was wrong. I only nodded and said, "Nothing." What was killing me was that if I had had the guts to ask, I knew Clayton would tell me everything. Honesty was his most unmalleable trait. But I was a coward. I would not have known what to do or say. That night I slept in his arms, but made no attempt to rouse him.

The next day Clayton received an unexpected phone call from another old friend. The friend was a very famous film actor whom Clayton had known in San Francisco before he had become a movie star. He had, in fact, been a lover, sandwiched somewhere in between Ken and me. He is still popular today, and his Italian-American good looks have never deserted him.

I had never fully believed Clayton and was consequently very much surprised to see the actor actually show up at our house for dinner that evening. Clayton had wanted him to stay over with us, but he had a room at the

Huntington Hotel. He said he was only in town for one night and that the hotel would be a more comfortable arrangement for everyone. Upon his arrival I immediately fell into a kind of worshipful stupor, staring nervously at the face I had seen on the screen so many times. He, on the other hand, seemed perfectly relaxed with me.

Over the dessert — pecan pie, an abomination Clayton was inordinately fond of — I was suddenly conscious that Clayton's friend was making passes at me. I guess I had been too awestruck to take account of this earlier. Clayton seemed not to notice. With cooler calculation than I'd had in me with my Parisian friend Marie, I began returning the attention. When Clayton stepped out of the dining room for a moment, I even let him drop his hand into my lap as he whispered, "I think you're really hot. Do you think Clayton would mind if we got together?" I blushed without answering. I had gotten an instant erection. He rubbed it. "Of course, he doesn't have to know."

In spite of the undeniable magnetism between us, our guest left our home a little drunk, but otherwise undebauched. I made an overture to Clayton. His rebuff was, I suppose, as affectionate — and definitive — as it could be. I was furious.

"*Porca puttana! Che cazzo fai!*" I yelled at him. "Has your little friend Robert sucked you dry?"

Clayton stared at me. "So that's what's been bugging you. It's time we had a talk, Luca."

"You don't deny it then!"

"Deny what? Listen, I never vowed to be sexually monogamous."

"For Chrissakes, Clayton!" I had picked this up from Ken. "Why do you always use words I don't understand?"

"I never promised you I wouldn't have sex with other people. I never tried to keep *you* from other sexual experiences. That has nothing to do with our love."

"What love? You don't even want to fuck anymore — at least not with me!"

"That's not true."

"Are you going to tell me you haven't been fucking that goddam Robert?"

"If you want to hear it, okay. Yes, I *have* fucked Robert. Now is that what you wanted? You're acting like you won't be happy till you've made me hurt you. I wasn't making a big deal of it precisely because I didn't want to hurt you. But it was stupid on my part. This has got to be talked out."

I was not listening. Clayton had spoken the truth with a minimum of rancor, but — as much as I had expected the confession — I was still shocked. The hurt seemed to sting deep inside me, stunning anything reasonable I had left to say. I thought, instead, of the meanest thing I could say.

"What do you two do, anyway? You fuck him while he tells you how great that *crap* is that you write?"

I was sorry to see that this had little effect on him.

"Let's not fight like this, Luca. Cool off a bit. Then we've obviously got a lot of things to discuss." He turned away from the bedroom.

I grabbed my coat. "I'm not discussing any fucking thing!" I hurried past him. "If you want to reach me, I'll be at the Huntington Hotel. You know which room!"

I did go to the hotel and I did fuck Clayton's friend, angrily. And though my rage diminished to some degree the purer hedonism of my lust, I did have a pleasurable time. Had it been under different auspices, it would have been even more fun. He is a sexy man, I was horny, and there was a strong attraction between us. It may even be that I used my anger exactly in order to fulfill a guilty sexual fantasy. But lying on top of him afterwards I could not help thinking about other things.

How. . .*easy* it had been to fuck him. I knew I would

never fuck him again. I did not love him. I did not care about him. Was it this easy for Clayton to fuck Robert? Or me? Were we all just holes to be mechanically entered and uncaringly fucked? I thought of my longing for Clayton. How different it was. I sensed all at once the fundamental difficulty in holding a man, in keeping him in your emotional grasp, when you feel your sexual power is passive. It seemed my sexual duty to arouse *him*; that is, it was my duty if I expected to be sexually satisfied. To make a man want to fuck you again and again over a period of years, to be more than just a "hole," you have to make yourself special to him. Was I still special to Clayton sexually, or were other holes easy, more desirable, substitutes for me? I knew only too well that fucking someone could be an unbelievably mindless act. Were Clayton and I now to have a sexless "marriage"? Would I ever feel the excitement of him inside me again?

I thought for the first time about what it was like to be a woman in bed. Psychologically, getting fucked is a profoundly different interaction from fucking. The complementary desires that define the interaction necessarily require opposite views of that sexual relationship. I had never understood this before. Only a man who likes to fuck and be fucked could understand these divergent roles. The power exercised by each can be compelling, but the "woman's" position is the more precarious, depending as it does on a consistently erotic and almost magical sensuality. The active role, while drastically limited by sometimes capricious variations in desire or biological function, is simply. . .performed, and nothing more. I wanted to cry rather than think I was not still titillating to Clayton, that it was not me, me, Luca Savelli, whom he desired, who stimulated his biology as much as his soul. Instead of crying, I fucked the movie star again, and fell asleep.

At four in the morning I returned home and got into

bed next to Clayton. I knew he was awake, but he said nothing. I laid my hand on his bare stomach and he covered it with his own. Then he released it and turned on his side, away from me. I forced myself not to cry.

The subsequent week was hellish for both of us. We said very little to each other, each one's eyes averting the other's, our paths through the house plotted with cautionary avoidance. We did not want to face each other. Not yet at least. The wounds were too fresh. We slept together, but did not cuddle one another or lie too close. We scarcely touched. Until one night Clayton drew me into his arms and made love to me. His tenderness seemed to reach down and grab me back from some dark abyss I was falling down through. And when he brought me to orgasm with his kisses and his pumping inside me, I groaned both with passion and sadness.

He lay next to me after he had come, softly panting into my neck. He was still half hard inside me, ready to go at it again as soon as he caught his breath. But I pulled away from him, unwilling to go on. Not because I had had enough, but because it all seemed so hopeless. I turned my back to him and lowered my head into my chest. What does one fuck do? I thought. What is it supposed to heal?

"Luca, tell me what's wrong. Please." he said, putting an arm around me. I shook my head. The register of his voice changed, dropping in pitch, rising in urgency. "Don't despair of my understanding," he pleaded. "I couldn't stand it."

"It's just that I thought we had something special," I finally said, hollowly.

He took one of my hands and wrapped it around his balls, as he had done once before. "Everything I have is yours, Luca. If you want me to be monogamous, I'll do it. If you want me to be goddam celibate, I'll try it."

I felt like I had asked him to cut off his balls. I did

not want that. I did not want to cut off my own balls. The lines of love and trust that we had drawn, which had seemed so clear to me when I was trapped in Trento and which had appeared then unattached to sexual exclusiveness, were once more fuzzy and confusing. I did not know what I wanted. No, I *knew* I wanted to feel loved by Clayton, desired by him.

I turned over to face him. "It's not that, Clayton. But I've got to feel that I'm the *one*." And before I knew what I was doing, I was crying and telling him all the things I had been feeling: my feelings of worthlessness, my jealousies about his own increasing prominence, my need to be sexually desired by him, my contradictory worry that this was the only thing I had to offer him. And when I had confessed all these deficiencies, I told him about my months in Trento, and my work as a "model" in Milan. I told him everything. He held me in his arms as I sobbed convulsively. He kissed me over and over, soothing me, "Didn't you realize none of it mattered? Didn't you know I'd always love you? The pain's gone. I'm here. You're here. We both survived. Love's the only thing that ever mattered."

When I had stopped crying he got up out of bed and went to get a copy of *Kidnapping of a Modern Hero*. He crawled back into bed, took me under an arm, and said, "This is a passage that several critics have cited for its notably maudlin sentiment. This is after Andrea's been shot by the squad of 'rescuers.' It's the hero's last lament for him."

I laid my head on his chest and listened to him read, the sounds resonating through his warm flesh.

" 'Andrea, Andrea, you were the best in me. And what did I trade you for? Money that cannot buy a heart as close to mine as yours was. Fame that cannot budge loneliness. Power that is powerless in the face of death. Andrea, you should never have forgiven me. Mine was an act undeserving of pardon. You should have gone on hating me. Or is that forgiveness your vengeance? Your mercy may have brought you peace. For me it has become a torturous punishment for love abandoned. You *loved* me, and I traded the best for something that is not love, is not life, is . . . gone. Oh, Andrea, do not forgive me, do not forgive me. The day I said I could replace your love, I condemned myself to a life without mercy. Andrea, I love you. Do not forgive me.' "

He paused after the reading.

"I wrote some of that when you were still in Trento. It was supposed to go into a letter I sent you. But it was too dark. I couldn't pass my grief onto you like that. Do you understand? The love I give you is because of *you,* not because I'm a good guy who just happens to love everyone. Anything you've done for that love, anything I've done, belongs to you and me, and only to you and me." He kissed my forehead. "Your *love* is perfect."

I understood. He did not mean that we could not see each other's defects. But we had given the best of ourselves, our love, to the other, and that unfaltering love exalted our own values as individuals, made noble everything that would have otherwise seemed so selfish. I had thought myself so worthless, so debased, so pitiable, so poor in every quality except my love for Clayton. *But this love was the best in me.* I had given another human being love, and whatever my failings as a person, Clayton had seen the caliber of my love as *his* worth, and mine. And if my love was the self-worth of the human being I loved, how could I deny my own importance?

I tightened my hold on Clayton. I felt his silent tears moisten my face. I thought, as I had never before, Do not let me die in this man's arms now! I have so much more love to give him!

Robert was never seen around our house again. Clayton did not speak of it. Knowing him, I am sure their sexual relations came to an end at once, though if Robert had ever been a true friend Clayton would not have hesitated to see him again socially. I had not handed any ultimatums to Clayton. His breaking off of their affair was voluntary, a response to his own sensitivity, their dalliance now contaminated for Clayton by my hurt.

We both felt chastened. We promised to try to understand the other's sexual needs and desires, even when they might lead us to other partners once in a while. But we swore never to flaunt these experiences, unmindful of the feelings of the other. We agreed to bind ourselves in a monogamous *trust* that declared to the other, "You are the *one.*"

After our reconciliation I reread Clayton's books. I felt that I had missed so much. They were not easy reading for me. I was, of course, in no position to judge their literary merits, or even their English grammar. I was lucky to comprehend them at all. Novels always seem gratuitously turgid to the foreign student culling unknown words for a trip to the dictionary. But I read them in their entirety for the first time. And I understood. It gave me a new feeling of kinship with Clayton. I knew the writer of those words as no one did.

The books, though, had also made me feel woefully ignorant. I felt as though I had let my education leak into a bottomless well, beyond recovery. I had once been a good, if hardly brilliant student, but my complacency about my intelligence had made me dull, stupid. Selling clothes was doing nothing for my intellect. At my current rate I was liable to end up little more than a fashionably dressed vegetable. I thought it over carefully, then went to Clayton for advice.

"I think I should go back to school," I started. "What do you think? Is it possible? Anyway, it would be good for my English."

"Great idea!" he said. He had just come in from running errands. He set down a bag of groceries. As always, he had the last surprise. "Of course, it would be easier if you were a citizen. How would you like to be legally adopted by a widely disrespected, but disarmingly horny American writer? I've talked to a lawyer and I think we can swing it.''

I could not digest the full import of his suggestion at first. I helped put away the groceries while Clayton elaborated. As I listened, I wondered if the man I was listening to really knew how completely my life was his.

X   Jewels of the Universe

I was twenty-five when I enrolled in the University of California at San Francisco. It had taken a great deal of wrangling to get my transcripts from the University of Trento accepted by UCSF for credit. Fortunately Clayton knew someone in the Admissions Department. In America, I was learning, as everywhere, it helps to know the right person in the right place at the right time.

I continued to work part-time at Wilkes Bashford, but most of the expenditures for my schooling were covered by Clayton. Convinced now that I was contributing to our lives, I did not mind Clayton's loving subsidization of my education.

I had enrolled under the name of Luca Savelli, though by the end of the term my legal name would be Luca Savelli Hayes. It was a name I never used, and no one, least of all Clayton, begrudged me the pride I had in my original Italian name. The *soprannome* "Luke" was the limit of my

Americanization in this regard. I was, in my own mind at any rate, still thoroughly Italian, and, indeed, earned my scholastic honors with what I would have thought at one time was typical Italian aplomb, stretching my education at the university over a period of six years. I discovered, of course, that this apparently lackadaisical pace is even more common among American students, whose freer attitudes often embolden them to return to the classroom *long* after others would have given up.

My own extended studies did, however, pertain as much to the language barrier I was still working against in my first years at UCSF as to the "unruffled" industry, *alla italiana,* which I brought to my pursuit of a degree. My imperfect English permitted only a fairly light study load in the beginning, although even this proved grueling. The first two years, in particular, were very rough, as my months away from college had rendered my mental faculties as imperfect as my English. My memory was as rententive as a cracked sieve. Plowing through the simplest textbook was time-consuming and, at times, pointless.

That I was not satisfied with a B.A. in English Literature, but was pushing ahead first towards a Master's also accounts for my lengthy course of studies.

Meanwhile, Clayton's career skyrocketed. I like to think it was the comfortable and settled homelife we provided each other that led to his prolific success. His fortunes were inseparable from our happiness. As I plunged deeper and deeper into textbooks and Shakespeare and Jane Austen and Henry James and Emily Dickinson and Gore Vidal, the more inspired Clayton's writing became. He never won a secure place in the hearts of the critics, but their former enmity seemed worn down. The disreputable author of tripe had become, however deplorably, a distinctive mainstay of the American literary scene.

Each year saw a new novel, most of them best-sellers.

His countless short stories were eventually collected into three volumes. Paperback rights and sales, which had been a sizable portion of Clayton's income since *Organ of Conceit,* was an ever-expanding source of revenue. He occasionally wrote articles for magazines, and even worked a brief stint as a book reviewer himself for a short-lived city magazine in San Francisco.

And if today his work is spoken of with an impatiently dismissive air by most "authorities," he has also acquired an impassioned chorus of hagiolaters who feel that there is an intellectual and lyrical purity in Clayton's work. I do not set myself among them only because my own view is more subtle, more unapologetically subjective, more intensely irrational. Ever since the night that Clayton read to me from *Kidnapping* I have not been able to read any of his work without conscientiously rooting out its message for *me.* Yet the unassuming beauty I have found in his writing is, for me, not an element subject to analysis; for me, the beauty lives in my heart, too personal to be analyzed. My ability to *describe* that beauty, though, did form the bulk of my Master's thesis. The thesis happened to be one of the first in the country to take in the work of Clayton Hayes.

Clayton's star, seemingly forever on the rise, guided him at last even to Hollywood. Hollywood the business, not Hollywood the town. He had been asked several times to adapt his novels into screenplays by the various persons who had bought the film rights. But he always declined, saying he could not bear to trudge through the same stories and the same characters *again.* He insisted that he had nothing fresh with which to tell the story again; he considered this essential to a successful film adaptation. One had to have a different perspective from the original author's in order to produce something interesting.

With this in mind, he did persuade a producer acquaintance to buy the rights to a short story by Tennessee

Williams, "Two on a Party," with the promise that Clayton could write the screenplay. Clayton did, the producer did not like it, and when the script was eventually nominated for an Academy Award, stripped of everything Clayton had written though his name still appeared in the credits, he was relieved to see another film receive the award. Clayton resisted all further temptations to involve himself in film-making after that.

My own peculiar attitude towards his work may be summed up by admitting that my favorite novel of his is one of the last, *The Piper Dances.* I am not enamored of this book for its mastery of the English language or its realistic characterizations or its accomplished storytelling. But it is very special to me nonetheless. The book is two novels in one, the first story ending abruptly with a combination earthquake, tidal wave, hurricane and electrical storm that destroys all the characters of the first story and clears the set for the second story to commence. This was in fulfillment of the cataclysmic deus ex machina Clayton had, in frustration, been threatening to use for years. The book was a genre-straddling, satirical coup that was a favorite of Clayton's too. Such daring on his part was in keeping with what had evolved as my own, perhaps puerile, opinion of what a person's life work shoud be: *play,* a children's game to fend off demons with anything that will leave the emotional field open to more rewarding enterprises — like love. I remember Clayton and I were especially happy together during the writing of *The Piper Dances.*

Not that it is easy to isolate an "especially happy" phase in all those years. I mean only that we were more affectionate with each other, as sometimes occurs with people who have lived together for a long time and suddenly re-realize that they truly love the person next to them. It is like falling in love again: one's sense of wonder and desire is renewed. This happened often for Clayton and me.

Contentment became a way of life. Love had long ceased being a cause for self-immolation. Passion was no longer incinerating, but fiery with a life-giving force. And the arguments we did have had none of their old lashing violence.

The one thing most people find difficult to believe is that Clayton and I enjoyed sex together, regularly and enthusiastically, even after nine years of living together. I cannot explain it, but we were never bored with each other's bodies, which we had come to know so well. This did not prevent us from having sex with others, and maybe our relationship was even aided by our willingness to experience other people. But neither of us ever had "affairs" as such, and our "extramarital" activities were never openly laundered. If I found a fellow student at the university a good lay, or if Clayton was enticed by the beguiling beauty of a young man in New York or Los Angeles, where I imagined leagues of mesmerized sycophants languished expectantly, quivering beneath his sexual/literary aura, who was to say that these were not also life-giving?

We had discussed three-ways, but we both allowed that we were too selfish to share either the stroking we got from each other or the stroking we benefited from in the arms of outsiders. There was one exception to this general policy — or rather one and a half. The "half" had been Claire. One night Clayton and I had taken her out drinking to try and help her forget a boyfriend she had just broken up with. We failed miserably. Upon returning to our house with her she seemed as distraught as ever. Afraid to send her home so upset, Clayton pulled me aside and suggested we have her sleep with us.

There was nothing sexual in our embraces that night, and when Claire at last fell asleep between us tearfully murmuring what great friends we were, I leaned over and kissed Clayton. His sensitivity with my friend, as with so many things, had touched me where mere sympathy could never have reached its pallid hand.

Our more complete sexual triangle took place in Hawaii. It was one of our favorite vacation spots, and in 1976 we bought a condo in Wailea on the island of Maui to use for our frequent visits there. Before then, though, during one of our first stays on the island, we had met a young tourist from Houston. We had both found the man handsome, intelligent, and good company, but it was obvious that I was more sexually attracted to him than Clayton was. In turn, Clayton was more appealing to him than I was. For the week of his stay there the three of us spent most of our time together, snorkeling in Honolua Bay or body surfing near Napili Point or dining in Lahaina in the evenings. We became a frolicsome trio recognized all over the island.

On his last night in Maui it was again Clayton who proposed to me that we sleep with him. His idea was more a gesture of friendship that sexual desire. But this time the embraces were definitely erotic for me. And I suspect that Clayton did enjoy watching me fuck our friend (a logistical problem: three-ways are inevitably two people having sex, while the third one watches, more or less), though not enough to ever request a repeat of the triad with anyone else. Afterwards, the young man blissfully slept between Clayton and me, his arms and legs clutched about Clayton, mine about him. Again I had to kiss Clayton, this time with more passionate gratitude for the generosity of his understanding.

In the morning we drove the young man to the airport, assuring him it had not all been a "mercy" fuck. In his eager affection he bought us two fresh flower leis in Kahului before flying off. We hugged him good-bye as he put the leis around our necks, and on the drive back to our hotel the scent of plumeria filled the air-conditioned car. I held Clayton's hand in mine as he drove, saying nothing . . .until I kissed his hand and sighed, "How can anyone live without you, Clayton?"

The most memorable and enduring friend to come out of our many stays in Hawaii has been "Sugar." He was forty-three when we first met him, tall, thin, and somewhat birdlike, with a long beakish nose and receding chin, and a goose's neck forever twisting and bobbing the head atop it. One could see that he had probably been very cute in his youth, with puckish good looks. He is also one of the most demented queens I have ever had the pleasure to know. His fey, epigrammatic humor seems to thrive in a world of its own, unseasoned by the sanity of pessimism.

His real name is Timothy Cane, but everyone on the island calls him Sugar. The first time we saw him he was walking by himself on the beach wearing a colorful straw sunbonnet and a pair of cut-off jeans, and swinging a plastic bag full of ice, scotch, club soda and glasses. When he came to where we were lying on the sand sunning, he stopped short and lowered his sunglasses.

"There *is* something new under the sun! There *is!*" he squealed, then marched away down the beach without looking back.

At the time Clayton insisted that this little performance had been provoked by my bathing suit. I had, in the European style, always worn swimming briefs that Clayton called "G-strings" and which I must admit received a number of scandalized stares. That I had a body deserving of such exhibition, Clayton claimed, was the only reason I had not been hooted off the beach. On the other hand, Clayton always wore the kind of baggy swimming trunks that I thought did his own considerable endowments a disservice.

Later in the week we saw the same queen at Hamburger Mary's in Lahaina. He marched up to us, drink in hand, and without any pretense to shyness declared, "You are not only the two hottest men on the island, you are *the* jewels of the universe. You *must* be lovers.''

"You've found us out," I said, hugging a beer bottle.

"Thank God!" he cried. "Now I can rest in peace knowing that in five years you will have hurt each other terribly!"

When we informed him that we had already passed this number undaunted, his eyebrows did a crazy little dance high above his eyes. Finally he lifted his hand to us as if to have it kissed and said in a frail Southern accent, ''Whoever you are, I have always depended upon the gullibility of strangers."

Sugar was in fact from Memphis, but retained this richly affected voice steeped in mint juleps, black-eyed peas and pork gravy only for its entertainment value. He was a relatively successful painter who had been living on Maui for years. He had a house up in Napili Point where he spent most of his time painting colossal tropical canvases. We learned all of this that evening, interspersed as it was with the sort of wildly irrelevent, parenthetical comments so typical of Sugar.

He had read most of Clayton's books, but when Clayton introduced himself he feigned a mildly overdone gasp of surprise. "Of course I'd read that you had a beautiful young Italian lover — but, my god, this is *criminal!*" And when he heard that I was working on my Master's, he exlaimed, "A *brain*? But you *can't* look like that and have a brain! It's like I told my mother. She used to say, 'Sugar, don't laugh. Laughter gives you *ugly* laugh lines in your face.' But she could afford not to laugh. She was beautiful. I *told* her, 'Mama, you can't think yourself *not* beautiful and not laugh.' "

A sad-looking little man came up to him at one point and Sugar made an exaggerated display of fussy affection, chiding him for not calling, promising to get together for drinks. As the man waddled away Sugar turned to us and warbled, "I can't *stand* her. But whenever I have to suffer with someone I don't like, I find it best to be effusively civil. Yes, sincerity has its place — but let's not be too candid. Candor should be *charming*."

Sugar was always a charming companion during our stays on Maui. He loved to have us up to his house or drive us around showing us the sights. ("Lahaina! Lahaina! Enchanting, historical Lahaina! That T-shirt boutique has been there since 1973.") Underneath all the saucy humor was a heart of extraordinary sweetness, and in a moment of repose he might turn to Clayton or me and ask for a kiss. "Give us a little kiss. Sugar's feeling a little low." And in bestowing the kiss, we knew it was treasured for the simple friendship it betokened.

I still make a point of visiting him whenever I go to the island.

Clayton and I traveled extensively together in those years. I often went with him on his lecture tours just to see different areas of the country. We went to visit Claudia in England several times, her family growing eventually to include two daughters and a son. I was never sure who got the most out of our visits, me or Clayton. We both seemed to absorb so much warmth from my sister's presence that these relaxing stays at their home near Oxford, where David teaches now, became a welcome respite from the States that both of us depended on. She was more than a gracious hostess; she was the soul of compassion. And when she gently explained to her younger daughter that Uncle Luca and Uncle Clayton slept together because love never sleeps, and that when two people love each other like Luca and Clayton or Mummy and Daddy, sleeping together is one expression of that love, I felt conscious all at once of how boundless my respect for her was. *Claudia, ti voglio bene.*

And of course we made many trips back to Trento.

There, at my mother's house, the subject of our sleeping together was simply never discussed. Sometimes we joined Claudia and David and the children at their summer home near Lake Garda, but more often we stayed in my old bedroom. The first time, we had had to move Claudia's old single bed in with mine and put them together under a double sheet. They remained that way for us on all our subsequent visits.

I was glad to see that my mother kept up a lively interest in her social circle. Outside of work her schedule seemed to be a constant round of calls paid and repaid upon friends and family. She never remarried, but has not wasted away in the absence of a husband. She has many male friends, though none of these appears to be a romantic liaison. But who knows. She does not tell me everything. A mother is not obliged to tell her son everything, as she loves to remind me. I tease her about her men friends, but she only laughs and says that her children's happiness is enough for her. "What could a man give me now?" I sometimes sense that my father's suicide is still a troublesome memory for her.

When she retired she began to travel herself. She came to stay with us once at our cottage in San Francisco. She could not understand why we had not gotten one of those big fancy American houses she had seen in the movies. Surely Clayton had the money. I explained that it was *home* for us, and this she understood. At the end of her visit she bought us a huge Swedish ivy that still hangs near the window of the bedroom.

Trento itself changed little. Most of our old friends were gone. Claudia and Alessandro, of course, but Michela, too, had moved away, to Milan with a job in an advertising agency serving the fashion industry — one of the better ones, I'm happy to say. Fabio, I knew from letters, had gone to live with a popular young Italian film actor in Rome. They had met while the actor was touring with a play in Trento.

Their relationship, needless to say, had been a very hushed affair. We visited them once in Rome at the apartment they maintain in the outskirts of the city. Fabio was as open and funny and wonderful as ever, but I found the actor rather pretentious and insincere with Clayton and me, and perhaps a bit jealous. After trying to impress us with his acting credentials, or at least with all the people he knew in films, on both sides of the camera, he then complained that Fabio was putting on too much weight. They have, nevertheless, managed to live together all these years. We did not visit them again. Fabio and I continue to exchange cards from time to time, but I have not seen him in years. During our visit in Rome I remember him saying that they should put a sign up at the city limits of Trento: Dante's "*Lasciate ogni speranza, voi ch'entrate.*" Abandon all hope, ye who enter.

But Trento had in fact begun to have pleasant memories for me once more. Walking down its streets with Clayton I was comforted by the sight of familiar walls, familiar faces. And that same arm on my shoulder. In the squares we could see the same men standing in the exact same places we had seen them stand years before. "La Loren," the madwoman of Piazza Duomo, still rambled about the square muttering to herself. The young men still lolled in intimate groupings near the central phone office.

What changes there were were minor. A new shop, an ancient building renovated, at last a laundromat. One evening Clayton and I were walking down the middle of the street heading towards the Cantinota Restaurant when we heard the buzz of a motor behind us. We both assumed it was a Vespa, or some such motorbike, coming up to pass us. Neither of us could help bursting into laughter when what pulled around us turned out to be a motorized wheelchair speeding past us at about twenty miles an hour. It whizzed away into the distance and disappeared around a corner, its wheels screeching.

But these were changes that only emphasized so much that had not changed. Dante's face had not moved from the mountain. And what had not changed seemed to speak to Clayton and me, seemed to say to us: Each year has forged a link you never guessed existed. We had shackled ourselves together tighter and tighter, closer and closer, but there was something increasingly easy in our indivisibility. The chains did not rankle. The ties were liberating, were reassuring. . .were love.

One of the few disappointing trips Clayton and I ever took was an excursion back to Louisiana to see his family. I would not call it a catastrophe; I have made more disastrous journeys. It was merely that the members of his family seemed to exude some ineffable, clinging vapor of inhospitality, enshrouding themselves in a dank, queerly luminous atmosphere of guarded pride and imagined slights — just as the blue fog of summer irradiates the twilight hours on certain San Francisco hills. Unfortunately, there was nothing picturesque about these relatives. For me, none of them was much worth remembering; for Clayton, they were all aggravatingly unforgettable. (For the curious, a more detailed if caricatured portrait of his clan may be gleaned from Clayton's bucolic farce *The Marquis of the Bayou*. While not providing much emotional sustenance, this background of Louisiana lowlife was a rich source of material for his stories.)

What always struck me as strange was that none of the misfortune his family had suffered had brought them any closer together. I do not doubt that his parents loved him, or that Clayton, as their only surviving son, was precious to them (I can honestly say no one seemed dearer to them). But one could have surmised nothing of these feelings in their behavior. Affection would have been alien in the territory upon which they transacted their relationships. In this landscape everyone appeared emotionally displaced. Clayton himself confessed after our visit that it would probably be another eight years before he worked up the stomach to see them again.

His mother, a phenomenally nondescript woman, was kind to me in a stiff sort of way. Her kindness seemed at first only to be relief: upon meeting me she did not even bother to whisper as she told her husband, "Well, Floyd, at least this one's white. We can be thankful for that." She nagged Clayton about everything, from his clothes ("I think those jeans are too small for you, Clayton. Your butt's stickin' out like the back of Daddy's pickup!") to paternity (When *are* you gonna marry and give me and your father some grandchildren?") to literature ("I tried to read that last book of yours, Clayton, I *did* — but *Lord*, when are you gonna write somethin' decent?"). There was, in fact, a complete set of Clayton's books in their dining-room cabinet. I dared not be condescending about their not having read them. I had been neglectful myself for so long. But in their indifference to his work there was a claim upon their son that was both voraciously selfish and coldly unparental.

As for the question of grandchildren, Clayton tried to explain time and again that he preferred men sexually, and that unless human biology had drastically altered, neither I nor Clayton was about to bear any offspring for them. She would make no attempt to hide her disapproval, but instead clicked her tonque tragically and said, "I know, Clayton, but that don't mean your children won't be normal."

She was, on top of everything else, a ruthless cook. Clayton and I finally decided to take our meals in restaurants after one particularly bad lunch of bacon fat, macaroni, and canned peas.

Mr. Hayes was a severe old man of few words who even as he approached seventy still made his regular shrimping forays out into the gulf. His brusquely taciturn manner was occasionally preempted by a gregarious species of misanthropy. He hated everyone and everything. When he was not out on his boat he seemed forever preoccupied with a wide circle of friends and, unavoidably, his innumerable relations, but he never had a kind or appreciative word to say to or about any of them. He always had a beer in his hand, which is to say he was always in some stage of drunkenness. He quarreled often and boisterously with Clayton's mother. Indeed, I was astounded at how much they had to argue about considering how much time they spent apart. It appeared that, despite Mr. Hayes' weeks at sea, familiarity had bred with a vengeance.

Clayton's father barely nodded at me during our stay in their home. He spoke to me, if at all, about Italy, which he said he had a desire to see. But then he would turn around and say something outrageously bigoted about Italians, or at least about the Italian-Americans he knew in Louisiana. His only remark about my relationship with Clayton was once when he noticed us exchange one of those flagrantly intimate looks that couples cannot help but exchange. Without looking up from his beer can, he mumbled (with what was, after all, unerring irony for him), "It looks to me like someone got up on the wrong side of the bed."

More irritating for Clayton was his father's request for a loan to buy a new shrimp boat. Clayton's parents were in fact very well-off financially, and Clayton had never curtailed his natural generosity with them. The loan, however, was meant as a test of Clayton's "loyalty" to his father. As a play on Clayton's guilt, his father at last mentioned the loan he had wired to Trento years before. Clayton angrily pulled out his checkbook and wrote a check for three times that amount, which he had long ago repaid.

"Here!" he shouted at his father, "take this and do what you like with it! But don't you *ever* call me your son!"

His father took the check and tore it into pieces. "You think just because you're the only son I got left you can buy my love?" he said.

Clayton was so flabbergasted by this ludicrous turnabout in his father's gamesmanship that he laughed. But it was not a gay laugh.

Their wretchedness as a family may simply have been the measure of their bad luck, but Clayton was not disposed to take it philosophically. We cut our trip short, and after visiting his grandmother in New Orleans, a bright and fascinating old woman who was the one relative of his we both liked, we flew back to San Francisco. When we got back he immediately contracted to have the cottage remodeled. It was a statement of his love for me: You give me what nobody else does. One more invisible link had been forged.

In San Francisco my friendship with Claire also ripened over the years. I could not begin to gauge the full extent of her influence on my life. She was the one chiefly responsible, of course, for sabotaging my own bigotry towards Italian-Americans and Southern Italians. Her most pervasive effect on me, though, has been in a general lightening of my heart through her rollickingly funny companionship. At times sharply witty, at times shame-lessly corny, at times simply crazy, her effervescent humor has had the thankless task of buoying my sagging spirits more often than I care to remember. After Clayton, she is the person I have had the most good times with. And when times got bad, it was Claire I counted on to make me laugh.

She taught me to speak a pseudo-English that we have since used as a means of exasperating strangers in the street or in shops and restaurants. "Fort were toke ishamble a cone sax," Claire will say to me. I reply in the negative. "Note, to cam biddle shore in rinking." The American ear tends to be maddeningly intrigued by these sounds, perking up to odd words that at first resemble English so much. We have overheard full-scale disputes as to the exact identity of this language break out among San Franciscans eavesdropping on our manufactured tongue.

Claire is more accustomed to resorting to simple Italian in any situation that calls for furtive expression. If she is treated rudely in a cafe, she may receive her cup of coffee with her most winsome, sneaky smile and in a softly dulcet voice tell the waiter, "*Grazie, testa di cazzo.*" It sounds so sophisticatedly gracious when she says it. Thank you, dick-head.

She is intimidated by nothing, nor does she grovel for accolades, or even acceptance, from those who some might deem her social betters. She does not have a lot of phony manners, and no one would think of her as especially cultured. But she is always herself. I once went to meet her at the elegant Redwood Room of the Clift Hotel for a drink after work. I found her quite unconsciously creating a scene by sitting at her table boldly reading one of San Francisco's trashier tabloids — the kind given free to tourists. On the front page for all to see were several naked women in various seductive poses, and the unrelated headline, "Angie Dickinson Eats Shit!"

"Luca, it's incredible!" she called across the cocktail lounge as soon as she saw me. "It says here that Donna Douglass, you know, Ellie Mae from the old 'Beverly Hillbillies,' was once arrested for giving head to this girl in the bathroom of some gas station down in Van Nuys."

I tried to ignore the offended glares of the other patrons as I made my way to her table.

We went together once to a new "relaxation" salon that had opened in San Francisco. The place was called "Soma" and offered for the first time anywhere sensory deprivation tanks for public rental. You paid so much to float in heavily salted water at body temperature in your own individual lightproof, soundproof tank. They looked like big washing machines. We had recently seen the film *Altered States*, which featured just such a tank. After being deprived of all sensory stimulation, the star of the movie came out of the tank a Neanderthal. We did not have such high hopes for ourselves, but we were eager to try out the "void."

I came out of my dip into sensationless nirvana feeling very relaxed, if not of an altered state of mind. Claire, however, informed me that she had spent the entire time splashing around inside the tank singing to herself, her repertoire including the Gershwin tune, "Soma-time, when the livin' is easy, Fish are jumpin'. . . ."

Clayton's thirty-ninth birthday was coming up and Claire helped me plan the surprise party I was throwing for him. It was her idea to have the Chinese specialties called Dim Sum catered in. Dim Sum, for those who do not know, consists of a variety of little hors d'oeuvre-like snacks that people normally make a meal of in Dim Sum restaurants, where the dishes are served from carts laden with a multiplicity of choices pushed about by waiters and waitresses. Claire rented a very old-fashioned waitress uniform for the occasion, complete with white cap, and hauled the trays of food about our cottage all evening honking in a clipped Chinese accent, "You want some of dese? Or some of dose? Or some of dese and Dim Sum of dose?"

I was thirty-one when Clayton turned thirty-nine. Most people could not tell the difference in our ages just by looking at us. Clayton had kept himself extremely fit. I had become as proud of his youthful sexiness as of his literary fame. Friends and strangers alike still eyed us enviously when we walked into rooms. It would take monumental false modesty for me to discount all the tales told of what a handsome couple we were and the startling effect we sometimes had on people. But our public conduct together was never affected, and whatever physical beauty either of us possessed was enhanced dramatically by our undisguised feelings for each other.

My birthday gift to Clayton that year was a leather-bound copy of my thesis. "Clayton Hayes: The Popular Novel as Spiritual Balm." It was the first he had learned of its theme. And, for once, the surprise was all his. It had not been easy keeping it a secret. I had had to do most of the writing outside the house, while putting off his interested inquiries with discreet assertions of academic privacy — which of course only fired his curiosity more. At last holding the thesis in his hands, he looked from its title to me, and back to the title again, in stupefied silence. Then he kissed me as tears, proud and grateful and loving, filled his eyes.

We had already planned a visit to Trento after Clayton's birthday that fall. The day before we left, Claire dropped by to say good-bye. I was packing. She seemed rather harried and made the sign with her two hands that says, *"Due palle cosi"* Two balls like this. It means that one is fed up, or that someone or something has been a pain in the ass. Although it refers to the testicles of male anatomy, it is not an uncommon gesture or expression among Italian women.

She explained that it had been a rotten day at work, then added, "But I still had time to get you a little going-away present." She often did this for my longer trips. I politely told her she shouldn't have, and then accepted the small gift-wrapped box. I was shocked to see that it contained handkerchiefs.

When she saw the look on my face, she cried, *"O, Dio.* I'm sorry Luca, I forgot." *Fazoletti* are never given as gifts in Italy. They carry with them the specter of grief and weeping. I am not superstitious, but a lifetime's habit of neither giving nor receiving hankerchiefs had to be consciously set aside. I handed her a coin, a custom that follows on the other.

"You see, it doesn't matter," I said, trying to allay her concern that she had brought me bad luck. "The superstition means nothing if I pay for the handkerchiefs."

Her distress was not pacified. "*Che scema*! What an idiot I am! I'm sorry, Luca. The thing is, I *know* the tradition. I just wasn't thinking."

Her face did not lose its worried look all evening.

XI   Now, Voyager

I realize that in writing of my mother's "house" I have perhaps misled the reader to believe that it is a separate residence...in actuality, a house. My family home in Trento, however, is instead a large flat in an apartment building of six units. The apartments might more properly be termed condominiums, since all the residents own their own units. This is a quite conventional housing arrangement in Italy, at least in the North, where the majority of middle-class families are able to afford their own apartments. Another large number of people rent their flats, while a small minority of relatively wealthy citizens own private, individual houses or villas.

We discovered upon our arrival in Trento that winter that an older cousin of mine had just lost her husband to a heart attack. At the same time a flat in my mother's building was being sold. As the sudden death of her husband had been very traumatic for my cousin, she had spoken to my mother about moving into her building so as to have the solace and support of her aunt close at hand. Her own mother was dead and her father was already saddled with the family of the woman he had remarried. My mother, while willing to give moral support, was not close enough to the cousin to ask her to move into her own apartment, especially as the cousin still had two children at home with her. Besides, as I have noted, my mother had already established a life very much her own and I doubt she would have surrendered her life-style to anyone. She wanted to share her home and time only if it did not infringe upon the one luxury she had become attached to, independence. Having her niece in the apartment upstairs was a compromise they were both amenable to.

But because my cousin had not been left very well provided for by her husband, getting the money to purchase the flat was a problem. Not surprisingly, she approached Clayton for financial assistance. She did not know him well, but had of course heard of my "good fortune" (*zio americano* — American uncle — refers to any rich friend). Clayton was not at all reluctant to listen to the request, nodding favorably as my cousin nervously made her pitch. He told her he would see what he could work out.

I mention all of this rather unimportant matter only because it is the only thing Clayton and I argued about on that trip. I thought he was letting himself be taken advantage of. I was, indeed, quite angry with my cousin. He said he did not mind helping our relatives, meaning my relatives were his, as long as there were real need involved.

Before any of that was settled, we agreed to visit overnight with my cousin Franco at his home in Folgaria. Franco had married many years earlier and had a couple of small children as well. Clayton and I were not particularly thrilled about spending so much time with these relatives, but Franco had been so insistent, and we had put off his invitation during so many stays in Trento, that we felt we could not say no again. The only recompense accorded us was Franco's assurance that his father, crazy Uncle Ugo — no saner and still frustratingly hearty — would not be joining us.

Franco came to pick us up in his car toward dusk. I did not want to deprive my mother of her car and we did not want to bother with renting one. Franco was elated to see us, as always, and treated us with a respect that bordered on worship. To him, we were the perfect romance vicariously participated in, the embodiment of some secret life he had only dreamed about. Or so I thought.

The drive to Folgaria is normally little more than half an hour from Trento. At Franco's urging we consented to take the longer route that day. It is a road that winds precariously through the mountains and adds about twenty minutes to the drive. Once we had set out on it Clayton and I were glad Franco had persisted, as the panoramic vistas seemed more spectacular with each bend in the road. I had almost forgotten how scenic my province was. There had been an early and heavy snow that winter and the white-capped mountains loomed majestically on the other side of the steep drop to the valley below, while the car hugged the narrow, icy ledge of a road cut into the snow-covered rock.

As he negotiated this demanding route, Franco suddenly announced that we would be making a brief detour. He wanted to stop in the village of Nosellari.

"Why?" Clayton asked in Italian. "Is there something worth seeing?" He was sitting in front and had to turn around to look at me in the back seat. I shrugged.

"I want you to meet someone," Franco said, smiling mischievously. "I want you to meet a friend of mine."

"Who?" I asked, barely remembering the name of the town.

"A friend," Franco said. And pointing between me and Clayton he explained, "A friend like you and Clayton. A boy. I love him very much and he loves me." As he continued to gesture with one hand, the car hit an ice slick and Franco had to grasp the steering wheel quickly with both hands to keep us on the road without slamming into the mountain wall. The swerving loss of control only lasted a moment, and then Franco went on gesturing with the free hand. "He and I, we make love together."

"The same boy?" I exclaimed.

Franco had to think a second before he could figure out whom I was alluding to. When he recalled his confession to me from years before, he shook his head. "No, no, this is a different boy. I really love this boy."

I was dumbfounded. Nosellari is a tiny town without as many as two hundred inhabitants, and that Franco had managed to find *two* homosexual lovers among its population amazed me. I began to wonder if there was something in the local drinking water. Or what, exactly, was Franco's penchant for boys from one small, obscure Italian village. It seemed a most unlikely fetish.

I must note that Franco had retained his good looks, even if he had also retained most of his not so clean or appealing grooming habits. There was still something irrepressibly sexy about him. I could see that if anyone were going to make a career of seducing backward mountain boys, it would be someone like Franco. Intelligence had never corrupted his desires.

"What about your family?" I asked, thinking at the same time, There but for the grace of Neptune. . . .

"Oh, my wife knows. She's met him. I explained it to her. She understands. She accepts it. It's not the first boy I've had. But I really love Angelo." Then he winked and threw in the apparent non sequitur: "Manuela is pregnant again."

"And what about your father? Does he know?"
Clayton asked.

"*Me ne frego!*" Franco bellowed. I don't give a fuck!
But there was, in reality, something so docile about this
aggressive boast of independence from crazy Uncle Ugo
that one just knew that the fact of such affairs had never
been brought to his father's attention. Poor, sweet Cousin
Franco.

"Anyway, Angelo is the most beautiful boy I have ever
known. He's seventeen and he's got the face of an angel —
no kidding — a real angel." He unnecessarily advised
Clayton, "Angelo, you know. . .angel. The same word in
Italian. It's a boy's name too. And this boy is a real angel.
And so beautiful. Wait till you see him. I tremble just to
touch him."

Franco then said something I don't remember, but
which made me think at the time that he was hinting at a
sexual four-way with me, Clayton, him, and the boy from
Nosellari. With Franco it was hard to be sure — there was
always something lascivious in the curve of his lips.

All at once the car skidded across ice again. Unable
to control the car, Franco cursed a terrified, "*Madonna!*"
Then, with a sickening lurch, the car went off the edge of
the road, off the mountain, and plummeted into midair. I
can remember seeing blue sky through the windshield, then
a bank of rocks and snow swing eerily into view. Then I
was aware of nothing.

The next thing I remember was looking down the side of
the mountain at the car another fifty meters below me. It
had crashed head-on into a slab of rock jutting out from the
mountain. The slab of rock was now pounded free of snow.
I had somehow been thrown from the car. I must have fallen
about ten meters. I was lying in the snow among leafless,

gnarled scrub. My right leg was twisted under me. It had been the first part of me to break the snow and hit bedrock.

I was at first afraid to look to carefully about me. I was scared of what I might see. For a moment my eyes rested upon the open copy of E.M. Forster's *A Passage to India*, which I had been reading, wedged in the snow. I tried to move, but the pain in my leg shot tears into my eyes immediately. My whole body shuddered in agony. I had to catch my breath. At last I summoned the courage to call out. "Clayton! Clayton!"

There was the faintest glow of sunset in the sky now. I could make out a dark hulk in the snow above the car. It moved. The figure of a man slowly uncrumpled itself. My heart stopped, and then churned painfully against my breathless lungs. The man staggered to his feet. It was Clayton. He had evidently been thrown out nearer to where the car had crashed, but he seemed all right.

"Clayton!" I called again.

He looked around groggily. He could not see me. I called again. Looking up the mountain he saw where I lay and echoed my panic.

"Luca!"

The mountain between me and Clayton was much less precipitous than either the wall that stretched above me to the road or the sheer cliff below where the car had been stopped. He scrambled up towards me, shouting, "Luca! Luca! Are you okay!"

"I'm okay!" I propped myself up on my elbows. "Be careful!"

When he got to me he threw himself onto his knees in the snow beside me. "Are you okay?" he asked again. He put a hand to my face and pulled it back. I could see the blood on his fingers. My face must have been scratched by the shrubbery. Clayton was out of breath and heaving strangely.

"I think my leg is hurt," I said. "What about you?"

"Just a little shaken up. I'm okay now. Can you move your leg?"

I tried to shuffle my leg out from beneath me, but again the pain was overwhelming.

"It may be broken," Clayton said. He pointed to a flat shelf of rock nearby which was protected by a slight overhang and clear of snow. "I think I should try laying you out there."

"What about Franco?" I looked back down at the car.

Clayton followed my gaze and seemed to experience my own tremulous dread. We both searched about the mountain for some sign of my cousin. Then, after gathering his strength, Clayton said, "I'll go down and see." The strange panting which I had thought was simply his being out of breath had not subsided.

He rose unsteadily to his feet and trudged down to the car. The driver's side was not visible from my position. After a minute Clayton reappeared from behind the car. He paused, looking up at me and the climb ahead of him. He then painstakingly made his way back to me.

"Franco's dead," he said, again sinking into the snow beside me. Neither of us said anything for a long while.

"Are you sure?" I asked at last. Clayton nodded.

He shifted his body under mine so that I was able to lay my head in his lap. I buried my face in his jeans and he stroked the side of my bloody face.

I looked up into his eyes and they were calm and reassuring. For a moment. Then he looked at my leg and said, "I think we should try moving you over there. Then I can go up to the road and hail a passing car. I don't think the accident can be seen from the road." He was still breathing irregularly.

I nodded, though I knew it would be excruciating. I made what I hoped was a brave face and sat up on my elbows again.

"I'll carry you on my back. Put your arms around my neck and just let your leg hang." He turned his back to me and I leaned onto it, wrapping my arms together over his chest. He grasped my forearms in his hands and struggled to his feet.

The pain was so sharp I thought I was going to pass out.

"Hold on, Luca!" Clayton exhorted between labored breaths.

Because of our disparate heights, my legs dangled into the snow. He balanced the load as best he could and half-carried, half-dragged me to the little clearing of rock. I tried to stifle my sobs in his neck. Despite the debilitating exertion required of him, he continuously whispered the entire twenty or so paces, "It's okay, Luca. I've got you. I'm here, Luca. We're almost there. . . ."

Being set upon the ground proved even more torturous than being lifted from it. At last, though, both my legs lay straight out in front of me now. The right one looked oddly flat, but no fracture had broken the skin. The rock was freezing cold.

"I'll go back and get some of our things from the car." He coughed two convulsive, wincing coughs. He looked into his hand, then wiped it on his jacket. I could make out a moist smear of blood on the material.

"You're hurt, Clayton!" I did not attempt to suppress the alarm in my voice. "Stay here and rest. You're in no condition to go climbing all over this goddam mountain."

"I'm okay." He stood again. His rasping breath seemed to come increasingly harder to him. "I'll be back in a few minutes."

"Clayton. . . ." But I could think of no effective protest. And since he was still mobile, I knew he was right to do what he could. I watched as he went back down to the car. He was able to retrieve our overnight bag from the car with a minimum of effort as it had been in the back seat with me instead of in the trunk. He started back up the mountain, but then stopped short. He set the bag down and returned to the car. He disappeared behind the other side. After a few moments he came out from around the car holding Franco's coat. He proceeded back to the bag, where he stopped and knelt in the snow. He appeared to be rubbing snow on the coat. It occurred to me that he must be trying to clean blood off it.

At my resting place again, he took clothes out of the bag and tucked them between me and the cold rock. He put the bag itself under my head and softened the "pillow" with a folded towel. Finally he laid Franco's coat over me. The coat smelled of Franco, and for once this odor was comforting, as if his life still lingered about us.

"I've got to try and make it back up the road. Holler if you need me." His breath now came in short, shallow gasps.

"You've got to rest, Clayton!" I meant to sound stern with him, but I feared that it had only seemed liked whining. I took his hand and squeezed it. He leaned over me and kissed my lips.

"I'll be back in an hour or two at the latest."

He hesitated. Neither one of us wanted to be alone. But he was our only chance and we both knew it. He waited with me several minutes as the sky continued to darken. A few isolated stars pierced the frigid night, before clouds began rolling in. At last he started up the escarpment towards the road.

It was a sharp ascent, but not unscalable, even for someone in Clayton's weakened state. He navigated from foothold to foothold, from the handle of a bush to the handle of a cleft in the stone. He slipped a couple of times, but I did not worry as much for his falling as for the limits to which he was pushing his injured body. When I could no longer see him, I lay back to wait anxiously for his return.

Clayton made the trip between the road and my niche several times that night. It was not a much traveled road and a light snow had begun to fall, making it even less convenient to drivers. He was always hopeful, however, each time he set out again for the road, until he returned to me late into the night and said that he would settle in with me till daylight. There was not much hope of being found at the present hour.

"But they're sure to be missing us by now," he said, laying his warm body next to mine. "They'll be out searching for us at first light. It'll be easier then."

The numbing cold already had me shivering and chattering my teeth. Clayton, overheated from his climbs, pressed his warmth as close to me as possible. He lay his face against mine and cradled me in his arms. His warm breath, as erratic as it was, soothed me. And when the wind began to whip through the crevice we lay in and the pain in my leg made me moan, he pulled me to him tighter and murmured words of encouragement.

"You're going to be all right, Luca," he said, his own teeth beginning to chatter. "I'm going to take care of you. Just hold onto me." And all I could do *was* hold him more tightly.

At length, with nervous agitation, he began to speak of other things. He could not sleep and there was no conversation for us. Seeking to distract me from my pain, and perhaps to forestall despair, he turned to lighter, more distant associations.

"You know, this is really kind of romantic," he said with strained cheerfulness. "Even a little erotic. If it weren't so damned cold and your leg wasn't hurting, we'd probably be fucking right now. It's like that old movie, *Now, Voyager.* You ever see that movie, Luca?"

He knew I had not.

"It's this old movie with Bette Davis. You know who Bette Davis is, don't you?"

After all my years in America, in the gay community of San Francisco no less, I still had only the dimmest notion of who she was. I remember peevishly thinking the time inappropriate to start learning about her. I had no interest in old-fashioned American movies. Black and white films had always irritated me. But I answered.

"She's an American movie star, isn't she?"

Clayton seemed excessively pleased that I had responded. I realized only later that I must have been fading in and out of consciousness the whole time, and not from mere sleepiness.

"She's the greatest. I'll have to take you to a Bette Davis festival at the Castro Theater one of these days. Anyway, in the movie *Now, Voyager* she ends up going over a cliff in a car with Paul Henreid in Brazil and they have to spend the night together on the mountain. You see, they've just met on a cruise ship sailing down from New York. It's all very romantic because she's this very lonely woman whose had her life practically ruined by her very proper Bostonian mother, and he's unhappily married to a shrewish wife back in New York. Are you with me, Luca?"

I nodded. He kissed my cheek and whispered, "Good boy." I burrowed a hand through his layer of clothes and under his shirt to the warmth of his chest. I could feel the spasmodic inhaling and exhaling. For an instant there was the barest whimper of pain from Clayton, though I was not alert enough to judge whether it was the coldness of my hand or the tenderness of his flesh.

"I'll start from the beginning." Clayton pulled Franco's coat snugger about us. "Bette Davis plays this young woman, Charlotte Vale, a very repressed, frumpy young woman. Do you know what frumpy means, Luca?" He shook me. Of course I knew what it meant. I had a Master's in English Literature, didn't I? Why wouldn't he just let me sleep? He shook me again. I blathered mindlessly for a few seconds, then mumbled, "Dowdy."

"Yeah, and her dowdy old mother is Gladys Cooper, a really cruel and uncaring mother who has forced her daughter to become a neurotic spinster after destroying the only real love affair she ever had as a girl — with an officer on a cruise ship. It starts out with Bette Davis dressed in an old rag of a dress, looking even dowdier than her mother, even though they're rich, and sublimating some of her pent-up sexual frustration by carving little boxes. Her older sister-in-law, Ilka Chase, has sneakily invited a psychotherapist, played by Claude Rains, over to the house to see if he can help, but her mother disapproves of the whole business. She wants to keep her daughter an ugly, homebound spinster. . . ."

Mentally, I came and went throughout the night. But I heard most of the story. Clayton recalled the film in remarkable detail. He went over each scene with affectionate thoroughness. He even hummed the film's theme music to me. Occasionally he would tilt me toward him or whisper, "Luca! Luca!" into my ear to make sure I was still with him. And when I heard him repeat the line from the movie, "Don't let's ask for the moon; we have the stars," I was surprised to open my eyes and see the first glimmer of dawn in the sky.

I was also startled to hear the burr of some mysterious insect. Clayton heard it too, as he had fallen silent and cocked his head attentively. He gently released me from his arms and scuttled into the open. The sound of the insect was now louder and in the distance I saw a beam of light emanating from the direction of the noise. The whirring was like the rapid flutter of giant wings. Within seconds the thunderous creature revealed itself as a helicopter. Its floodlight swept across the mountain as Clayton waved and shouted frantically for its attention. The beam found him, after alighting briefly on the wrecked car. I remember watching Clayton hopping — almost dancing — in the snow, caught in the intense, radiant eye of the helicopter that roared above. It was an emergency helicopter of the mountain fire department. And then, the consciousness which had flickered uncomfortably all night extinguished itself, shuttering me in darkness.

I awoke in a hospital bed. White light streamed in through the white-curtained window and seemed to paint everything in the room white. My white plaster cast was in traction. There was a white, empty bed next to mine. A woman in white floated into the room and I had to shut my eyes against the glare. And fell instantly back to sleep.

The next time I awoke color had burst into the room. Flowers were strewn about the room in bright vases and my mother stood by my bed wearing a maroon dress and a heavy, deep purple coat. My Aunt Irene, two other aunts, an uncle, and several cousins were also in the room, diffusing its blinding whiteness. My mother's face was dry, but her eyes were red and swollen, and her expression a map of sorrow that not even my awakening could completely efface.

Aunt Irene, the only one unafraid to wear black into my hospital room, looked even worse, and it was to her that I first spoke. "I'm so sorry, Aunt Irene. . . ." My mother put her hand to my forehead and brushed back my hair as Franco's mother nodded, smiled wanly, and then collapsed into a nearby chair weeping. Two of our relatives swiftly hustled her out of the room as my mother took my hand.

"You're going to be all right," she said.

"How long have I been here?" I noticed that my plastered leg was no longer in traction.

"Three days."

It could have been weeks for all I knew. I glanced about the room again, sure that I had overlooked a face. "Where's Clayton?" I asked.

"He's in another part of the hospital, hon," she answered with fragile tranquility.

"What do you mean he's in another part of the hospital?" I did not understand.

"He's being cared for in a special room."

"But why is he in the hospital?" I was growing impatient and nervous.

My mother looked at me as though I were perhaps still out of my head. "Luca, he was hurt in the accident."

Only then, indeed, did it seem that my mind emerged from its fog. As much the product of a lingering hangover from medication as it was simple thoughtlessness, my confusion was instantly overpowered by a rush of adrenalin. Unhappily, upon attempting to bolt from the bed, I discovered that the adrenalin had done little to restore my weakened muscles. I feebly wrestled against my mother's restraint before collapsing back against the pillow, exhausted.

"You've got to stay in bed or you're going to hurt yourself even more. There's nothing you can do for Clayton right now. The doctors are taking care of him." She endeavored to take her most authoritative tone with me, but the unmistakable note of sympathy in her voice did not allay my panic.

Physically I was still useless. "How badly hurt is he?" I was finally able to mew.

"I don't know. . .but the doctors are taking good care of him, don't worry. He asks about you of course. Even when they first brought him back from the operating room he was mumbling 'Luca, Lu—' "

Her eyes suddenly revealed a panic all their own at the realization that the wrong thing had been said. She laid a hand on my arm. It was too late.

There ensued another, more obscenely comic battle over my desire to go to Clayton. This time I surprised myself with a surge of energy that had my arms and one good leg flailing all over the place. And what I could not accomplish with my body I attempted to remedy with my voice. Screaming at the top of my lungs at my poor mother, I demanded to see doctors, demanded a wheelchair, demanded to be taken to Clayton.

A rather frail-looking nurse who hardly appeared up to the task scurried into the room and tried to calm me. She told me that Signor Hayes was in stable condition and that I was better off relaxing until the doctor gave instructions allowing me to resume normal physical activity. I still floundered about trying to get me and my broken leg out of bed. My mother asked the nurse if I shouldn't be given an injection or some kind of sedative.

My threats to murder the nurse, my mother, the doctors, and anyone else who got in my way having failed to work, I had to decide on a different tack — more especially as my strength was quickly wearing itself out. I assumed a more conciliatory attitude with the nurse.

"Listen, Signor Hayes is as much my responsibility as anyone's. I must see him. It's not right to keep him isolated from those who care most about him."

The nurse paused in her struggle with me. She looked at my mother, seemed to weigh some secret impulse, then left the room. When she reentered, I was thankful to see that she brought — not a hypodermic or a doctor or a thug of an orderly — but a wheelchair.

"I shouldn't be doing this. If the doctors catch me...."

My mother helped her bundle me into the wheelchair.

Dizzy from my tantrum, I let her gather my robe snugly about me and tie the cord. She informed me that the police had been waiting to speak to me about the accident. Several journalists were also hoping to interview me or Clayton. I asked her to track down the doctor tending to Clayton. She nodded as the nurse wheeled me out of the room.

The circuitous trek through the hospital's lesser traveled corridors was a disorienting series of stops and turns and slow approaches preceding mad dashes across passageway intersections. The journey was rendered all the more bizzare by a lapse of clarity on my part. It was almost as though I had fallen back into a semiconsciousness of half-real images and vague, volatile emotions. One moment I would be intent upon getting to Clayton, spurred on by an anxiety that was all too real. The next moment I would be distracted by an aged, immobile patient glimpsed through an open door, or the hollow sheen of the hospital walls. I became obsessed with the sound of the chair's wheels spinning across the floor, and only with an effort shook off the spiraling melancholy it seemed to provoke in me. Then I would have to stir myself again to my purpose, make myself more determined to see Clayton. The surreal effect of that memorable ride in the wheelchair imbued the mission with a unique quality of abstract but absolute need.

As the nurse hurtled me and the chair down the halls, my mind lost in its own otherwordly sense of urgency, I tried to make sense of what the nurse was saying. Everyone in the hospital was talking about us it seemed, and not just because Signor Hayes was a famous American writer. When we first arrived off the helicopter, Clayton had apparently insisted on making sure I was safely under the doctors' charge before he would leave my side, and then he himself had passed out on the emergency room floor. She did not know the extent of his injuries. He was in an intensive care unit where no one was admitted except for very short visits, one at a time. She had heard that my mother had been his only visitor.

Suddenly alert once more, I asked her name.

"Daniela," she replied, taken slightly aback by my question.

"Daniela," I said, shutting my eyes against the length of corridor ahead of us, "you must hurry." She quickened her pace. I listened to the wheels.

At last she wheeled me into a room with drawn shades. There were two beds in the room, but only one was occupied. I did not recognize Clayton at first, he was so changed. He looked thin and cadaverous. An intravenous tube was taped under his nose. The funereal light and strong odor of medicine in the room cast an impermeable gloom upon everything. We were all trapped in a shadow.

"I'll be outside," Daniela whispered, and left me by the bed.

I was afraid to speak. Clayton's eyes were closed and his breathing was still uneasy. Horror-stricken that he had lain like this for three days — alone, separated from the person he had worked so hard to save, probably unaware of how I was doing — I was sapped of all the fortitude with which I had braced myself to get to him. Clayton, who had lain with me on a cold rock for so many hours until we were rescued, had been permitted to languish without one word of encouragement or one smile of support from me. What he had suffered I was too ashamed to imagine. I felt as though I had been forced to acquiesce, however unknowingly, in some peculiarly vicious form of medical treatment, a treatment based on the clinical infliction of loneliness.

This disturbing thought appeared to jar Clayton to consciousness. He opened his eyes and stretched out a hand to me. "Luca . . . ." he whispered hoarsely.

I took his hand in both my hands and sobbed into it quietly, uncontrollably. In anguish my mouth bit at his knuckles. I felt his ring, the ring I had given him, cold against my teeth. He put his other hand on my head and repeated my name softly.

I looked up after I had stopped crying and saw that he was smiling, though there were tears in his eyes too.

"I asked to see you," he said weakly, "but they said it wasn't possible. They said you were in another ward. How are you doing?"

I wiped my tears on my shoulder and told him I was okay. Indicating the cast on my leg, I smiled and shrugged. I wheeled the chair closer to the head of the bed and touched his face. He took my hand and put it to his lips. He kissed my palm and the ring he had given me. I laid my fingers on his lips, their tips touching the plastic tube that led into his nostrils, and let them rest there as we looked into each other's eyes.

"How are you feeling?" I asked.

"Okay, considering. I'm a little messed up inside, I guess. They had to cut me open. I hope you don't mind a few scars." He smiled again. His voice was so breathy and insubstantial it seemed to come from another world, carried on a haunted wind.

I lifted my body with my hands on the armrests of the chair and cantilevered myself onto the side of the bed. Leaning over I was able to kiss his lips. I set my cheek against his and whispered into his ear, "I love you, Clayton."

He kissed my cheek and started to whisper something back. But overcome either with emotion or the discomfort of my being pressed so close upon him, he merely kissed my cheek again, held his face against mine, and sighed deeply, regretfully.

I pulled back and tried to remain seated on the edge of the bed. This was an awkward position for both of us. I lowered myself back into the chair and took his hand in mine again.

"Actually, the only thing that's really bothering me right now," he said, "is this damn catheter they have stuck up me."

Not utterly oblivious to any further danger I might be putting him in, I debated throwing off his covers and simply pulling out the catheter right then and there. I was about to get Daniela's advice when a doctor blew into the room, blustering in an angry, impenetrable English. He strode to the bed, literally snapped Clayton's hand out of mine and began to push me out of the room. It was to become the first of many scenes with doctors during my stay in the hospital.

I was able to stop the good doctor dead in his tracks with a brilliant string of Italian invective. Unfortunately, getting him to oblige me in any other regard after he realized I was Italian proved a more arduous undertaking. His Italian was no more civil, if more comprehensible, than his English. Upon regaining his momentum, he shoved me out the door and into the hallway. I considered jamming myself in the doorway with my cast, but, after one last glance back at an alarmed Clayton, I figured that what had to be said had best be said outside the room.

For a young man who was not so young any longer but who was still not thoroughly used to compromising either his pride or his vanity, it was unsettling to have to work so hard to bring some imperious force into my manner. Never had impertinence seemed like such a deliberate performance — or such a chore. It was a measure of my fearful concern for Clayton as much as the infirmity of my physical state. By the time I collected my wits and interrupted the doctor's tirade (he now stood berating Daniela, who had waited meekly outside the door), I found myself having to control a wobbly vibrato which had crept into my voice.

"Doctor," I interjected, "what about the catheter?"

He stared at me blankly. Evidently Daniela took that

as her cue to be dismissed, for she turned and disappeared down the corridor crying.

"The catheter?" the doctor barked. "That's no business of *yours*. What do you know about catheters!"

Disheartened by the brusqueness of his condescension, I nevertheless persevered in getting an explanation for the catheter. But when I suggested removing it and replacing it with a plain, old-fashioned bedpan, I'm afraid the yelling match recommenced. Heads poked out of doorways. Nurses came running to see what the fracas was all about. Other doctors stood at a safe distance and watched.

I have never trusted doctors or hospitals, and this hospital — or at least this particular member of its staff — was doing nothing to assuage my general apprehension regarding the medical profession. But an impasse of sorts had been reached, as the doctor was not at all inclined to take me seriously, while I would not even trust him to push my wheelchair. I actually swatted his hand off a handle when he tried to turn me back towards my room. I wanted Clayton to be comfortable, and as disabled as I was, I was not about to be bullied by an abusive, uncooperative little quack. Infuriated, he finally set off down the hallway, heading, I was sure, to fetch the thuggish orderly I had expected earlier.

I called the doctor back. Reluctant initially to listen any further to me, he was somewhat mollified by a calmer, more contrite deference. I apologized for behaving so rashly in disobeying the hospital rules. I explained that Signor Hayes and I were very close friends and that the accident had very much upset me. I asked him what exactly was wrong with Clayton. The doctor still refused to discuss the situation with me. Then, relying on my mother's report, I just as calmly and rationally informed him that Signor Hayes was an important American writer, that a number of journalists, "members of the press from all over the world," were waiting to speak to me about his condition.

"If you see fit to complicate things for me," I said, "by not giving me access to Signor Hayes or by withholding any facts from me, I will have no choice but to have both myself and Signor Hayes transferred out of this hospital." My heart was pounding in my chest. Part of my excitement, I can concede now, was due to my own uncertainty as to how much of what I was saying was pure bluff.

"If I do have us transferred," I added more ominously, "the whole world will know why. You can be sure the story will not be flattering to you or the hospital."

He seemed to ponder this carefully. Whether my threats were effective because he believed I really could destroy the hospital's reputation, and his, or simply because he wanted to avoid as much fuss as possible, I cannot know. I do know that the trouble, whatever its precise nature, would only have escalated had the doctor not displayed less daring than I did. Nor could I afford to have a conscience about my little game of blackmail. On that score, I acted strictly in accordance with necessity. Had I to do it over again . . .ah, but to have to do any of it over again would be a pitiless crime in itself.

After a grimacing admonition not to interfere with Clayton's treatment ("You're not in a position to judge these matters"), the doctor hesitantly went on to give me a general account of Clayton's health. When I thought he was being too general, I probed with more specific questions. Ultimately, I received a detailed and — as far as I *could* judge — reasonably full and accurate description of his injuries and current condition. I was grateful to have the truth, but dismayed to learn the gravity of the situation.

Besides the relatively minor effects of exposure and a mild case of pneumonia, Clayton had suffered internal injuries. They had had to do exploratory surgery to find out the severity of the damage. His spleen had been ruptured and had to be removed. His liver had been torn and a cracked rib had partially punctured a lung. (When I heard this, I thought of how I had selfishly warmed my cold hand against Clayton's bruised chest.) The perforated liver was still hemorrhaging periodically and his lungs were fighting off both pneumonia and the breathless pain caused by the lacerating rib. I was relieved, though, to hear that the chances were one hundred percent for a complete, albeit lengthy, recovery. The greatest danger at that point, the doctor said, was from infection.

It was a miracle, he admitted, that Clayton had survived those first hours of internal hemorrhaging on the mountain.

The doctor also acknowledged that a condom catheter, one which fit over the penis like a rubber, would be just as efficient in Clayton's case and possibly less painful. He agreed to have it changed. (The original use of an internal catheter was never defended.) I asked how long he expected Clayton to be hospitalized. He said at least four weeks. I was suspicious at once. Although I am not opposed to socialized medicine in principle, it has been my impression that in countries where the state funds all medical care, doctors tend to hospitalize their patients much longer than competent care would seem to require. I mentally subtracted two weeks, thanked the doctor for his patience and the consultation, apologized again for my breach of hospital conduct, and then left him standing in the corridor as I wheeled myself back into Clayton's room without requesting anyone's permission.

I raised the window shade and returned to Clayton's bedside. I told Clayton that the prognosis was excellent, though he might have to remain in the hospital for two or three weeks. He was concerned about my encounter with the doctor, but I assured him that it had all been a silly little case of mistaken identity. I smiled and told him that it was all straightened out, even as I secretly steeled myself for what

I feared would be punitive reprisals by the hospital administration — or perhaps deliberate malpractice by a resentful doctor or two. I then took Clayton's hand again and settled in my chair for the long vigil.

I looked out the window and was surprised to see in the distance the building in which Clayton had formerly rented an apartment. We were in Santa Chiara Hospital in Trento facing southwest. I could even see the windows of the bedroom where we had first made love. I called it to Clayton's attention. He gripped my hand gently.

"When we get out of here," he said, "maybe we can rent it for just one more night." His eyes then playfully shifted back to the window, as they had once done during our English lessons when the dead pigeon lay on the opposite sill. "You see, Luca, there's always a bright side to look on. . . ."

I smiled and nodded. I had to smother the unpleasant memory of years before, at the apartment in Trento, when I had sat by his sickbed, his hand in mine. I told Clayton that when he was better we could just fuck right there in the hospital bed, my cast in the air, his oxygen resuscitating both of us. We laughed. A pale laughter.

Something else seemed to fall out of place. I kissed his hand and was suddenly seized by a cold terror inside. I audibly groaned. A thing vast and despairing had been sensed within the bounds of my affectionate hopefulness. Clayton looked at me, the alarm back in his eyes. Lowering my head and placing my forehead against the back of his hand, I told him that I was just a little tired. He shook my head with a mildly reproachful motion of his hand and urged me to go back to my room. He would be all right. I wanted to cry again.

"No, I'll be okay," I said, my head down. "I want to stay." He laid his other hand on my head and combed my hair with his fingers.

I believed the doctor — I had, in fact, no reason not to believe him — but in that faith there was concealed the darkest of uncertainties. I could not muffle the ugly, strident voices of doubt inside me, the voices that always speak of crisis and that, in that instant when I had kissed Clayton's hand, had pierced through with their bleak message: Gone. . .all destined to be gone. I told myself it was simple anxiety, a fear understandably produced by the trying days we had just come through. But as sensible as this sounded, I could not convince myself that Clayton and I would ever make love again.

This thought and others I put out of my head in the next couple of days. It was almost as if I *had* retreated to that earlier self, the callow, self-confident youth who had nursed Clayton in his old apartment. I can't even pretend that my dutiful attention to Clayton was not, in the final analysis, an act of selfishness. I did not want to be without him. That first night I spent in my wheelchair next to his bed. The only time I left the room was when a nurse came in to change his catheter. I took the opportunity to go and speak to the police and to some of the reporters. I gave them a brief rundown on the accident and on Clayton's condition. I told them he might be well enough and willing to talk with them himself in a few days.

I did not tell any of them that Clayton had saved my life. Nor was this reserve due to any guilt I bore for Clayton's injuries. Apart from the barest facts, any words I might have used at the time could only have belittled his sacrifice, coarsened it for the public. It would have seemed too much like soliciting outside validation for what was, and is still for me, a private act of very private significance. Clayton knew and I knew, and we both knew its name and its value. That was enough. No, I was not quite again that bold, impetuous Tridentine boy I had once been.

We were interrupted throughout the night by nurses

coming in to check on Clayton. I was brought dinner on a tray and he had the bag dripping into his arm changed. He was out of it most of the time. I was never told what kind of drugs he was being administered or in what quantity, so I do not know if his fitful consciousness was chemically induced or merely a consequence of the ordeal his body had been through. In any event, I was thankful to be able to wait there with my hand and a word or two whenever he surfaced from sleep into woozy wakefulness. He would look at me and smile, and once he said, "You look so sad, Luca. Don't be sad." And I smiled back at him, feeling all the sadder.

The next day he seemed better. He was awake for hours at a time and clearheaded. Despite the fact that I was allowed to spend most of my time in Clayton's room unmolested by doctors, I did have two more of my confrontations with the hospital administration that morning. After a great deal of arguing, and a bit of arm-twisting, I managed to arrange for a room down the hall from Clayton's. I had wanted to share his room, but no amount of pressure seemed capable of obtaining that. In the end, I accepted the practical inevitability of being with Clayton every minute of the day except when I slept.

My other run-in with the hospital involved the nurse, Daniela. I had to intervene in order to prevent disciplinary action from being taken against her. Countermanding a doctor's orders, naturally, is not a minor infraction, and I had to bring all my weight to bear (or, rather, all of Signor Hayes') in order for her to retain her job at Santa Chiara. I was even successful in keeping her off report. Later that day she came to visit us and I introduced her to Clayton. She laughed nervously and claimed that the worst she'd had to endure so far were some dirty looks from a few of the doctors. Then I found myself foolishly accepting *her* thanks for all she had done to help *me*.

My mother came and sat with us for a while that day too. Clayton took her hand and they exchanged a few words in Italian. I told her we would probably stay with her for several weeks after getting out of the hospital, until Clayton and I were ready to travel. Clayton laughed and told her that all we really needed was a good, home-cooked Italian meal. She promised to prepare us a regular feast the day we checked out of the hospital, and kept offering menu ideas for our approval.

I spent that night in my own bed. The following morning I was frightened to see Clayton looking worse. It was December 6, 1979. He had a fever and wandered in and out of consciousness with disconcerting unpredictability. He was delirious in the afternoon, mumbling nonsense as the sweat poured off his face. He was given large doses of antibiotics and by the early evening appeared to be in much better shape, physically and mentally. I read to him some of the telegrams that had come in. Claudia had wired, offering her home at Lake Garda for our recuperation and asking us to phone her in England at our earliest convenience. She would come at once to nurse us personally if she was needed. We had also received wires from his publisher, his parents, Ken, Sugar, Fabio, other assorted friends and admirers, including Clayton's actor friend whom I had once fucked — and even a very kind note from George.

I had received a wire from Claire instructing me to please let her know if she should fly immediately to Italy or not. I had already phoned her to tell her that we would probably be back in a couple of months and not to worry. In passing this news on to Clayton, I was puzzled to see his eyes mist over with an emotion oddly out of proportion to my remark. My mention of our eventual return to San Francisco could scarcely have been more offhanded. It is not impossible, of course, that I was willfully deluding myself in underestimating the importance Clayton attached to *home* in that particular moment, or the poignance that could be conveyed in so incomplete a sentiment as the name of a city thousands of miles away.

Nonetheless, he was in high spirits when I left him to go have dinner in my room. I was using crutches to get around and he joked that we would have to buy me a set of designer crutches by Armani or Valentino.

Back in my room I fell asleep after dinner while reading *A Passage to India,* which a member of the mountain fire department had graciously returned to me. I remember a weird little dream I had in that nap of a woman in a large, dark hat descending the gangplank of a cruise ship, friends saying good-bye to her, a young girl staring curiously at her.

I was awakened from my sleep by a breath in my ear. *"Vieni, Luca, vieni. Credo che sia gravissimo"* Come, Luca, come. I think it's very serious. It was Daniela. It took me a second to understand what she had said. I looked at her and then at my watch. It was almost midnight. Suddenly I knew what she meant.

I jumped from the bed and grabbed my crutches. I hurried down the hall with Daniela trailing behind me. I saw my mother standing anxiously outside Clayton's room. She had come to visit me and the doctors had shuttled her toward the more critical situation. She did not speak, but the hurt look on her face seemed to plead from me nothing so much as resignation.

I flew into the room on my crutches. A priest was standing near the door.

"Get the fuck out of here!" I was so angry I yelled at the priest in English. Bewildered, he staggered back against the wall.

A doctor and a nurse were standing over Clayton's bed. The monitors of his vital signs had been set up nearby and were beeping wildly. The doctor was giving him an injection. The nurse rattled the equipment at my explosive entrance. The doctor looked up. Jerking out the needle, he muttered something about it possibly being acute peritonitis. I shoved the nurse aside and moved in next to the bed, dropping my crutches in the process. They clattered to the floor as I perched over Clayton's comatose body. His breathing was even more irregular than it had been on the mountain. His face was inexpressive, yet somehow strained. It was as though we were all watching a sleeper having a bad dream, unable to wake him.

I took his hand.

"What's happening!" I screamed at the doctor.

At this Clayton's eyes opened and flashed clear and lucid for one moment.

"Luca . . . the bright side . . . ." he said, looking at me. Did he smile, or was the irony only in my misunderstanding?

Then his eyes closed as the monitors went into an electrical spasm. He inhaled with difficulty. The exhalation was an unnatural one, something being loosened from his lungs, from his body. I squeezed his hand. There was no response.

The machines were making a different sound now, a much quieter sound.

I took his shoulders and shook him. "Clayton! Clayton!" I looked up at the doctor, who gave me a hopeless shake of his head.

"Clayton!" I called again.

I threw my head onto the motionless chest to hear for myself that the heart still beat, still pumped life into his body. I heard nothing. I felt nothing. I would not believe it. I hugged him, certain I could will life back into him. His flesh stung bitterly inanimate against mine. Empty flesh, abandoned in an instant and already cool and artificial to the touch.

I stood up and looked from Clayton's still, silent

body to the faces about me. They too were still, silent, a little embarrassed. But they had life.

I pushed away from the bed and hopped crazily out the door. My mother was weeping softly in the corridor and tried to embrace me, tried to comfort me. I broke from her arms. I wanted to cry in only one person's arms, and his were lifeless now. I leaned with my hand on the wall for support and hobbled to the end of the corridor. I turned and ran to a set of French doors that opened out onto a terrace.

I went outside, my plaster cast thumping across the tiles. In the freezing night I looked around helplessly for something to hit, something to bang, something to throw. I picked up a deck chair and in my rage hurled it over the balcony. The violence of my pitch unbalanced me and I fell to the ground.

I looked up just as snow began to fall. *"Porco Dio,"* I cried. *Porco Dio, Porco Dio.*

XII   An Obligatory Dream,
a Human Calm

What foolish things most of us lose with our youth. An easier movement, a suppleness of mind and body, a range of daring not usually maintained into middle age. Maybe some physical beauty. Maybe some of one's certainty, that arrogance that says *I know*. If one is lucky, one may lose some of one's romantic ideals, some of one's vulnerability. I say lucky. Who wants to survive in a world of painful dreams and self-mutilation? The skeptical may ask what price resilience, but if one is to survive at all, one must come to believe that youth is merely another set of years in one's life, only as regrettable in their loss as the passing of this year or next. And, indeed, what foolish things pass with those years of youth! [The tone is a meditative one]

It seems I am going on like someone who feels he has lost the *best* with his youth. I do. I did. Nor am I too humble, alas, to admit that I feel cheated. I lost not just a lover, a friend, a feeling so very much like pure happiness that I could not have dreamed a more perfect joy. I lost a chunk of reality as indispensable, or as impossible to elide in its dispensability, as the free, hopeful yearnings of my youth. I cannot skirt the vacancy of emotion and perception left me, any more than I can reverse the course of time or deny the necessity of forgetting a reality that I lived and breathed — a reality that has shriveled, fallen, and decomposed. The reality died in a small town in Italy nine years ago.

I have worked hard to replace the reality with a quiet world of more pedestrian fantasies. I have contrived a plastic memory that bends and twists and misshapes itself to baffle the consciousness that sleeps beneath it, that no impolitic dream may fill in the missing images or rescind the sleep of regret. I veer towards wakefulness from time to time, but in my determination to tread a safe path through the solitary invention my life has become, I have managed to render the images of sorrow as evanescent as the splashed water about a pool under a Hawaiian sun.

To know that one has survived the worst along with the best sometimes makes one not proud, but simply apathetic. It all seems so. . .redundant. With or without love one goes on, through joy and pain. Why should one even *care* what it all means?

I had thought that no loss would ever cut so staggeringly close to what was vital in me as the death of my father. How could I imagine I would lose Clayton so soon, before I had given all the love I had to give? How could I have been so foolish as to think that the cleaving power of death would not visit me again? But that foolishness is all gone now, with my youth, along with the fatuous hope that life would deliver me from its own malevolence. Clayton will not come back to love me. And I cannot stop loving a man who is not there.

But if there is no effective imprecation against the darkness of loneliness, neither do the winds of reminiscence disrupt the stagnant equilibrium of shadow I have inherited. Of that I have made sure.

History is dead. In a dream the "past" is simply the illusory afterimage of something that came before.

Clayton's body was cremated and the ashes scattered over the Ligurian Sea from a boat I had chartered. Clayton had actually willed his body to a medical institute in the States, but they proved recalcitrant in arranging decent transportation for the body out of Italy. I was certainly not going to help them in their enterprise, no matter how worthy Clayton considered the cause. He and I had argued more than once about what was to me a gruesome disposal of human flesh. At the same time I was not about to let his parents prevail in their wish to have the body flown back for a burial in Louisiana. In addition to more obvious objections, a grave would have been too burdensome a reality. I have since caught myself praying (to Whom? to Clayton?) that he does not hold my final word on the matter against me.

In the end I took things into my own hands, literally, and filtered the ashes through my fingers, their weight- lessness sucked at greedily, first by the breeze and then by the heaviness of a sea that seemed to swell towards them, wanting him, wanting him more, wanting to draw the wispy remains of Clayton Hayes into one everlastingly serene illusion: that the end had been peacefully accepted.

My own desire for love seemed to disappear, too, into that blue water with Clayton, from where it has since emerged only in the body of a serpentine sexuality that is not love.

And yet it is not a wanton sexuality I have indulged, and if after fucking someone I sense that he lies beside me thinking it has *only* been a fuck, I shudder. The coupling of bodies in sexual passion is a warm if distorted refraction of all the more compelling affection I once knew. Its value is immeasurable for me, for sex has become in its own unassuming way a comma of sincerity, a compassionate pause in the somnabulist's walk. It has a reality of its own. There is nothing superficial — how can I tell them? — in my superficial tenderness. It is as deep and all-encompassing as the dream itself.

An American poet has written of the loss of innocence as a longing for "a dream to sift romance from destructability. . .all that heartache withered tearless long ago." I have come to understand the meaning of this lament. Romance is a kind of game, a game for the innocent. As one gets older one learns that for survival's sake there has to be a limit to the stakes involved. But once one accepts the limits, the purposefulness of the game is diminished. One learns there are some pains that are not worth the pursuit of love — and, oh, how worthless that can make love seem!

As I have aged I have grown to appreciate simple flirtation, enjoying the sort of attraction that tells me I am still desired while renewing my own sense of desire. But I am not oblivious to the heartbreakingly desperate futility of games of love. There is no "end" now to play the game to.

I have written earlier in this book that life *is* peril. And, in fact, when risk in abnegated one experiences a kind of death — or at least subscribes to life as a kind of hyp-notic trance, a fitful sleep. A human calm.

Everything I feel is dulled, and neither love nor terror can break through my protective shell. In regard to sex, I have with bitter irony discovered that a fundamental indifference is my most alluring feature to those still caught up in the consuming obsessions of romance.

The newspaper accounts of Clayton's demise reported death due to complications following an automobile acci-dent. Some geographically confused journalists stated that the accident had taken place in the Dolomites, or even in the Apennines. The more medically misinformed hinted at a long and scrupulously concealed illness of undetermined but terminal nature. AIDS, I know, has since been whispered. The death certificate read peritonitis. I would not consent, as legal next of kin, to an autopsy.

I have, I confess, always borne a certain resentment towards the doctors at Santa Chiara Hospital. My suspicions have been amplified by my own badly set leg, which mended poorly. I continue to walk with a slight limp that seems to worsen with each year — a limp almost as noticeable as my father's after his stroke. Otherwise I have preserved myself, in Californian tradition, with youthful vigor. To what end, as one may ask of most traditions, I do not know.

My days in the hospital after Clayton's death were spent in an antiseptic torpor. I neither wept nor verbally agonized over my fate, nor grieved in any other manifestly melodramatic fashion. I spoke and ate little. I did not often move from my bed. But there was nothing delicate in my despondency. It was nothing like the flamboyantly tearful moodiness of my first separation from Clayton in Trento. I at once committed myself totally to the dreamily sterile tranquility of an existence without Clayton. Energy was not to be wasted on draining, deceptive emotions. It was a trap. The specter of despair could not be allowed to terrorize me into thinking any of it was real.

I have to make it through till morning.

I accepted the countless condolences without tears, without warmth, without a dream of escape. I accepted the sympathy and heartfelt assurances of support as blandly as I accepted the furniture in my hospital room. I have learned to live with so much pain, calmly; it has all been perversely distilled into a sedative. I accepted and have continued to accept the occasional interviewer intent on a new perspective on the late popular writer, as though their attempts to understand mattered. (No one has yet compiled a real biography, and my reverential lassitude prevents me from commissioning one, or even authorizing one.) I have learned to accept unflinchingly the critical charges of mediocrity and banality leveled against Clayton's work. I have accepted that his work is, in truth, being forgotten. I have accepted without complaint the misrepresentations and out-and-out lies of others. I have accepted the well-meaning and not-so-well-meaning intrusions of public speculation into my private life. And I have accepted without rebuttal the muddled and amateurish psychological "interpretations" given to my relationship with Clayton. I have accepted the whole ugly nightmare as hopelessly as a doomed prisoner — no, not hopelessly, for there is always the hope that life will somehow find its destructive labors useless in the face of my resistance, loosen its hold over the dreamer and release me, its force dwindling before the pristine implacability of one who can no longer recall a reason to care.

After I left the hospital, but before the dispersal of ashes off the Ligurian coast, I conducted another, more personal ceremony. I hiked to the top of the mountain they call Dante and dug a deep hole with my bare hands. There I buried the ring I had given Clayton eight and a half years earlier. The site was in the middle of an unmarked, snow-covered clearing. I left nothing to indicate its location. I have never attempted to return to it. It is comforting sometimes to have the intensely meaningful layered beneath the unremarkable and ordinary. Secret power is often the securest.

What romantic foolishness there was in this rite I cannot judge even now. Maybe I only hoped to partake of some elemental strength invocable with mountains and rings and burial. But I can state unequivocally that it was the last act of my life to bear the vaguest intimation of the childish extravagance inherent in all romance.

I could not go back to live in Trento. I still visit

regularly of course. But the primary obstacle that makes Trento uninhabitable for me is *not*, oddly enough, the last calamity there, but rather those first six months I had spent there without Clayton after his return to San Francisco. The torment of those memories is even more intimidating than the two deaths that Trento has unfolded for me — while soon enough a third death, my mother's, will no doubt draw me back one final time into the cold grip Trento seems determined to extend me. Clearly, the egocentricity of my view places the spirit of my hometown in a somewhat diabolic light.

San Francisco is my home now. As it was with Clayton. I am close to him here without being threatened by more grisly associations. We were happy here together.

I was his sole heir and financially I was left with little to worry about. (I did give my cousin the money to move into my mother's building.) I took a position teaching Italian in a private Catholic girls' school because a life must be filled. And if it is not filled with the present, the past will seep in to wreak havoc with the sinister arsenal of memory.

The future is a pall that refuses to drop.

My friends are here in San Francisco too, of course. Claire remains the closest of them. She has stubbornly, after all these years, continued to harbor some guilt inside for the accident. I have told her that handkerchiefs are only handkerchiefs, and that foresight, if that is what it was, is not an act. But because of her guilt we do not discuss the accident. That we know what we know and do not speak it is solace for both of us. What expression could touch our bereavement anyway? Sometimes when Clayton is mentioned by one of us, we look at one another and the instantaneous sharing of a wound that will not heal is enough to remind us of the preciousness of our own friendship. Then we hug each other, and without a word she offers me, in the specialness of our affections, some of the specialness I lost in the Santa Chiara Hospital.

Alessandro I cannot bear to see very often, though when we do it is always on the most amicable of terms. Our relationship, however, is too strongly hinged on our memories of Clayton.

Sugar is still a friend whose company I seek out. I have retained the condo in Hawaii as much for his friendship as for the beauty of Maui. On my first visit back to the island after the accident, he met me at the airport and drove me in. He said nothing about Clayton and acted as though nothing had happened. His humor was perhaps gentler, but for the most part it was the same old Sugar. I was surprised to see him refrain from any display of sympathy. Then I realized it was his way of keeping his own emotions under control. When at last, at the end of my stay, he collapsed into my arms weeping, I was grateful for the chance to tell him how much Clayton had loved him.

My own tears had long ceased to flow so freely. I remember. And I do not remember.

For some reason I cannot fathom, Ken is the only one I can really talk with about Clayton. (His eyes were so puffy and sore when I returned to San Francisco in late January that I thought he would never look the same again.) We do not cry together or dwell on our loss. But in the evening, sitting in the cottage having a cocktail, I can talk about Clayton to him, and only him, in a manner that is not lachrymose or exaggerated or morbid. For a moment Clayton is real for both of us and unburdened of the gloomier character of dead, dead history.

For years I diligently left unreread all of Clayton's books — and more especially all the letters he had written to me during our one separation. One day, however, I had taken off the ring with the engraved trident, which I always wear, while changing the oil in my car. When I went to put it back on, I could not find it. After a frantic search that had me practically in hysterics, I found it lying on the dashboard of the car. Without thinking what I was doing, I immediately proceeded to the closet in my bedroom and to the sealed box that held our old correspondence. I rummaged quickly through the papers until I came across the letter I had received just before my humiliating telephone call back to the lecherous Signor Corsentino in Milan. I lifted the sheet of paper as if it were an ancient, priceless parchment decoding seven dead languages. It was the love letter I had never thought much of a love letter. I held it to the light of the window and read.

". . .I want you . . . Forgive me. . . ."

I cried as I had not cried since those last days with Clayton in the hospital. All the pain rushed back over me like the chill of wind that night on the road to Folgaria. I silently begged the God I no longer believed in to undo the suffering; to decree that the accident and the years of loneliness really had been only a long nightmare; to promise that as soon as my eyes dried I would awake and find Clayton next to me, his breath warm on my face. Barring that mercy, I pleaded for death itself.

Denied either of these amnesties, I begged for even worse: that my love for Clayton and the searing memory of that love would die, would exhaust itself and crinkle into ashes as easily dispatched as the handful of dirt I had tossed upon the sea years earlier.

I knew from long experience, though, that such prayers are never answered. There is no God to hear them. I wiped my eyes and went on with the safer, calmer dream of my own deliberate manufacture.

Would love be love if it were as fleeting as ashes in the wind?

One afternoon I came home from school and automatically switched on the TV. I busied myself, meanwhile, in the preparation of a little snack before dinner as the voices from the television kept me company. I was suddenly drawn to the screen by an unidentifiably familiar melody. I stood in front of the television watching a story being enacted that held, like Dante's face, some secret, unaccountable power beneath its innocuous flicker of black and white images.

A psychiatrist was telling a homely young woman that she was strong enough now to step out into the big world by herself and meet it on her own terms. He gave her a poem by Walt Whitman for inspiration: "Now, voyager, sail thou forth to seek and find . . . ."

I sank into a chair and scarcely blinked through the entire movie, through the blossoming of her womanhood on the cruise ship, through the car accident on a Brazilian mountainside, through the ritual lighting of two cigarettes in the man's mouth, through the elegant carriage of a woman battling against her domineering mother, through the lovers' estrangement and the mysterious wearing of a camellia corsage, through the adamant spurning of another's proposal of marriage, through the befriending of and vicarious devotion to the married lover's daughter. I sat motionless through the whole movie, undeterred by the hokey script or the dated look of the black and white film. Yes, I did blink, many times, to clear the tears from my eyes.

And when a man and woman looked out the window across the trees to a sky full of stars and the woman said, "Don't let's ask for the moon; we have the stars," I could only discern the actors through the blur of tears flooding my eyes. I wept helplessly in the chair until, once more, the dream of forgetfulness reestablished its dominance, and I went to eat my sandwich.

On my last visit to Trento to see my mother I went to a new bar near her house. It is also near the *distretto,* and its patrons are mainly the young men from the army base and older men, not unlike myself, who may be depended upon for at least a free drink. It is the kind of bar where young men may be met and their company enjoyed, with or without more serious intentions — though the scent of money and pleasure intermingle in the air like the curls of cigarette smoke. Eroticism is as palpable as the undisguised bulges in the young men's jeans. And if two apparent strangers leave the bar together, no one is derisive. It is, quite simply, the closest thing these days to a gay bar in Trento.

I was sipping a vin brulé there one evening when I recognized a man entering the bar. He looked several years older than me. He was fat and flabby, with a jowly, rippled face and stooped shoulders. The eyes, behind old man's glasses, were tired and emotionless except for the pathetic gleam of lust in them. It was my old childhood friend Francesco, whom I had never let kiss me. I had heard that he had married and had several children. He did not recognize me. I did not greet him, but watched as he briefly, vainly cruised about the room looking for a likely pick-up. His glances returned by no one, he sheepishly departed by himself.

I do not mean to sound smug about his seeming lack of fortune. And my own presence in the bar was not so innocent either. *I* did not leave it alone. But I cannot help grading my life against one so transparently unfulfilled. Lost, grieved, mourned beyond all sensibleness — but I did have the *best*.

Maybe it is for this reason that the dream is not an unhappy one. I live and know a joy of sorts — the joy that comes from having known what nobody else can know, a knowledge that sometimes make me smile to myself. There is a kind of contentment in my passionless dream (or passionate in only the most sensual and transitory of senses). I can laugh, too, even if all the laughter has the sad ring of that September in Trento with Clayton. I laugh and I hear the echo of laughter from a distant room. But why shouldn't I laugh? I am free to do whatever I like, though it all seems strangely perfunctory, as in a dream that the dreamer is conscious of and knows must go on. I may be said to be happy, as one may be happy in just such an obligatory dream, that must be dreamed though it has no meaning, is without symbols, has no interpretation. All the real dreams, the meaningful dreams, have already been dreamed...and understood.

Clayton's true legacy to me has been in the form of myth. There is an Olympian complexity and completeness in my image of him that transcends the merely factual events of my years with him. He is my Pantheon. In my personal mythology he has solved a riddle that no one before or since has been able to provide a clue to. And in my unconditional acceptance of the archetypal magnitude of Clayton's role in my life, there is a finality that no future can unlock. Must I confess, too, that each year ripped away from this no longer young soul only enriches the figurative absoluteness of that fable that is remembered love?

I could say with Jean Genêt that "the facts were what I say they were, but the interpretation that I give them is what I am — now." The paradox is that these distorted memories, from which I must even recoil at times, have formed their interpreter.

But my life is not over. I have only just turned forty and things may change. Who knows, I may even come eventually to some accommodation with the One who will not answer to the taunt Pig God. There is time. Even a dream is life. And the style of living I have defaulted to is one I am not inclined to repudiate, although I may periodically seek to reassess it.

For years I had no elegy for Clayton but the emptiness in my heart. The reticence of grief was its own commemoration. Now I have written this memoir. Now I must sleep.

I must sleep now, perhaps to be awakened from time to time by the silent scrawl of words upon a lifted page, by the gray light of Bette Davis in an old movie on the television screen. Or by the unintelligible chatter of voices on a city bus.

L.S.H.
September, 1988
San Francisco

A friend has recently brought to my attention a more authoritative and definitive explanation for the origin of the place name Trento. Its etymology seems to lie embedded in the prehistoric linguistics of northern Italy, the form TR being a pre-Indo-European root devolving to such words as TRansit, TRaverse and TRansport, and evident in such comparable words for a thoroughfare as the Italian sTRada, the German sTRasse and the English sTReet. The root, in fact, would seem to signify any strategic point of necessarily common passage.